Lust, Lies and Love

Quinton Simpson

Lust, Lies & Love

Lust, Lies & Love

First Published for:

Maximize Publishing Inc., Michael McCain &

For Author Quinton Simpson

ISBN-13:
978-0692677964

ISBN-10:
0692677968

Lust, Lies & Love

Lust, Lies and Love

Quinton Simpson

Lust, Lies & Love

Biography

Born in Thomasville, Georgia, Quinton A. Simpson enjoyed his upbringing in the south. He grew up in a small town known as Meigs, Georgia. He attended Thomas County Central High School from which he graduated. He later moved to Albany, Georgia where he began writing what now is Lust, Lies, and Love. Quinton also is an upcoming fashion and jewelry designer/event planner. He believes in giving back to the homeless. He has worked with different charities including The National Kidney Foundation and The Cancer Society. His past life, friendships and relationships inspired him to write his first novel. Quinton Simpson is a developing novelist, poet, and entrepreneur that is using his love of writing, creative arts, fashion, consulting and design to shape a brighter future for himself. Quinton enjoys participating in philanthropy and charitable causes that empower those who need it most.

Lust, Lies & Love

Introduction

I walked into the supermarket to pick up a box of condoms. I saw this young man that caught my eye. I knew I had to have him. He was tall, sexy, and handsome. As I was leaving the supermarket, the young man stopped me and gave me his number. When I got home, I called him because I wanted to get to know him. We met up and went to dinner. We had a wonderful time. His name is Mike Smiley, which I thought was a very nice name. Later that night, we went back to my place for drinks and a movie.

After the drinks and movie, I went to take a shower. I got out of the shower and walked into the room with my dick hanging out. I was hoping Mike was ready to put my dick in his mouth. I wanted to feel that warm, gentle and wet feeling all over my dick. As I walked into the room, Mike was already on his knees giving my friend Fred some good head. I couldn't believe my eyes. I wanted to feel that amazing rush. After Mike got finished giving Fred some head, Fred and I had some wonderful sex. A couple of days later, a guy by the name of Calvin came over. He said he was a longtime friend of Tom. We started to talk. We were both giving each other the eye. Minutes later we were making crazy love. The sex was so amazing and lovely. When we got finished having sex, I laughed in his face for about ten minutes. Calvin couldn't take the dick and I was fucking him stupid.

"Why are you laughing?" Calvin asked with that just-fucked-and-can't-take-it look on his face. I respond breathing heavily and drenched in sweat. "I was laughing because you were crying and begging me to stop." Calvin didn't think it was so funny. His feelings were hurt so he got up looking crazy and left. I didn't give a damn about his hurt feelings. When Calvin left the house, I got into bed and went to sleep. Calvin gave me some wonderful sex and put me to sleep.

The next day, I went to work and called Calvin. I wanted to know how was his body feeling, but he didn't answer. I felt bad because I shouldn't have laughed at him. When I got off work, I went home. When I walked into the house, I saw Tom on his knees sucking Fred's little dick. I watch the both of them for about thirty minutes. I loved it. Later, I joined them. The three of us had a wonderful time. They made me feel like a king. I was so proud of Tom for giving me a great gift. Later that night, we all met up at a party coincidentally where Tom and I first met. Tom's my boyfriend that I care for so much. I don't love him, but I do care for him. Tom isn't worth my love. When we got to the party, I saw a lot of fine dicks. I wanted to take them all home. I left my friends in the party room and went to the bar for a couple of drinks. I walked into the bar and met his guy by the name of Sam. He was a lawyer in New York. After a few drinks, we left the bar and went to take a walk in the park. What a blast we had. After a walk in the park, we went back to Sam's hotel. Dinner was great. After dinner, the two of us laid on the bed and watched too. It felt so great because Sam was a real man who knew how to treat a guy. We cuddled into the early morning which was great because he only wanted to be held and loved.

The next morning, the both of us got up and went to work. I couldn't stop thinking about Sam. He was loving and caring. When I get off work, I gave Sam a call because I wanted to meet up for dinner. When he came over, I prepared dinner and wine for him. I knew he had a long day at work. He sat down and began to eat and drink. I went into the bathroom and ran a nice and hot bubble bath for the two of us. I think we both earned it. When the two of us got into the bubble bath, Sam began to rub me down with his soft hands. I loved it so much. Then he begins licking me from head to toe. He kisses me with his soft lips and gives me the best sex I have ever had. The dick was so good. He had my mind and body going in circles.

When I woke up the next morning, Sam had to leave because of work. I called the other guys over to see how the party was. Everyone came over except for Tom. He heard about Sam and me. I really didn't care about Tom's feelings. He was so boring. I had to get some new black dick. The guys said the party went very well, but Tom didn't have a great time because I wasn't there. I thought that was funny.

The only thing Tom can do for me is to give me some great sex. I treated Tom with respect and showed him love, but he took me to hell and back. I could have killed Tom. He thought the world of himself. I had to let him know that I didn't. The guys and I went out for lunch. I invited Sam to come because he was a really nice guy. When Sam got to the restaurant, everyone started to look crazy because they knew Tom and I was still in a relationship. I didn't care what the guys thought.

Sam met the guys but didn't care for them. They were so rude and hood. We left and went back to my place because Tom was out of town for work. I was so happy. We begin to talk and one thing leads to another. I was feeling that entire eleven and a half inch dick in me making me feel like a real man. We did it all, and I felt so good. Tom doesn't make me feel good as a person. Mike and Fred began a relationship that I thought was crazy because we all were sex partners. Then again, that's the past. I am happy for them even though Tom and I were together.

I was really feeling Sam. He meant a lot to me. I finally got the nerve to call Calvin because I haven't heard from him since the last time we had sex. Calvin wanted to meet up and talk, but I wasn't with the talking. I wanted some sex. That's what I got because Calvin was missing every inch of it. When we got finished having sex, he expresses his love for me and tells me that I mean the world to him. I started to cry because I was feeling him so much. I began to think about Tom. I love the things that Sam does for me. I told him let's get together and be lovers. He was so happy, and I thought it was funny because he knew I was lying.

Later that night, Tom came home from out of town. He was so tired. I ran him a hot bubble bath, cooked him a dinner, and put on some nice, slow music. We took a bath together and had the most powerful sex. I felt bad because Calvin and I just had sex an hour ago before Tom got home. I sat Tom down and told him everything about Sam and me. He didn't believe me because he said I am always lying to him and that he is not leaving no matter what. I called Sam and told him about it because Tom is young, dumb and stupid.

Sam thought it was crazy that Tom didn't believe me. Sam and I met up because he was home. He needed a place to crash. I invited him to move in with Tom and me. I talked Tom into saying yes because Sam really needed somewhere to stay. The both of us helped Sam move in. It was crazy because Tom started to have a second thought about Sam moving in. I didn't care what Tom thought because Sam wasn't going anywhere. Sam and I were getting closer as friends and Tom didn't like it at all. He thought we were spending too much time together.

I invited all of the guys over for a spades party. So everyone could get to know each other and have a nice time, but things didn't go well. Tom was still upset about Sam living with us. It really didn't matter how he felt because Sam and I were good friends. After everyone left the party, Sam and I had wonderful sex while Tom was in the bedroom sleep. I had to be extra quiet because I didn't want to wake up Tom. I couldn't be extra quiet though because the dick was so good. After Sam and I finished having sex, I took an amazing bath.

After my bath, I went into the room and fucked Tom so good because that's what he wanted. I was thinking about Sam while I was fucking Tom. I told Tom I enjoyed the sex, and he began to smile because he thought I was telling the truth. What Tom didn't know was that I was thinking about Sam the entire time. Tom left and went back out of town for work. I invited Calvin to come over to talk about him and me because we really needed to get things in order. He began to express his feelings. I wasn't feeling it because I am in love with Sam. He means so much to me. Fred and Mike

Lust, Lies & Love

weren't happy with me because they think Tom and I should try and work it out. I thought about what the guys said while Tom was away, but it didn't settle in because of my love for Sam.

I called Sam and told him what Fed and Mike said. Sam told me to do whatever is right in my heart. He didn't want to come between Tom and me. Sam really wants to be with me. I felt so sad because I am stuck between the two.

Tom just got back home. I told him everything. He said that he is not letting the relationship go. No matter what. Tom and I called Sam over to the restaurant so we could all talk. The three of us went back to the house for some hot and steamy sex.

Tom didn't want to have a threesome because he wasn't feeling it. When he saw Sam and I making wonderful love and how Sam was sucking and licking my big dick, it made him mad as hell. He decided to join making Sam and I feel like kings of the castle. Tom enjoyed all of it because I was enjoying it. Fred and Mike came over after the three of us had sex and we had a sit-down talk. When I got up to go to the bathroom, I notice that Mike was looking at me while I was in the bathroom.

Lust, Lies & Love

As I was walking out, Mike pushed me back in and started to unzip my pants down. I tried to move him, but I couldn't. Mike took my dick out and began to suck. I was so surprised because I thought he would never do anything like that. I enjoyed it so much. His lips felt like feathers. His mouth was warm. His tongue was lovely. That was some kind of head he gave me. I wanted to stick this dick in him until his belly felt weak. Mike sucked my dick until I came in his mouth choking like a bitch.

After we finished having sex, the both of us went back into the living room and joined everyone. We didn't want anyone to think anything. The head game was so lovely and nice. When everyone left the house, Tom and I thought things over and realized that we were going to be together no matter what. When we were getting ready for bed, the phone rang. I wasn't going to answer it until I looked at the caller ID and noticed that it was Mike calling. I picked up the phone and began to talk because he had something heavy on his chest to tell me.

When we met up, he wanted to talk about us getting together, but I couldn't do it. I was still feeling Sam, but I was in a relationship with Tom, who I didn't love anymore. I wanted to call and tell Fred, but I couldn't. So I called Calvin and told him about it because I knew he will come over and talk, give me some good head, and let me fuck him. He's my sex toy and play bunny.

After Fred and Mike left the house, I called my friend, Calvin, because I wanted more sex. He doesn't mean anything to me. Calvin came over and started to take off my clothes, lick me from head to toe and suck my dick. He gave me the best head of them all. I put him in the buck. He couldn't take it yelling for me to stop because it was hurting. I laugh because he wanted his 12 inch dick. Calvin started to cry because it was hurting so bad. I didn't care. He wanted it, and I gave it to him. Calvin only meant a lot to me when it came down to sex. I know he will give it up to me and only me after everyone told each other how they really felt about one another. I thought it was time to treat everyone to dinner. Things were getting crazy in our lives.

When we were getting ready for dinner, Fred pulls me off to the side and asks me what was wrong with Mike because he has been acting funny. I didn't know what to say because Mike and I had been having sex for quite some time. I told Fred to sit down to talk because I felt so bad about the things I was doing.

A week later, Tom had to leave for three months for work. He was so mad because I couldn't leave with him. I was so happy because it was more dick for me while he was gone. That was the happiest day of my life. Sam and I are going to have a wonderful time. What a wonderful three months we are going to have. After Tom left, I called Calvin and Sam over. I wanted to have a threesome. I knew they were ready and willing to do whatever to make me happy. I went to the door because I heard a soft knock.

When I open the door, it was Calvin and Sam. They came into the house for drinks and some talk time. We started talking and drinking for about an hour. A couple of minutes later, Sam takes his dick out of his pants and puts it in Calvin's and my face. Calvin begins sucking Sam's dick because he was really horny at the moment. I begin to laugh because I knew Sam was going to fuck the hell out of Calvin. Calvin can't take dick.

When Sam started to give Calvin the business, I joined in a few minutes later because I was ready to get my dick sucked and get fucked by my baby Sam. I love him the most. We had sex for about two hours. I felt so scared for Calvin because Sam and I gave it to him hard. He could barely walk. He left the both of us. We began to laugh because we already knew he couldn't take it.

I called Fred and Mike because I was going to get a haircut, and I wanted them to join. It had been a long time since we have seen each other. They met Sam and me at the barbershop. When we got inside, we notice that everyone turned their heads toward us. I thought it was because we were all laughing and talking loud. I step outside because my barber wasn't there. I notice that it was a guy standing by our car talking to someone about coming to pick him up. I asked him did he need a ride. He said yes. I gave him a ride and he took me down this long dirt road. He asked me do I suck dick. I began to laugh. I didn't want to do it, but it was so big. I couldn't help but to suck it. I felt all ten and a half inches down my throat. He had me shaking and crying, but it felt so good.

He later fucked me until I couldn't be fucked anymore. The dick had me going insane. I got myself together and took him home. I had to pick up the guys from the barbershop. When the guys got into the car, I told them what happened between the guy and me. They were mad because they all wanted some dick. So I took them all down, one by one. They all had tight asses and deep throats which I loved because it took longer for that rush to come. When it did come out, it went all over their faces and mouths. It felt so good. I needed that rush.

I called Tom after everything was over and done because I wanted him to know what was going on with me. All of the guys left except for Fred because he wanted to talk about the way Mike been acting with him. Instead of talking, one thing led to another. I took off Fred's clothes and started licking him from his lips to his stomach. I had his body shaking like a newborn baby. I later started licking his dick up and down. When I was sucking his dick, I couldn't stop because it was so good. I deep-throated his dick like it was candy in the candy shop. Then he took his dick out and put it in my ass. I lost my breath for a minute because it was so big.

After he got it in good, he punished me for making him wait for so long. I couldn't do anything but lay there. He was working my body to the max. It hurt for a minute, but I began to get used to it. When I did, it was on.

Lust, Lies & Love

I didn't tell Tom because he didn't care about me having sex with other men. That's what I loved about him. All of the guys were into having sex parties. That's what they love doing.

When Calvin had his first sex party, he invited all of the guys over. They went crazy because it was very young dicks there. They knew what was about to happen. I couldn't do anything but laugh because I had my eye on two young men that I knew wanted some good dick. I took them in the room and helped got the both of them naked. I was so ready to fuck the both of them. They are young and don't know any better. After they were undressed, I started to play with their dicks. I let them suck on my dick at the same time. I was ready to put my dick in their tight assholes. I made them lie on the bed and get into position. I was ready for some good ass. I knew they had it.

When I put my dick in the first young man, he started to cry because he wasn't use to dick. I still didn't stop fucking him because of the crying. He was begging me to stop because he couldn't take it. I was still going in it hard. I had to teach him about playing with a grown man. He was crying like a baby. The dick was too big and painful for him to take. His body was in so much pain. I later began to have sex with his friend, who I enjoyed the most. He was a ride or die dude that would do anything to please you. He sucked my dick, took down my cum and licked every part of my body. What a freak!

Before the young boys left the house, they wanted me to call the rest of the guys up for dinner and drinks. So that's what I did because I wanted everyone to meet our new friends. Their names were Matt and Jack. Everyone came over except Fred. He couldn't get over the fact that I didn't want to be with him. We all got together and played a game of spades. We had three different types of drinks. We were all having a blast until Fred walked in and started to go crazy on me. I didn't know what to do because Mike was there. I didn't want him to know what was going on between Fred and me. I took Fred into the kitchen and had a long talk with him because he was so rude for going off on me in front of company.

I finally got Fred to settle down and relax. I introduced Fred to the new guys. Things were better after that. We played cards all night. No one was ready to go home. I took Jack and Calvin outside. I wanted to introduce them to each other. Calvin was ready for love. I thought Jack would be best for Calvin. I left the two of them outside.

An hour later, Jack came into the house and told me to come outside because he and Calvin needed to talk to me. They were feeling each other, but at the same time, I wanted to have sex with the both of them. I knew it wouldn't work out. I told the two of them to follow their hearts and that everything will fall into place. I believe that is what they are going to do. They are so in love with each other. When the both of them returned to the house, we all begin to clap. Everyone was so glad to see Calvin happy. Everyone left the house except for Calvin and Jack. I told them to spend the night and get to know each other better. They agree. I was so happy for them. They are really trying to find love. Sam and I went back into the room when everyone left because we had a lot to talk about. I told Sam that I loved him. I was going to leave Tom alone for good. That is only if he wanted to be with me.

He said yes. I got on the phone to call Tom. He really needed to know what was going on between Sam and me. I told him that Sam and I are together. He didn't get mad at all because he knew something was going on between the both of us. I felt bad for only a minute. I didn't want Tom to be sad and lonely. I called Matt and told him that I had someone for him. I think it would be a good idea for him to come over and meet the guy.

When Matt came over, I had dinner with him because Tom was two hours away. I didn't want him to be waiting with nothing to eat. When Tom got to the house, Matt was acting weird because Tom and I were once lovers. I told him to be cool because it doesn't bother me. After I helped everyone find their lovers, I knew it was time for Sam and me to take a trip to enjoy ourselves. We went to Mexico for one week. It was the best week ever. I was finally with the love of my life.

When we arrived home, the two of us had sex for days straight. My body was so tired and weak. Sam drained me. I couldn't do anything but sleep. I was so in love with Sam.

When everyone got to the house, we all sat in the living room and talked about what happened at the club. Calvin had to leave a little early because his job called him to work. Jack decided to stay because of the drive. He didn't want to travel alone. When Calvin left the house for work, the three of us decided to have some fun. Sam and I had a wonderful time playing with Jack. He knew how to suck a dick and how to make love. We had sex with Jack until the early morning. It was wonderful. We didn't want to stop fucking him, but we did because we knew he couldn't take it anymore. When Sam and I finished fucking Jack, he went into the bathroom and showered. Jack had a long night with the two of us.

A week later, everyone came over to have a lover's sit down talk, which I thought was nice because we never did anything like it. Everyone got along very well. At the end of the sit-down talk, we all took a night out on the town and partied like the rock stars we are until Fred started to fuss about Mike drinking too much. Mike tried to fight everyone because he didn't want us to help or talk to him about his drinking too much.

Hours into the night, Mike broke down and came to me because he wanted to talk about his problem. As we started to talk, everyone started to come around because they wanted to be there for him. We all left the club in one piece, which I couldn't believe because Mike was acting so crazy about people trying to help him. He gets better in the end. Everyone went their own way except for Calvin and Jack. They didn't feel like driving back home. We invited them over for the night.

Lust, Lies & Love

Jack got up the next morning for work. So Sam and I had breakfast. Matt and Tom came over to the house to check up on us and to see how Jack was doing. I went into the kitchen to go and get Jack. When the five of us got into the living room and took our seats, things began to get weird. Tom wanted to know did I ever love him and asked why I let the relationship go. I told him that I didn't love him anymore.

It was time for me to move on. He had this look on his face like what the hell did you say. Tom was very understanding. That's what I loved about him. I am always going to care about him because I knew that he was always there for me no matter how I treated him. He didn't want to be with someone else. Tom didn't seem to get it. I tried many times to leave him, but he didn't want me to go. He always told me that we were in this thing for good. I will always love Tom. Now it is time for me to be happy and move on.

Lust, Lies & Love

Chapter 1

Calvin and Jack were both from Atlanta, Georgia. They have three wonderful kids. Calvin was an army man. Jack was a singer. Their relationship was very weird. Jack invited a couple of the guys over to their home. They wanted to have a sit-down dinner. We started to sit down at the table and talk about our lives. As we began to talk, there was a knock at the door. Jack got up from the dinner table and went to answer the door.

It was Sam. I was so happy to see him because he's been gone for about two months. I couldn't believe he came to the dinner party. Jack was a wonderful singer. I wanted the guys to hear him sing. I asked Jack would he perform for everyone. He said yes. When Jack begins singing, tears started to run down many faces. His voice was powerful, sexy and amazing. They guys didn't know that Jack could sing. They were so amazed. When he finished singing, we all got ready to hit up the town.

Calvin and Jack paid for everything at the bar. We all went back to the house. I notice Calvin was flirting with Sam. That rubbed me the wrong way. I asked a couple of the guys to come outside with me. I couldn't believe Calvin would do anything like that. I informed the guys what was going on. They told me not to worry because Sam loved me. I was a lot better after they told me that. I still wanted to kill Calvin because he tried me the wrong way. After I got over everything, we all went back into the house. Jack and I gave everyone a hug because it was time for us to leave. We got back on the bus. Jack went to lie down and went to sleep. I put a blanket over him. He had a long night. I wanted him to enjoy his sleep.

The next day we arrived in Miami, Florida, which was the next tour city. It was so many people at the hotel to greet Jack. The fans were going crazy. We couldn't believe it because Jack hasn't been in the music business that long. Everyone went to the hotel after the meet and greet. The hotel rooms were lovely and amazing.

Lust, Lies & Love

Whenever Jack and I were settled, I called Sam to see how things have been going. He said okay and that he really missed me. I can tell in his voice that he was sad and ready for me to come home. I wanted to cry because I was missing my better half.

Before we got off the phone, Sam told me that he loves me and to take care. I thought that was so sweet. Jack was sitting on the edge of the bed looking crazy. Why I don't know. I took it upon myself to go into the bath. He needed to release some stress. I put candles all over the bathroom before letting Jack enter. I had the bathroom lit up with candles and rose petals. Jack finally went into the bathroom. He was so shocked because he never thought I would do something like this for him. He deserves it. We took a nice bubble bath. I had more in store for Jack.

When Jack got out of the bathtub, I put rose petals all over the bed. In the middle of the bed were a bottle of wine, a plate of strawberries, and a can of whipped cream. I laid Jack down softly onto the bed and started licking him from his toes. I stopped at his dick. I sprayed the whipped cream all over his dick then licking it off with my tongue. I went up to his lips and started kissing him with strawberries tasting the juice all down my throat.

Those lips had me stuck. I later turned him over onto his back and began to lick him up and down. I worked my way down to his ass which was so sweet. I opened his ass and went to work sucking his asshole, licking on his thighs, and rubbing his body. I couldn't control my lips or my tongue. I so loved it. Jack's body was so soft and smooth. I fucked his ass so gentle. Jack's ass had me, Cumming, back to back. It was hard for me to hold myself. That bitch ass had me weak as hell.

When we woke up the next morning, room service was already ordered. We only had twenty minutes to eat because we had to leave for Tampa. The driver was so sexy and good looking. I wanted to eat him up. I went to the front of the bus because I needed to talk to the driver. As we begin to talk, I notice his dick was hard. The print looked big, but I needed to see the real thing. I kept talking and talking.

My lips were dry so I licked them. Mr. Bob, the driver, asked me did I need some chapstick. I said yes. HE went into this pocket to get it, and I see his dick moving. When he took the Chap Stick out, I said thank you. I used it and gave it back. He told me to put it back into his pocket. As I was reaching into his pocket, he grabbed my hand and made me touch his dick. That's when Jack walked up. He didn't think anything of it. He was just checking up on me.

After Jack left the front of the bus, I unzipped Mr. Bob's pants because I wanted to see his dick. I took his dick out. It was huge. I had a surprised look on my face. I said to myself. What a big dick! I got on my knees and started sucking the head of his huge dick. It was so big that I couldn't go all the way down. I was rolling my tongue all around it. I was hoping he didn't wreck. Mr. Bob was shaking like crazy. Ten minutes later, he came everywhere. The poor driver had to pull over so that he could clean himself. A couple of minutes later, we started back rolling. An hour later, we arrived in Tampa, Florida.

That was the longest ride ever. The driver stopped on the side of the road to take a break. He opens the door because he heard a knock. It was Sam and Calvin who got onto the bus. They surprised the hell out of us. We didn't know they were coming. We were so happy to see them. It had been a while since we've seen them. The tour was taking a lot out of us. We needed the love. The four of us really enjoyed each other. We couldn't spend that much time with Sam and Calvin because Jack had to perform within a couple of hours. Sam and Calvin came to the show. They had first class seats which was the best. Jack's song meant so much to him. He was so proud of Jack. What a job well done.

After the show, we all went back to the hotel. Management wanted to talk with Jack and me. They thought it would be a good idea for the both of us to move to LA. We wanted to know why. Jack's agent said it would be good for him. He wanted Jack's career to blow up. Jack said yes. I didn't have a choice, but to say yes. This was something that I loved.

After we left the conference room, I didn't know how to tell Sam about the move to LA. I got Jack to tell him because I didn't know how he was going to take it. Calvin was so happy with the move. I was hoping Sam was going to be okay with it as well. The change would be great. He wasn't happy. He just started working again and didn't want to start all over. I took Sam off to the side and talked with him.

Later that night, Sam told me that he thought about what I said. He wanted the best for the both of us. Sam thought it was a blessing that Jack and I were asked to move to LA because he knows things would work out for the better. I didn't think yes was going to be the answer.

That night we all got together to celebrate. The club was calling our names. So many people were dancing, drinking and having fun. I knew we were going to have a blast. Calvin and Jack started out with two drinks. Sam and I only had one. We all went on the dance floor. Everyone was dancing like old men moving from side to side. My head started spinning. I went to sit down because I wasn't feeling well.

By the end of the night, I began to feel a lot better. Everyone was still on the dance floor. Now they were moving like drunken old men. It was so funny. When we left the club, it was around five in the morning. I was ready to go. We all went to the burger house. We needed food to help us sober up. The food wasn't good, but we needed it.

The next day, we left for LA. We thought that maybe we will have fun before we left. There was a big table in the hotel room. We started to play strip poker. It was crazy. We were drinking like crazy. Everyone wanted to lose because they all wanted to get naked. What a sex party we were about to have. Dicks were about to be slinging everywhere. I was ready for it. Sam was the first person to lose. He didn't want to win because he knew his dick was going to get sucked good. I was the first person that had to get down on all fours. That dick was big, long and fat. My mouth was dripping. I couldn't wait to put that dick in my mouth. We all stop playing poker. The guys were ready to fuck.

Before we got ready to have fun, Jack's manager called me. He wanted to make sure that we had everything ready and packed. Before the manager was finished talking, I hung up the phone so fast because I was ready to fuck and get fucked. All of the guys were sexy as hell. I wanted to fuck all of them at the same time. Calvin took out that fat dick. I went crazy. I bent over and touched my toes. Calvin put that dick deep inside me. I began to throw it back. Then he started to fuck me hard as hell.

My ass was hurting like crazy, but the dick was so good. I couldn't stop throwing this ass back on it. After Calvin doing me from the back, he told me to lie on the bed. He put my legs behind my head. My arms were behind my back. I thought I was ready. Then he put his big dick in this wet ass of mine. I was moaning like a baby. I couldn't believe my ass was wetter than the overage pussy. I was riding that dick as if it was a horse. Calvin came back to back. This wet ass was too much for him. I got on my tip toes and starting bounding up and down. That dick was losing its mind. Calvin was weak as hell. Something came over him. He started fucking me like his best friend had died. My asshole was in so much pain. I was taking that big dick. My ass felt like it was ripping. I wanted to fall out.

After Calvin finished fucking me upside down and stupid, I laid down. He wanted more sex. Sam and Jack joined Calvin for a threesome. Sam and Jack both laid on the bed naked waiting on Calvin to come into the room. Sam started eating Jack's ass from the back. Calvin finally arrives in the room and opens Jack's ass and started fucking him good.

They had a party going on. Jack was moving like a worm. Calvin was fucking Sam like the dog he was. The three of them were doing some hardcore xxx shit. Sam and Calvin were doing Jack like he was nothing. Calvin held Jack down so that Sam could fuck his insides crazy. Words could not express the look on Jack's face. I felt so sorry for him.

After they finished fucking him dumb, we only had two hours left before it was time to leave for LA. Jack could barely walk. I had to help him to the shower. He began to moan and cry because he was in so much pain. The two of them had fucked him silly.

Jack got out of the shower an hour later. Now it's about time for us to leave. As the bus was pulling up, Jack couldn't walk by himself. His agent got off the bus with a scared look on his face. He wanted to know what was wrong. We told him. He couldn't believe his ears. Jack's manager thought he was married because of the way he talked about Calvin. Jack never said Calvin's name when he talked about him around his manager or agent. He always referred to Calvin as his heart. Everyone was there for Jack.

As I was going to sleep, I couldn't stop thinking about Jack. My buddy was so out of it. I didn't like that. I wanted to take a walk around the park because my mind needed a break. After clearing my mind, I went back into the house because I needed to talk with everyone. Calvin stood up in front of everyone and told us that he had to leave for six months. The army called him. Jack was hurt because they were just starting to work on their relationship. I felt even sorrier for him now than I did when he was butt-fucked hard and made crippled. Mike and Fred asked all of the guys to help plan a party for Calvin. That's just what we did. Fred invited over three hundred people. This was way too many people for a going away party. We managed just fine.

As the party started, I notice Calvin and Jack were in the corner crying. I went to see what was going on with the two of them. They were crying because they didn't want to let each other go for six months. I told them to go into the room because we needed to talk about Calvin leaving.

When we got into the room, Jack was looking so sad. I started to hug and kiss on him. I was trying to make him feel better. I think he was getting hot because he was feeling all over himself. So I began to take off his clothes, start licking his body up and down with my tongue and blow into that sweet ass. His ass was rubbing all against my lips making my dick hard and ready.

I turned Jack over on the bed and began to play with his fat ass. That ass was wet and sweet. Jack stood over me and spread his ass open. He bent down on my face, and I fucked him with my tongue. Jack had my mind gone. Calvin was looking at Jack and I while we were having sex. He was jacking his dick and moaning out loud. I was getting turned on because the moaning sounded so nice. I couldn't stand to see Calvin in the chair jacking off so I went over to him, got on my knees and put his dick in my mouth. I felt every inch of it down my throat. He had me gasping for air. When Calvin took his dick out of my mouth, my throat felt wrong. I put his dick in my tight ass and began to ride. What a great feeling!

Calvin and Jack went into the kitchen because the guys were waiting for us to come back. I stayed in the room because I needed some rest. I woke up an hour later. By this time, everyone was getting ready to go to the airport with Jack. It was time for Calvin to leave. Jack cried all the way there and back. He didn't know what to do. I made several calls to different recording studios in the attempt to land an audition for Jack. I thought he had an amazing voice.

When we arrived at the house, I told Jack about the guys listening to him sing. He was so happy to perform for everyone. It was time for Jack to hold his own. Singing was his love and passion. Jack was very nervous to sing for the recording agent. I encouraged him to do it because I was confident that they would love him just as much as I do. So he went in to sing {what song did he sing???}.

When he was done, the agent told him that they would give him a call if they liked him. I called Calvin because I thought maybe he should know what was going on. He didn't sound like he was happy. Calvin likes all of the attention to be on him. I thought it was so rude of him. Jack has been trying to get signed for many years but hasn't had the support. I was trying to explain to Calvin that it is hard to get into the music business. I also explained to him that he should support Jack's dreams. Calvin wanted to be the man of the house. Jack wanted to put his dreams on hold because he wanted to make Calvin happy. I told him not to do it. "Live your life for you and follow your dreams." He thought about what I said and made it happen.

Lust, Lies & Love

CHAPTER 2

A couple of months later, I got a phone call. I was the recording agent. They wanted to sign Jack with their company. I couldn't believe what I was hearing. I immediately called Jack and told him to meet me at our favorite bar. He thought that something was wrong. When Jack got to the bar, he was looking so worried because he didn't see a smile on my face. I told him to sit down. "I just received a call from the recording company." His eyes got big, and he started to sweat. I started crying for him because he has been through so much. I started crying. "Why are you crying?" I replied, "I am so happy for you." The agent called me to sign YOU, not anyone else, but YOU. Jack looked at me with a blank face. He didn't know what to do or say. He was speechless.

Lust, Lies & Love

We went back to the house and called the guys to inform them of the great news. They were ecstatic as I knew they would be. I told Jack to call Calvin. Things are much better now. Calvin told Jack that he loved and realized that everything wasn't all about him. After talking with Jack, Calvin asked to speak to me. I was curious as to what he had to tell me. My mouth drops open as Calvin is telling me that he bought a house for Jack and himself. I was bawling like a baby. All of their dreams were coming true. I didn't tell Jack because I knew he was going to cry. I wanted it to be a surprise. Jack thought something was wrong.

All of the guys came over to Jack's and Calvin's place. We finished telling everyone about the music deal. They thought we were playing until we let them listen to the recording. No one could believe it. This is something Jack has been waiting for. We couldn't wait to celebrate. Calvin flew home some days later. He wanted to surprise Jack. When he arrived, Jack was so happy to see him.

As planned, Calvin surprise Jack with the house. Tears started to flow. We had a party at the house. Everyone came out to enjoy the fun. Over the loud music, I hear the telephone ring. It was the agent from the recording company. He tells me that Jack has to leave Atlanta and head to New York for a month. Calvin was hurt when he got the news. He didn't want Jack to leave, but he knew he had to. Jack left three days later. His agent was ready to start recording.

When Jack left for New York, Calvin took it very hard. He didn't want to be alone. I went over to his house because I knew he needed someone. I went to have a talk with him about Jack leaving. He couldn't do anything but cry. I began to hug him. Then I started kissing on his neck and loved all over him. His body was getting nice and hot. He wanted some good dick. I was going to give it to him. I loved that way he smelled and taste. The head of his dick was sweet. His asshole was so tight. His balls were amazing. The sweat off his body turned me on. He made my body melt. He is such a powerful man.

When Calvin went back to work, he was missing Jack like crazy. Jack called to get Calvin to come to New York. This time was different because they didn't invite any of the guys to tag along. They needed some alone time. The guys all understood of course. Reunited in New York, the Calvin and Jack went on a lovely date and did what lovers do. I was happy for the two of them.

The guys called me to plan something for those love birds. We all agreed to have a recording party for Jack when he arrives back home. The planning went very well. We invited everyone in the music business. Jack was clueless about the party. We wanted it to be a surprise. When they arrived, Calvin told me that he bought Jack a black on black Benz.

The next day it was time to party. I couldn't wait because I was ready to see the look on Jack's face. His manager and agent were also coming to the party. We blindfolded Jack and told him that we were going somewhere he always wanted to go. He was nervous. When we arrived at the venue, we took off the blindfold and surprise Jack. He was in shock.

Later that night, Calvin pulled up in the Benz that he bought for Jack. We wanted to do a grand reveal. I took Jack outside to see his gift. He started to cry. He never thought Calvin would do anything like that for him because things haven't been the best between the two of them. I was so happy for the both of them. Just when Jack thinks all of the surprises were over, the guys announce that they bought them a trip to Italy. With that jaw-dropped, mouth-opened and shocked-beyond-belief look, Calvin and Jack were at a loss for words.

When the party was over, everyone went home except for Sam and me. We stayed the night with Calvin and Jack. The four of us went into the living room for drinks. It didn't help that we were already drunk. I had to stop drinking because I was horny as hell. My dick was hard and stiff. I wanted some sweet ass. I called everyone into the room because I wanted to watch a movie. Things went from watching a movie to fucking. That was exactly what I hoped to happen. I took off Sam's clothes and started sucking his big dick. He put all of that dick down my throat. I took it out of my mouth and put it in my tight ass. Sam bent me over and started fucking me from the back. I began to run, but he held me down and fucked me insanely well. My asshole was sore and weak. I couldn't move afterward.

Calvin and Jack began to fuck after getting turned on from watching Sam and I do the do. Sam took his dick out of my ass after fucking me like a horse. Then he puts in it Calvin's and Jack's mouths. They were sucking like children with lollipops. I didn't want to take the dick out of their mouths. Slobber was running down the length of Sam's dick. Sam fucked both of them nasty. I couldn't do anything but look and enjoy. I loved it so much.

After the mini sex party, I went to sleep. We were all tired and no good. I wanted to stop having sex with all of the guys. I couldn't bring myself to do it because the sex is so good.

Jack woke everyone up the next morning. He had to leave and go back to New York. He didn't want to leave. His manager called him that morning insisting that he come to New York right away. We all took Jack to breakfast. Sam and Calvin left the breakfast shop to find Jack a gift. Jack and I decided to go back to the house. We had to take care of some unfinished business.

Jack started to kiss my lips. His lips were soft as a feather. His eyes were glossy. His tongue was longer than that of a lizard. He had my head in a black bag. The kiss was so good. I couldn't think straight at all. I held Jack in my arms, kissed him with my love and didn't want to let him go. Sam and Calvin eventually arrived at the house. They came into the bedroom and saw that we were in bed. They didn't get mad. They thought it was so sweet, but I think Calvin was a bit upset. Jack and I always had sex. It was amazing. If anyone knew how to dick me down, it was Jack. He always fucked me good when he didn't want to do Calvin. He always called me. He knew daddy ass going to give it to him good.

Calvin took Jack to the airport now that it was time for him to leave for New York. Sam and I drove back home. We had guests that would be arriving soon. I couldn't stop thinking about Jack. I knew he was in a relationship, but he meant so much to me. We had great things going, great sex, went on great trips and shared great experiences together. People always thought we were a couple. I always knew Jack wasn't happy with Calvin. He played the I LOVE YOU role in front of people. When we are together, it is the opposite. Jack wanted to be with me at one time, but I knew he wasn't going to leave Calvin. Calvin was young, dumb, and didn't mean anything to Jack. Jack was once my pride and joy.

When everyone found out about Jack and me, we had to let the friendship go. Calvin started asking too many questions about us. I never gave him a straight forward answer. We were falling in love with each other. Sam was asking me all kinds of questions because I seemed sad. I told him what was on my mind. He was like I understand. "I'm in the picture now. You cannot help who you love." I thought about what Sam said.

A couple of hours later, I got over it. Our guests finally arrived. They were some old friends from out of town. We all sat, ate and talked as old friends do. I haven't seen them in so long. I called Calvin to come over because he was acquaintances of one of the guests. I dinner was great. The wine was wonderful.

Calvin moved in with Sam and me. He didn't want to be at home alone. We were happy to have him. I knew it was going to be more dick and ass for me. I had this Cheshire cat kind of grin on my face. We allowed Calvin to have our bedroom. We wanted him to feel at home. Jack called the house. I told him about Calvin moving in with us. He thought it was a good idea.

Jack came home early. He had to prepare for a promo tour. The tour will be held overseas. Calvin was happy that Jack was home. He was only staying for two weeks. The guys wanted to make it the best two weeks ever. They had all types of events planned. We wanted to enjoy ourselves. Calvin and Jack called us every day during their trip. I wanted to know why. They were supposed to be enjoying themselves.

Jack's manager called me while he was on his trip. He informed me that the tour may not happen because the ticket sales were so low. I didn't tell Jack about the message because the manager was supposed to call me back with an update. Two days passed with no update. I called Jack's manager and asked him about it. He said that everything was good and that the tour was a go. That was what I wanted to hear.

I waited until Jack got back to give him the news. He was so thankful that everything went through. His life was about to change from this point forward. He was about to deal with fame, traveling the world and meet all kinds of people. I was praying that he was able to manage all of this on his own. At times, I think that maybe all of this is too much for him, but I knew he will make things happen.

Jack left three days after his trip. His manager called me to work as Jack's assistant. I went crazy with excitement. I started to scream. Now I can share the success with Jack. Everyone came into the room insisting that I tell them what I was screaming about. When I told them, they couldn't believe it either. Sam was elated until I told him how long the tour was going to be. It was a three-month long tour. Sam didn't want to hear it, but I could care less. I wanted the extra money. I was going to make a great assistant.

We were ready to leave for the tour. I started having second thoughts about taking the job. I didn't want Sam to leave me over it. If it is meant to happen then it will so I no longer pondered the idea. My life and career were more important than a man. I called the agent to get an objective opinion as to what I should do. He told me to do the right thing and to do what is going to make me happy. Before I could call Sam and tell him what was on my mind, he called me and told me to take the job. He knew that it would be good for me. I was looking over my life.

We left a week after the call. We were only there for three days when the guys flew over to see us. They stayed for two days. The following day, we were scheduled to be somewhere else. Jack was so scared to go on tour. He never performed in front of thousands of people.

Our first stop was in Orlando, Florida. It was over eighty thousand people at the first show. Jack began to shake and sweat. He didn't know what to do. There were so many people. Jack performed very well. I shined behind the scenes as the great assistant. Things were much harder than we thought, but we managed to pull everything through.

After the show, we did a little meet and greet. We had so many fans, and it was only the first show. We were working our way up. Jack was tired and sleepy so we went back to the tour bus. I made sure Jack took a hot bath and went to sleep. I wanted to fuck him in his sleep because he was looking so sexy. I wanted to eat him up.

A couple of days later, Calvin flew in for the last show and to take Jack back home. The tour drained Jack. He made it through like a champ, though. I was so proud of him for doing such as a great job. With taking on this big role, I was ready to go home. I was missing Sam and the guys. We haven't seen each other in a couple of months. I couldn't wait to enjoy them.

As we were leaving the tour, I got very teary eyed. I was already missing the fans, the fame and the awesome time we had on the tour. Jack was the best friend ever.

Lust, Lies & Love

CHAPTER 3

Mike and Fred moved from Atlanta, Georgia to New York. Fred was offered the position as a charge nurse at one of the largest hospitals there. When they arrived and settled in their new home, the both of them were really scared. The city was much faster and larger than they anticipated. Within a couple of weeks, they became very familiar with the city and the way things worked.

Mike and Fred invited all of the guys to New York. Everyone met up at our place before we left. When we got into the car, Calvin started acting crazy because he didn't want to go to New York. So we all told him to stop acting that way for the simple fact that Mike and Fred are looking forward to each and every one us to come and have a really great time. Jack was able to convince Calvin to take the trip.

As we boarded that plane, we all began to get nervous and frightened. We were thinking that the plane was going to crash. Whenever we made it back to land, we were relieved knowing we made it safely.

Mike and Fred had an amazing home. We all had our own room and bathroom. Everybody was going out of town. This made Jack feel bad. I decided to stay with him. I wanted everyone to have a blast.

When everyone left the house, I went into the bathroom to make Jack a hot, bubble bath. He wasn't feeling well. I helped him to walk to the bathroom and took off his clothes. He got on his knees and started sucking my dick. Thirty minutes later, I took my dick out of his wet mouth and let him lick on my musty balls.

What a nasty bitch! I made him get up and go back into the room. I smelled his body. I can't stand a stank dick bitch. His tongue smelled like shit and old milk. I wanted to beat that punk ass because of the smell. I had to sit Jack down and tell him. Dude step your game up because your balls are musty. Your ass smells like old pussy. I hate nasty ass men that don't clean themselves. That is a turn-off. Jack went into the bathroom and took a bath. Now he smells like peaches and cream.

When he got out of the bathtub, I picked him up and placed him on the edge of the table. I lifted his body up and put my dick inside him very slow. Going back and forward for about ten minutes, I wanted him to get used to it. When I felt that he was ready, I started fucking the hell out of him as punishment because he knew to be clean when I am fucking him. I had his legs around that back of his neck handcuffed together.

I wanted to punish him for being stupid. He started yelling at me. It was hurting him a lot, but I didn't care. That ass was mine for that night. I got it how I always wanted it. I shot cum all over his face and mouth. That was what I needed. His body was so weak. He showered again before the guys returned. Just when Jack was getting out of the shower, Calvin and the guys walked into the house. They were drunk as hell and needed to take a bath.

I went into the room where Sam was. He was passed out. I turned on the shower and put him in it. He was horny as hell. His dick was sticking up on hard. His nipples were hard. His body was looking good and tasty. I pushed Sam on the bed and started to suck his dick. I was sucking like it was my last. His dick was expanding in my mouth as I felt his body get weaker and weaker. He got up and told me to bend over. I did just as he demanded. He fucked me from the back as if I was a bull. He was going in harder by the minute. I couldn't feel anything but pain. He was fucking the hell out of me. He had me screaming to the top of my lungs. I took it because that's what I wanted. He had my legs feeling tired. My mind was completely gone. When we got finished doing the grown man, I couldn't do anything but sleep. The sex was amazing and powerful.

The next morning, Mike and Fred prepared breakfast for the eight of us. Since we were all together, I decided that this would be a good time to ask the guys about their night. To no surprise, they wanted to know what Jack and I did last night why they were out. I said nothing. I told them that we watched TV because Jack wasn't feeling well. They thought it was sweet that I stayed at the house with Jack. I wanted everyone to get out and have some fun. I thought it was a wonderful idea because I fucked him crazy. He loved every minute of it.

Lust, Lies & Love

Mike took us all out to dinner. Fred couldn't make it. He was on call. We dined at Jay's Steak House which was perfect. The food was great. We had a blast. As we were leaving the restaurant, Mike received a phone call from the hospital notifying him that Fred passed out during his shift. We didn't know what to do. We had to stay strong for Mike.

We made it to the hospital. The nurse was standing outside the room because Fred's body had begun to shut down. Mike started to cry. We didn't know what to do or say. We walked into his room. His body looked so bad. They had tubes all in him.

A week later, Fred started to make progress. We were so relieved and thankful. We thought he was going to die. We stayed an extra week to help Mike with Fred's care. I wanted to nurse him back to health. Two days before we were to head home, we walked around the city and had a nice dinner. Fortunately, Fred was able to join us again.

We all went back to the house because everyone was getting tired and hot. Mike and Fred wanted to prepare drinks for us. As we began to drink, I notice Fred looking at me. I turned my head acting like I didn't see him looking. I wanted to fuck him on the table while everyone watched. Mike wanted all of the guys to go out to this new club called Club Yo Yo, which we thought was a funny name. Fred didn't want to go because he wanted some of this good dick that was going around. Everyone started to get dressed except Fred. He said he wasn't feeling well.

I told Mike and the guys that I would stay with Fred. They thought that it was a wonderful idea. I couldn't wait for them to leave because I was ready for some good ass. Fred gave Mike a hug and a kiss before he left. When they got into the car and drove off. I began to kiss on Fred making him hot and horny.

He began to take off his clothes and play with himself. My dick got rock hard. He got on top of the kitchen table and put his legs up in the air. I began to push the head of my dick into his sweet hole. I ram my dick deep into his ass making his insides feel like a wreck. He started jumping on my dick as if he was a monkey. His ass was very wet. My dick was enjoying it. I put him in the buck. He started to moan. He was loving it.

After I took my dick out of his ass, I put it back in his mouth. He was sucking as if he was a baby. He didn't want to let it go. I cum in the nasty bitch's mouth and made him get up. I went to take a shower and went into the living room to watch television. Fred was still on the kitchen table moaning and playing with his ass. He wanted more dick. I went back and gave him more. He took it like a pro. I loved it even more the second time around.

By the time everyone got back from the club, the both of us was asleep. That ass put me to sleep. This dick knocked him straight out as well. We all got up the next morning and went home. Fred was feeling a lot better. I was glad to see a good recovery. It could have been worse, but everything went well.

As we were leaving to go back home, Mike and Fred began to cry because we have so much fun. They couldn't believe everyone came to see them. Fred went back to work three weeks after we left. Mike was so glad to see Fred doing better. I got a phone call from Fred asking me to come back to New York for three days and to not tell Sam. He didn't want Sam to know because he wanted me to come alone. I didn't make the trip because Sam was going out of town for three weeks for work. He wanted me to go with him. I couldn't say no to the love of my life. Fred didn't get mad because he is very understanding. I wanted to hook up with Fred because his dick was ready.

Lust, Lies & Love

I knew that ass was on deck. I didn't sweat it because I knew round three was coming very soon. His ass is so wonderful. That mouth is even more amazing.

After Sam and I arrived home from our trip, Mike and Fred called because they wanted to come and visit. We were happy to have them. Sam went to pick up the both of them from the airport. When they got to the house, the two of them went straight to sleep. The flight had them tired. Sam had dinner waiting because we knew they wanted something good to eat. Mike and Fred woke up and were ready to eat. We all caught up on good times because we haven't seen them since we left New York. Mike took the four of us to this local store that sells movies, sex toys, and games. It was very weird because Sam and I had never been in a store like that. The things we saw were crazy. Mike and Fred bought a lot of sex toys. I already knew they were freaks. I wanted to use the toys on them at the same time.

As we were leaving the store, Mike received the call of his life. It was a call from the Hospital which employs Sam offering him the position he so desired as the Director of Nursing. We were so happy for him because this was something he always wanted. I took everyone out to celebrate. Mike got so wasted that he didn't remember getting the job. Fred picked up Mike and put him in the car.

When we arrived at the house, Fred put Mike straight into bed because he was so drunk and out of it. Things almost got out of hand. Fred was mad at everyone. I couldn't believe it. I attempted to keep Mike from drinking so much, but he wanted to celebrate his new position. After everyone sat down and talked with Fred, he understood what we were talking about. Mike sobered up the next morning and began to laugh because he didn't remember a thing that he did or said the night before. We thought it was funny and crazy. We all were so proud of Mike and Fred.

I didn't want to go back home because of the love they shared and how they treated everyone. They came a long way. They were about to break up because Mike wanted to have a threesome for his birthday. Fred wasn't having it at all. Fred was really upset because he couldn't believe Mike would ask him something like that knowing that they were trying to fix their relationship. Mike called and informed me about the threesome. I loved the idea. I told him to make Fred happy and not to upset him.

Lust, Lies & Love

Two hours later, Mike called me because he had something very important to tell me. When he started telling me what was going on, I realized that he wanted me. He said that he wanted to come in my room on a lonely night and put rose petals all over me starting from my head working his way down to my feet making me feel like a real man. He wanted to put whipped cream on my dick and balls, lick my balls and wrap his tongue around my dick. He is such as nasty freak. I was loving Mike at that moment because I knew it was going to be nice.

Minutes later, Fred was calling because he was so upset with Mike about the threesome. I told Fred that it would be perfect and that I will be the third person. His face lit up with a very big smile. He wanted some more of this big dick. I took a flight to New York some days later to share my love with Mike and Fred. That was what they wanted and needed.

When I arrived in New York, we went straight to the house making no detours. I went to the bedroom and lay on the bed. Mike and Fred came into the room, pulled down my pants and started to suck daddy's dick. Fred moved Mike out of the way and started riding my fat dick. I was in happy land. I threw my dick into Fred's tight ass. When I took it out, Mike put it into his mouth and rolled his soft, wet and thick tongue around it. My eyes were rolling into the back of my head. I couldn't do anything, but lay there. It felt so good. I put some strawberry juice between Mike's ass and licked it out. I didn't want to stop licking. I made his body weak and loose. He was speechless. This tongue had him going crazy. Fred was getting very hot as I was licking Mike's ass. I told him to bend over so that I could cuff his hands to his ankles and fuck him until he couldn't be fucked anymore. He told me to fuck him hard. I found that very funny. I put it in and started fucking him. It was so hard. He was yelling and crying because it hurt so badly.

I hit him across the ass and told him to take it. You're a man. You should be able to take the pain. He was such as bitch. His body began to fall and rock. He started to bleed so I stopped and shook my head. The little bitch couldn't take pain or dick. I un-cuffed him and helped him put into the shower. He needed the shower badly. Mike was tired and sleepy because I ate and fucked that ass so good.

When Fred took as shower, I left New York and went back to Atlanta. Sam was coming home in two days. I needed to be there. Mike and

Lust, Lies & Love

Fred call me the next day and thanked me for coming to New York. We had a blast. I was ready to get back home. I was missing Sam so much. I knew daddy was missing his little, sweetheart. Mike and Fred got married on Mike's birthday, which I thought was very nice. I was so amazed when the both of them called and asked me to be the best man. I thought my ears were playing tricks on me, but they weren't. The honeymoon took place in Spain. They stayed for two weeks. The city was so beautiful. Sam didn't go because of work. I really wanted him to come and join the fun with us.

When I got back to the States, Fred bought them a house and a new car. Mike was in shock. He couldn't say anything for ten minutes. After the awe-struck silence, he thanked his hubby and told him that he loved him. That is what you call real love. I stayed in the new house for three days. I had to return home because my baby was on his way back. I wanted to tell him all about the wedding and the trip. I made it back home safely when Mike called. He was telling me how he couldn't believe what happened. I was happy for the both of them and how things was going. This is what you call true friends.

Lust, Lies & Love

Even though I fucked the both of them, I had to admit that I was lonely. We all became closer after the marriage. We started to understand each other more. We meant more to each other. They will always be my friends. I almost lost Sam because he always thought that Mike and I had something going on.

Although his suspicions were true, that doesn't change the way that I feel about him. I always told him that nothing was going on and that I was in love with him and only him. He meant the world to me. I also had to make me happy and do me because I wasn't always happy. Whenever Mike and Fred came into my life, things got so much better for me. They gave me the world and more. I wanted to let the sex go between the three of us because they were married. I knew it wasn't right. I am going to miss the sex, but I needed to let it go. I called Mike and Fred to tell them about the sex thing. They were ok with it but didn't understand why because they thought we were going to continue to make each other happy. I thought about it hard and called them back. I didn't want them to be mad. I invited them over later that night.

When they arrived, I was sitting on the couch naked as a Jay bird. Mike came over and sat beside me. Fred was standing up with his dick on hard. I knew it was about to go down. My dick was hard as fuck. I was ready to put it in Mike's mouth. Fred came over and started sucking my dick. He was deep-throating my dick like a real bitch. I took my dick out of Fred's mouth and stuck it in Mike's ass. That ass was so tight and soft. Mike had me shaking like a fucking baby. His ass was so good and wet. Since they were married, I was going to nasty fuck them.

Fred had to leave early because his job called him. He didn't want to leave because he knew things were about to get hot. After Fred left the house, I undressed Mike. I started licking up his thighs and working my way to his lips. I sucked on his thighs until his body began to shake. I played with the head of his dick and began to make love to him. His body began to fold. Mike's ass was the best ever. Mike had me cumming as if I was running well. He took all of my cum and more down his deep throat. I was really enjoying him.

After we finished making love, the two of us took a shower. We decided to go to a party. I knew it was going to be a sexy party. People only had on underwear. I was ready to fuck something. My dick was getting hard. I was ready to use it. The ass was everywhere. I started walking around because I wanted to meet new people. They were all nice and freaky. I knew it was time to party. I went into this room where people were sucking and fucking. I had to join. I pulled this guy out of this threesome and pulled out my dick. He began to suck my dick. His mouth was so wet. His body was soft as a baby's. I had to fuck him. I took my dick out of his mouth and eased it into his ass. His ass was tight and pretty.

Dude had my mind gone. He rode my dick so good. I couldn't do anything, but lay there. His ass was off the chain. I took my dick out and started slapping him across the face. He was loving it. I fucked the young man really good. He didn't want me to leave, but I had to go. Mike was in the main party room with everyone else. Mike was having a blast. He was also horny as fuck. That was exactly how I wanted him to be.

We left the party and went back to my place. Sam was sitting on the couch looking sexy as fuck. I jumped onto my baby's lap and started to bounce up and down. His dick was hard as fuck. I got off of him. We all went into the dining area for dinner. My baby cooked an amazing meal. The wine was a great choice. The three of us sat around the dinner table and talked about our lives. I really didn't say anything about my life because I was so stuck in between the two. I had a lover and a friend. Sam loved Mike and Fred. He just didn't like that was going on with Mike and me. Mike had the best ass ever. I couldn't let it go. Fred was cool with our fucking around.

After everyone left the house, Mike and Fred went to the Florida Keys to take a break from everything and everyone. We all thought that was a good thing. Three days later, Mike and Fred called Tom and me because they were thinking about moving to the Keys as well. I didn't want it to happen because they would be far from us. I knew they had to do whatever to make them happy.

I called all of the guys and told them. They weren't all that happy. We all understood why they wanted to make that move. Fred got a better job. He really needed the extra money. I got over it. Mike and Fred had a lot going on in their lives. Their marriage was open. Mike did whatever and whoever. Fred stuck it out because he wanted his marriage to work. I felt sorry for Fred at times. Mike was faithful when he wanted to be. Fred was still there knowing what was going on.

A week later, Mike called me because he wanted all of the guys to come to the Florida Keys. I was ready. I called the guys up. They were happy. We all met in Atlanta and headed to the Keys. I knew we were going to have a sexy party. I haven't had good ass in so long. I Knew Mike had it.

We arrive in the Keys. Mike and Fred were at the airport. I was so happy to see them. When we got to their beach house, they had the dinner table loaded with food and fruit. Everything was prepared and ready to eat. After everyone finished eating and drinking, they took us on a tour of their home. It was something out of a fairytale. The view of the beach front was amazing. There was sand everywhere. They had their own private beach. We were having a blast. We had dinner on the beach which I thought was lovely. The sun was about to set. I was ready for some midnight ass.

Mike and Tom had on a pair of boy shorts looking right as ever. I wanted to fuck the both of them. I left the beach and went back into the house. Mike came into the house to get some extra towels. His body was looking sweet. I had to have it. I called Mike into the bathroom and told him to help me zip my pants down because the zipper wouldn't come down. He got on his knees and fixed the zipper.

My dick came out of my pants. He went to work on it pulling on my dick with those soft and silky lips. I was getting weak as fuck. I got Mike up and told him to sit on my face. That ass was so soft. I put my tongue in his tight asshole. He began to ride my face. Mike's ass was so good. He got up and lay on the bed. I watch him finger fuck his ass for about five minutes.

I couldn't take it anymore. I know it was time for me to fuck the hell out of him. I put whipped cream all over his body. I started licking him with the tip of my tongue and made his body feel good. Sweat was dripping from everywhere. He couldn't stop moaning. I was fucking the stupid bitch so smooth and gently. He couldn't get enough of this good dick. His toes began to curl. His body folded. I Knew I was fucking that punk bitch good. My dick was feeling so lovely.

After we finished having sex, I sent Mike back outside because he was supposed to bring everyone towels. When he got up, his body began to shake. Mike was so weak. Everyone wanted to know what took so long when he finally made it outside. He told them that he had to find them. Fred was like I should have told you. They were upstairs in the back closet. I made it outside. The guys were drunk and horny. I was ready to fuck whoever. We all went back into the house and started taking our clothes off. All of the dicks were big.

Calvin came where I was and started sucking my stank dick. I didn't shower after I fucked Mike. I let him suck it. Slob was dripping so badly. I made him eat my sweaty ass. His tongue had me going crazy. I didn't feel bad about letting him suck a dirty dick. He wanted it so I gave it to him. When I put my dick into Calvin's tight ass, his body began to fold. I fucked him as if he was nothing. The bitch needed to learn.

When it was time for me to cum, I put it all down his nasty throat. I didn't care about him. I just wanted a nut. Tom watched me fuck Calvin. He was cool with it because that was the type of person he is. I got Mike and Fred to run the train on Tom. They fucked him so good. His asshole was jumping like crazy. His body couldn't stay still. I told them to fuck him as if they didn't know him. That is exactly what they did. He was so sore and could barely move.

When they finished, I Knew it was my turn. Tom told me that he couldn't go another round. I took my dick out and put it in his mouth. He sucked on it for about ten minutes. Later, I put his legs behind his neck and started eating the hell out of him. He couldn't do anything, but moan.

My tongue was so powerful. He was shaking so badly. When I got ready to put my dick in his ass, he was like he couldn't take anymore. I put it in any way and fucked him like a dog. He was crying. I started to fuck him harder. I didn't care how his body felt. I wanted me some ass. That's what I got. When Tom got out of the bed to go to the bathroom, he fell down. His body was tired and weak. I felt like he didn't enjoy my sex when he fell down so I put him back on the bed and fucked him until he couldn't move. I got off of him and went to sleep.

The next morning we all got up. Tom was still asleep. I started jacking my dick and came all over his face. He woke up with the white face. I couldn't do anything but laugh because I knew he was entirely too weak to wash his face. He walked into the kitchen. Everyone started looking crazy. I told them that it was dried soap. Tom said sure. "You know what it is." I wiped it off of his face because it was time for us to leave the Florida Keys and head back home. Mike and Fred didn't want us to leave because we were having so much fun. I really enjoyed myself. They treated everyone with respect. The both of them mean so much to us. Whenever we needed anyone to talk to they were always there. We love these guys so much.

Now it's time for everyone to go home and get back to their lives. I hope Mike and Fred enjoyed the Florida Keys and stay there. The both of them believe in moving. They are so nice and amazing. I can't wait to visit them again. I'm really going to miss them. Everyone started crying when it was time for us to leave. We are really true friends that mean so much to each other. Those guys are the very best.

Matt and Tom were two of the most amazing people I ever met. Tom is a teacher. Matt is a real estate agent. Both of their jobs are based out of Atlanta, Georgia. Matt has two wonderful children. Tom stopped working as a teacher because he wasn't making enough money. Eventually, he went into the porn business. Teaching wasn't getting it. He had to do something that was going to bring the money home. Matt didn't approve of the new job change. Matt called me so we could go to Tom's first show.

As I was getting dressed, my phone began to ring. I looked at the caller ID and noticed it was Tom. When I answered the phone, Tom proceeded to invite me to the show. Matt arrived at the house to pick me up. Before we could leave, Matt pushed me on the bed and started to pull down my clothes. I tried to push him away because I didn't want to be late for the show. I wanted some of that mouth and ass, but I knew we had to be somewhere. I stopped pushing Matt away and let him put that warm mouth on this dick.

He had this dick hard and wet. I put him on the floor, tied his legs behind his head and fucked him crazy. I had that wet ass talking back. That throat was so deep. He couldn't take all of this dick. I fucked him only with the head of my dick because he kept running when I tried to push the whole thing in. I tied his body down with a couple of ropes and fucked him stupid. His body was shaking like he was on drugs. I was loving that ass and mouth. He knew how to use the both of them.

CHAPTER 4

After I finished fucking that horny bitch, we both took a shower and left. When we arrived at the club, we didn't get out at the same time because Matt was too sore. I wasn't going to help him out. Tom did a wonderful job. The three of us went out for a late night snack. We all enjoyed ourselves. When we got back to Matt and Tom's place, I was ready to get into the bed and crash. They wanted to talk about the show and our plans for the next day. As they began to talk, I started getting horny. I took my dick out and put it in Matt's mouth. He was sucking it like dick was going out of business. I took my dick out of Matt's mouth and put it in his ass.

As I was hitting him from the back, I noticed a strange smell. It smelled like shit and musty balls. I took my dick out of his nasty, low down, simple-minded bitch's ass and told him to go and take a bath. I don't like fucking nasty niggas. Tom was so upset. He already knew I don't like nasty ass. Tom made it up by getting up on the table, placing his body on the edge of it and spreading those left to the max. I took my time putting this dick in his soft ass. He started to moan. It made my dick get even harder. I start slapping him across the ass. "Whose ass is this bitch," I said through clenched teeth. "Mmmmmm. This is daddy's ass." Tom said between moans. I took my dick out of his ass. Tom wanted more of daddy's dick so I put it in his mouth and fucked his mouth until I had to cum. He swallowed my large load.

After Matt finished getting himself together, we all went out for breakfast. I couldn't stay with them too much longer because I had to return home. I arrived home and got settled. I began missing the guys a lot. They were so nice. Tom didn't stay in the porn business. Things started to get very dangerous. Matt was so glad that Tom didn't stay in the business. Six months later, he went back to teaching.

Real estate wasn't going well for Matt. He didn't know what to do because they just bought a house. When Tom told me about

Lust, Lies & Love

Matt's job and about everything else that was going on, I called to chat with my good friend, Lee. Lee has been in real estate for about twenty years. I knew he could help Matt. I told Matt where to meet Lee. After their meeting, Matt called wanting to thank me for helping him out. Things started to get a lot better. Lee helped Matt sell three houses that went for 3.5 million dollars apiece. I was happy for him, but naturally things started to get a little crazy. Matt started to get the big head.

Tom had to remind him that without the help of Lee and me, he would still be struggling. I thought things were getting better for them. Matt eventually had to sell his house for a bigger one. The kids had to move in. I called some of the guys up because Matt and Tom had so much going on. I thought they could help cheer him up. We went out to the club and drama came our way.

One of Matt's ex-boyfriends happened to be there. We didn't know it until Matt introduced him to everyone. Tom was very upset because Matt got up from the table. All of the guys had to calm Tom down. He was about to fight Matt and the ex-boyfriend. We got up and left the club. It was just too much. We left Matt with his ex and went to the house. Tom was still upset. It was so hard to talk with Tom about Matt.

Matt didn't come home until the next day. Things got out of control. The ex came into the house with Matt. Tom asked Matt what was going on with him and his ex. Matt told him that nothing was going on and that they were just good friends. I didn't believe it. I felt very sorry for Tom because I knew Matt cheated on him. I pulled the ex aside because I wanted to know what was going on with him and Matt. He told me that they were only friends and that he still has feelings for Matt. When I heard that, I knew that love was still there.

After we finished talking, I started to worry about Matt and Tom's relationship. They haven't been together that long. I couldn't stop thinking about the conversation that I had with the ex earlier. I called Matt to clear things up. He thought it was a great idea to meet at his place. When I arrived at Matt's place, the ex introduces himself as Mark. He cooked a very nice dinner. The wine was tasteful. As we ate and drank, Mark started to pour his heart out about Matt telling me that his feelings have always been there. He admits that he is in love with him. I was so shocked because I didn't know he felt that way about Matt. He began to cry. The poor thing didn't know how to handle the situation.

I knew Mark was hurt. I began to rub Mark's hand and gave him a kiss hoping he would feel better. Instead, things got heated. Mark started kissing me from head to toe stopping at my dick. He was sucking on it with his waterfall mouth. He had my body shaking. Then he began to suck on my balls. I was enjoying it. I bent him over and started to play in his ass with my thick, long, lizard-like tongue. His ass was sweet and tasty. I took my time eating that ass. I love the way ass taste and smell. It gets me so hot and horny. I love when the sweet juice starts dripping from everywhere.

I picked Mark up into the air and started fucking him upside down. His ass was moving like water. His legs were shaking like a dangling flower. My dick was feeling like a king. I put him down so he could ride my dick. He is such a young freak. I laid him down and made real love to him. I took my time by licking his body, sucking on his soft feet and loving his wet booty. We made awesome love. I didn't feel bad about having sex with Mark. He was already in a relationship and so was

Matt. He understood that he needed to move on and let Matt enjoy his life with Tom.

After everything was over and done, Matt and Tom went on vacation. They went to China for two weeks. I thought they needed a break. They had so much going on. I heard from them after the first of being there. They were having a blast. Tom called me because he thought it would be a good idea for all of the guys to come visit China. Everyone was ready to go and party.

When we made ground, Jack got a phone call from his job saying that he was needed at work. Calvin stayed in China. Jack left the next day. Matt and Tom had everyone spoiled. They bought us whatever we wanted and put us in one of the most expensive hotels. The six of us went out on the town. Words couldn't express how nice it was. We didn't stay out late because we wanted to enjoy one another. Tom started to cook dinner as everyone else stayed in the living area. He called everyone into the kitchen for dinner. It was really good. We drank shots of patron. We were beyond wasted. Matt told everyone to come into the bedroom. I knew it was about to go down.

Four of the guys were taking their clothes off. Calvin unzips his pants and puts his dick in my face. I wanted to throw up. His ass smelled like raw meat. His body looked like a hot mess. He kept asking me can he suck my dick. I didn't want to say yes because I needed to take a shower knowing my dick was musty. My balls were stank. This musty dick was all in his mouth and ass. I had to tell Calvin to deep throat this musty dick. I told him to let me feel the back of your throat. "Let my dick juice flow all in your mouth," I told him as I was about to bust a nut. The other guys sat back and watched. A couple of them were playing with each other. I thought it was hot and sexy.

Since Matt and Tom were good to us, I wanted to give them some of this good dick. That's exactly what I did. I laid down on the bed while Tom climbed on top of me. I placed his ass on my face. I open up his butt cheeks and put my tongue all in it. He had a really wet ass. I couldn't stop eating it. I wanted to drain his ass. After Tom got off my face, I bent him over and started eating him from the back. My lips were getting weak, but my tongue was getting stronger. Those thighs were soft and sweet. His toes made my tongue fold. I taste every part of his body.

I approached Matt. I got on my knees, pulled down his zipper and put his dick on my lips.

Lust, Lies & Love

The thickness of it felt so wonderful. The movement was great. I got on the head of his dick and bounced up and down. It hurt like hell. The head of his dick was so big, but I still enjoyed it. Matt was fucking the hell out of me. He had my ass so wet. I didn't want to let that dick go. He really knew how to make a man feel good. The three of us went to sleep after having wonderful sex.

When we all woke up the next morning, the other guys cooked breakfast. We packed put clothing and left China. Matt and Tom left the following week. I got back home and was so upset. I didn't want to leave China nor did I want to leave Matt and Tom. Matt's job started to pick up. Tom got a raise. The kids were happy to be living with them. Whenever Tom and Matt made it back to the States, they were happier than ever. Matt meant so much to Tom and the kids. He thought that he couldn't make it through without them. Everyone planned a surprise birthday party for Tom.

Matt had a total of five strippers and one human birthday cake. The party was so nice, but Tom didn't seem to be happy. One of the strippers happened to be Mark, Matt's ex. I told Tom not to be upset. Mark works for the contracting company who hired strippers for the party. As the party went along, Tom started to feel a lot better. We had a long talk during the party. All of the strippers came up to me and began to dance all over me. My body began to get hot. I took the underwear off one of them and started to play with his dick. I rubbed my lips across his dick, licked his balls and sucked the head of his dick. He threw me on the stage. He got on top of me and started grinding on me.

My dick got hard as fuck. I wanted to push that bitch nigga off of me and fuck him to death. He got on the pole and put his fingers in his ass. He was moaning like a baby. I took those same fingers that were in his fat ass and sucked them. Then I licked his sweet and tight hole. I had that nigga's body weak as hell. We were fucking in front of everyone. Sam wasn't mad at all.

When we returned to the house, Matt and Tom couldn't believe their eyes. They never knew that I had it in me to have sex with a stripper at a club. Everyone was talking about it, but I didn't get mad because I love sex. If I want it, then I am going to get it. I told Matt and Tom that I was sorry for having sex in public. They forgave me. I went back home the next day. I had to take care of home and work. Matt and

Lust, Lies & Love

Tom let the other guys stay a couple more days. Tom sent me flowers for being a good friend. The real estate business began to fall. Matt didn't know what to do. He just sold three homes over 3.5 million for each. He was confused. He didn't know where things went wrong. Tom call me crying and sad. They just bought a home. I told Tom to tell Matt to leave the firm and to join my friend's firm. He wanted the best for his family so that's what he did.

Four months later, things began to get better. I was back happy for them. Tom always talked about these suppose-to-be friends. You never see them. You only hear from them. I think they were considered more as the downfall of friends. Whenever Matt and Tom was going through, you never hear from them. I thought it was a little weird. I always told Matt and Tom to choose their friends wisely. Everybody isn't your friend. The both of them thought about what I said.

Tom called me the next day crying because it was so hard for him to let his suppose to be friends go, but he had to do it in order to better his life and his relationship with Tom. Tom arranged a small social gathering for Matt because Matt changed jobs. Things were getting better now. Matt and Tom stopped going on trips and having social parties. The kids were getting older. They were trying to save money. They never know when things were going to go sour. I think it was for the best. They guys started a group club. We put money in his jar every month. Whenever we reach our goal, we will surprise Matt and Tom.

We all went on a trip. The trip took Matt and Tom by surprise because they have always wanted to go to Spain. That's where we went. The both of them began to cry. They have been through a lot. We wanted to help them. The kids didn't come because of school. They guys and I only stayed for three days.

We wanted them to enjoy the rest of the week. They didn't want us to leave. Tom was trying to get a teaching job in Spain. They made more money, and the schools were better. Real estate makes a lot of money in Spain. The cost of living was also cheaper. They called the other guys for their opinions. They wanted them to move because things will be better for the both of them. Neither one wanted to leave us. We all thought it would be best for them to move on with their lives.

Whenever they got to the States, we all had a blast. Sam and I threw one of the biggest going away parties. We invited two hundred plus people. They were shocked. We had everything they wanted to eat and drink. We got wasted. Their party was perfect.

An hour later, I began to get sleepy. Matt and Tom told me to go and lie in their bed. I got out of the bed and went to take a shower. My body was hot because of the drinks. After I got out the shower, I decided to lie back down. I didn't have on any clothes. Tom came into the room and saw me without any clothes. He began to rub my body down with baby oil. He started blowing all over my body making me horny. My dick was getting hard. My ass began to get wet. He demanded me to play in my ass. The feeling was wet and nice. I was making myself weak.

Matt came into the room and saw Tom rubbing me down. He took my fingers out of my ass and started to tongue fuck me. It felt so good. I couldn't move my body if I wanted to. Tom put his dick inside my mouth. Matt put his big dick in my ass. The both of them fucked my crazy. My ass was pounding. My mouth was hurting. I took those dicks like a pro. Matt fucked me so hard. I couldn't move or talk because I was in so much pain. After Matt took his big dick out my ass, he began to suck on my sore asshole. Those lips were soft and lovely. I didn't want him to stop. We all went into the shower then. I dropped down to my knees and started sucking both of their dicks at the same time. They had me choking. My eyes were filled with water. After I took their dicks out of my mouth, I went to bed. I couldn't take any more dick. The two of them fucked me so good that I wanted more, but Calvin couldn't take it.

We all got up the next morning and went to breakfast. Matt's and Tom's emotions started to flow. They were sad about leaving. I didn't want them to go, but I knew they had to go. All of the guys went out to dinner before they left. We threw them a going away dinner. The dinner went very well. Everyone was crying tears of love. I think we were the best social circle of friends. You couldn't get it better than us. We all drove out to the airport. Everyone wanted to say goodbye. Matt and Tom got on the plan with tears in their eyes. Those were tears of we-will-miss-you-all-and-we-love-you tears.

Two weeks later. They call saying that everything was going well with the kids and them. I was proud of them. They went from the top to the bottom. With the help of the guys and me, they are back on the top.

Two months later, Matt and Tom had to leave Spain. They were moving to Paris. Tom got a teaching job that paid ten thousand more than he was already making. The four of them didn't want to move, but the money was sounding so good. Tom left the family a week early to find a place to live and to start work. Matt stayed behind. He took on the responsibility of selling the house. They needed the extra money.

Two weeks before Matt got ready to leave, someone bought the house. That made things even better. Tom loved his new job because the pay was more. Matt started his own real estate business. He sold four houses in two weeks while living in Paris. A couple of them were thinking about buying a vacation home. Sam and I were also thinking about it, but we didn't know what to do. By the time I called the guys to inform them about the trip to Paris, they were already packed and ready to go. I couldn't believe it because we always have had that slow one in the group. I was the slow one on this trip. Sam was about to join us. We were so happy. Matt and Tom sent a limo for us. When we arrived at the airport and go out the car, I noticed that Sam wasn't with us. I open the car door. He was asleep. I woke him up. I didn't want my baby to get left.

We all went to sleep on the plane because we had a long day. Tom was at the airport to pick us up because Matt was at work. Paris was so beautiful. Words could not express how beautiful it is. Matt and Tom had a seven bedroom, six bathroom house. I wanted the house for myself. When I got into the kitchen, there was a personal chef cooking dinner. The aroma of the food he was preparing tickled my nose. The chef let me sample the meal he was preparing for dinner. The people who lived across the street came over for dinner. It was a family of four. I didn't get them at all. I can say they were very respectful and nice.

As we were sitting at the table, the wife began to sing and dance. I thought she was a little crazy, but everyone else enjoyed it. She told us to call her Mrs. Cee. She was the Queen of the Nile. The guys started to look at each other crazy. Everyone started talking. Mrs. Cee wanted to talk to Sam about her husband. She began to tell him that she had a strange feeling and that she was not pleased with it. She believed that her husband is bi-sexual. She insisted that she would get a divorce if this is true. She expressed how she could not live with the thought of him being with another man. Sam began talking more seriously with her. She began to cry. He heart never lied.

Sam pulled her husband away from the other guys. The three of them went into the living room. Sam started telling Mrs. Cee's husband, David, what she was telling him. David couldn't say anything. Without judgment, Sam sincerely encourages him to talk to his wife about the issue because it's really hurting her not knowing of his sexual preferences. He agreed to tell his wife whatever she would like to know. Mrs. Cee apprehensively approaches David very closely with tears in her eyes.

"Are you bi-sexual or not?" She asked quietly looking down at her fingers.

"I don't want to hurt you, but yes I am," He replies with a big sigh. "I've been this way for about five years."

Mrs. Cee turns toward me and asks. "Do you know of a divorce lawyer? If you do, I need to know how soon we can start filling out the paperwork."

David's mouth drops open as he heard the words come out of his wife's mouth. He couldn't believe his ears. "Honey, I am so sorry. I should have told you before we got married."

He regained composure instantly, furrowed his brow and pointed down at her. "I am not leaving my marriage or my family. Make whatever arrangements you have to, but I'm not going anywhere. This marriage is going to work. You will give me another chance." He said as if trying to instill fear into Mrs. Cee.

David's massive voice caught the attention of the other. I couldn't do anything but cry because this is the same reason my mom left my dad. He was cheating on her with another man. My mom was hurt, but she stayed married to him for seventeen years before she left. I told David and Mrs. Cee about it.

After revealing that news about my parents' marriage, they decided to stay together and work things out. We finished talking, and they thanked me for sharing my hurt with them. David knew their relationship was coming to an end but wanted to thank me for saving his marriage. If I had not intervened, their marriage would have ended very badly.

We went into the kitchen where the other guys were pretending not to listen to what we were talking about. They wanted to know what was going on and what took us so long. I told them that we were talking about having Tom and Matt and welcome home party. I laughed on the inside. I went into Matt's and Tom's room. I wanted them to know what we were talking about. They thought it was so nice of me because David and Mrs. Cee had been going through a lot. I walked out of the room and went into the kitchen to make everyone drinks. Mrs. Cee began to sing and dance. I knew she was feeling better.

As the drinks started to come, everyone began to party like crazy. David was so wasted that he didn't know where he was. Mrs. Cee told me to take him into the guest room. She was trying to have a good time. That's what I did because she needed to have some fun.

Whenever I took David into the guest bedroom, he began to fall over and started acting crazy. I had to go and get Matt. When we both arrived at the room, David was in the shower. I thought he was so drunk that he couldn't move. I stayed in the room while Matt went into the bathroom to check up on him. Matt came back into the room and asked me to help him. I was thinking to myself to help with what. I realized wheat he was talking about. He needed help getting David into bed. As we were helping David to bed, I noticed he didn't dry off. His body was looking so lovely. I got a towel and started to dry his body off. As I was going down his body with the towel, my hand touched his dick. I removed the towel so I could see it. I couldn't believe my eyes. His dick was so huge. It left me speechless. Matt looked over at me and I started to laugh.

As we put him in the bed, I fell on top of him and started to suck his big, pretty giant dick. Slob was running all down my mouth. I had that dick wet as hell. My mouth was throbbing and my tongue was loving it. Matt was kissing on me as I was riding David's dick. I could barely ride it because it was so huge. David bent me over and started fucking me like crazy.

I couldn't take it. He didn't stop for anything. He kept fucking me harder and harder. I wanted to cry. Then he tied me up to the bed and fucked me stupid. My body was out of it. I didn't feel anything. He took control of me and my body. When he finished fucking me, Matt took over. My body was sore as hell. He tied my legs and arms behind my head. I couldn't move at all. Matt put his entire dick in me. He started to jump up and down. He had my mind going crazy. He fucked me like that for about an hour.

When I got out of bed, David pushed me back down and began to fuck me some more. I thought he had lost his mind because of the way he was fucking me. My body was just there. He had the biggest dick of them all. The two of them helped me take a shower. I returned to the living room where everyone else was, but they were all asleep. I had a hard time walking because they fucked me stupid. I was trying to help David out. I wasn't trying to fuck him.

Matt woke up the next morning with a big smile on his face. David started to laugh. The only thing I did was look. I couldn't move my head or my body. They fucked me so hard and good. Sam was the first person to wake up in the living room. He was like baby oh baby. I want some ass. My face turned blue. David and matt began to laugh. When Sam asked me for some ass, I went into the room where David and Matt were. I told them to keep it cute before Mrs. Cee found out. They stopped laughing and looked at me stupid because they didn't think I would do it. Matt knew that I would. I wanted to tell Sam, no, but I didn't because he deserves some. My body was hurting like hell, but I took Sam's dick for the team. I told Sam to let me take a bath first. Then I would give him some of this good ass. I had to sit down in the bathtub and soak. I was hurting just that bad. I stayed in the tub for about an hour. I had to get my body together.

After soaking my body, I felt so much better. I wasn't ready to fuck, but I didn't want to treat my man cold. So I gave him some of this sweet ass. I jumped on him and started to ride that dick. My body felt so good. I needed daddy's touch and loving. Sam turned my body upside down and started to fuck me. My arms and legs were going everywhere, but the right way.

He put me on the bed, opened my legs and told me to put daddy's dick in me. I had to put it in slow because it was so big. He took his time and made love to me. He was kissing and eating my ass so good. He made my ass so wet with that powerful tongue. I was shaking the entire time. Daddy knew how to work that dick. When we were done making love, I laid in his arms as he held me tight. I felt so loved and happy. I was beginning to love Sam even more.

There was a lot of noise in the living room. David and Mrs. Cee were fussing. She caught

Lust, Lies & Love

David in the bathroom sucking Calvin's dick. He didn't know what to do. Matt and Tom had to grab Mrs. Cee. She was breaking everything. They had to stop her. David couldn't believe his eyes. He thought he would never get caught.

Calvin was so nervous because David told him that he was no longer with Mrs. Cee. That's why he had David sucking his dick. He thought that David was single. Whenever Jack heard about it, he didn't get upset because they were both freaks. David called Sam and Mrs. Cee outside. He wanted to let the marriage go. Sam told David to try and work it out, but he wasn't hearing that. Mrs. Cee was also ready to let it go. David was not feeling women anymore. Sam called everyone outside. He wanted to talk to David about what happened, but David didn't want to talk. Mrs. Cee and David went home. We all got ready to hit the club.

Things began to get even better. People were buying us food and beer. We all got wasted and crazy. The crazy was in a good way. We didn't have to deal with drama. Sam had so much fun because he has not partied like this in a long time. He was drinking, dancing and partying. I was so glad that he had a blast.

Lust, Lies & Love

As we were leaving the club, I couldn't do anything, but think about Mrs. Cee and David. I want their marriage to work, but I think that it is coming to an end. Matt and Tom are trying to help them stay together. None of the efforts was working. It was not going to happen. David had taken Mrs. Cee through too much.

When we returned to the house, Tom told everyone to sit in the living room. He was really hurt because he really wanted things to work out for David and Mrs. Cee. Matt and Tom were the best friends I ever had. Whenever I wanted my dick sucked or wanted to fuck, I knew who to call on. I love these guys.

Lust, Lies & Love

CHAPTER 5

We're finally arriving home. Now it's time to party. I called all of the guys up because it's been a long time since we have seen each other. Everyone was happy to hear from me. I haven't seen the guys in over a year. I thought it would be a great idea for Sam and me to invite them over for dinner. Sam began to cook dinner and prepare wine. Everyone arrived at the house as Sam was finishing dinner. We were happy to see all of them. We sat down at the table except for Sam who was putting finishing touches on the food.

We began to talk about our lives and the events that took place in the year we were apart. Mike and Fred were still together, but things were not going well. Fred lost his job.

Lust, Lies & Love

Mike's income was barely paying the bills and making due. They didn't think they were going to make it. Life wasn't so good for them. They didn't have anyone to depend on. Everyone was busy living their own lives. I felt sorry for them because they were about to lose everything.

As Mike was telling us about everything, He began to cry. Tears started to flow down my face as well. I went into the bathroom and started texting the other guys. We needed to help them. I didn't want them to lose their home. We all pitched in and helped to save their home. They couldn't believe it because their bills were so high. We helped them pay all of them off.

After everything was over and done, it was time to hit the club. We stood in line for about two hours. My legs were so tired, but I wanted to enjoy my friends. After those long two hours of standing, it was time to get our drink on. It was so many people in the club. Men were everywhere. They were very nice-looking. We were having a blast. Things couldn't get any better for us.

When I saw a smile on everyone's faces, I knew life was getting better. The club was banging. The guys were getting wasted. Some of us were getting a little too drunk. I knew it was time for us to leave before things started to get crazy. We went back to my place.

When we entered the house, they guys hit the floor and went to sleep. Sam and I tried to get them up and put them in bed, but they didn't want to move. That was a happy moment for me because I really missed and enjoyed every one.

Sam woke up early the next morning to prepare breakfast. The guys love Sam's cooking and his amazing drinks. Everyone had a hangover. They barely ate anything. They wanted to go and lie down again. I told them to make themselves at home. I wanted to surprise they guys with a very nice gift because they have been so wonderful to me over the years. I just wanted to thank them all. I thought that I would play a three-day, four-night trip to Italy. That is where Matt's parents are from.

Before I finalized any plans, I have to talk it over with Sam. He thought it was a wonderful idea. While everyone was asleep and silent, I got on the phone and started making plans. I couldn't wait to go because we all needed a break. I was itching to tell the guys.

Lust, Lies & Love

A couple hours later, they woke up from a drunken stupor. I told them to come into the kitchen for something very important that I needed to tell them. They were all looking scared and crazy. When they sat down at the breakfast table, I began to tell them about the trip. Matt began to cry because he hasn't seen his mother in ten years. After he stopped crying, he hugged me, kissed me, and shook me. He just absolutely could not believe his ears.

Three days flew by. We were now flying from Atlanta and on our way to little Italy. The flight took forever, but I knew we were going to have a wonderful time. After we landed, Mat called to surprise his mom. The only thing you could hear was crying. I thought it was so sweet. Sam and I went outside of the airport to wait in the limo. When it arrived, they guys were shocked. Hey, thought maybe we rented an SUV. The idea was for everyone to ride in style.

On our way to the hotel, I noticed that Fred was looking at me in that I-want-to-sex-you type of way. I tried to play it off as if I didn't see him, but I couldn't. He licked out his tongue and started to put his fingers in his mouth. I knew from there it was going to be a good trip. I was going to have a good time fucking Fred.

By the time we arrived at the hotel and checked in, everyone was tired and jet-lagged. We got settled in and relaxed for a couple of hours. Sam wanted to take a tour of the town by himself. He has been so busy and wanted some time alone. I thought that was a great idea. I was ready to give Fred the business anyway. When Sam left, I called Fred and told him to come over so we could talk about Italy and Matt's family. He was so happy to talk about Matt's family.

When he arrived at the room, I was sitting on the bed to convey to Fred that I really wanted to know something about Matt's family. Then minutes into talking about the family, Fred began to kiss me from head to toe. I told him to stop because we didn't come to Italy for that.

Things began to heat up for the both of us. I push Fred into the middle of the bed and started taking his clothes off. He moaned softly. I slowly put my penis into his tight ass and fucked him nice and slow. He was pulling on my skin tight. I pounded him harder. I took my penis out of his ass and put it in his wet mouth. He was sucking like there was no tomorrow. He had my dick so wet. I grabbed his head and moved it up and down the length of me. I knew he was enjoying it.

We lay on the bed. I pushed his legs back and was eating him out. His ass tastes like strawberries and cream. I didn't want to take my tongue out. He legs squeezed my head, and his body was moving back and forth. I fucked Fred until he couldn't be fucked anymore. His body was sore. My mind was gone. We had some great sex together.

The Italy trip was far too short than I hoped, but we enjoyed every minute of it. We arrived in LA where Jack was. He was feeling a little better. He didn't have a choice but to get better. It was recording time. His all has to be in it. As I walked into the studio, Jack just broke down. His body would not let him operate.

Minutes later, he got it together. The recording was going well. He sang his heart out. The song had me crying. I was thinking about Sam. I enjoyed the music. Jack's management team was happy to hear he was going well. They loved the song. The album was ready for greatness. Everyone spent the night at the studio. We left around nine o'clock the next morning. It was very different for me because

I sleep at night, but with the business, you are up from the sun up to sun down. This is something that I have to get used to. I have a busy life. Indeed, I was ready to go back to the hotel. We only got three hours of sleep. I was so tired, but I know I have to make things happen.

Mr. Bob came into our room and told us that we had a meet and greet today. This is going to be another long day. Jack didn't get any sleep and was looking a hot mess. I had to clean him up before we went into public. He was already mad about our little tour bus. It was so small that if you turned around twice, you would bump into the wall or walk into someone. It was small for the eight of us. That was something that we had to deal with.

Because Jack was a new artist, his manager didn't want him to try and fly out a lot of his family or friends to every concert. He was just starting to make money. They didn't want him to go broke before he started making money. Jack agreed and was understanding. This meant that the crew couldn't indulge in the luxury of fame unless we paid for our own flight.

Two months later, we went on a world-wide tour which kept us busy and exhausted. Jack's vocals were not up to par at one point. A trip to the doctor's office to check them out assured us that there was nothing to worry about. He just needed to rest and not to use his vocals for a couple of weeks per doctor's orders. Jack didn't listen to the doctor. He had a show to do later that night and didn't want to cancel.

He did the show with pride. The both of us were missing our mates. It has been three months since we have seen them. We flew them out to Texas, which was our last city. They were like kids in the candy factory ready to eat us up. I couldn't do anything but run to Sam and jump into his arms. Jack started to cry.

He was so happy to see Calvin. He was telling Sam and Calvin about our hotel room. They didn't believe us until they seen it for themselves. Their eyes got big. They had a wow moment. Their hotel was the size of a house. It was twenty-five hundred square feet which were really big for a hotel room. Room service came to the room. The room service guy had two dozen roses and two bottles of wine. I thought maybe they had the wrong room until the guys told us that the roses and wine were for us. That was so romantic. The love came at the right time. We have been stressing and going through but we still made it.

Before we go to Texas, the four of us thought it would be nice to go to dinner. We needed to catch up on life. Also, we needed to talk about the months that we were gone. Things were so different at the dinner table because the other guys were not there. It's been a long time since we have seen them. I only talk with Fred and Mike once since we have been on tour. I really miss the other guys. They mean the world to me.

After we leave Texas, we will be heading back to L.A. I'm going to miss my Sam because we were going back on tour. This time, it will be for six months. We can't fly them out to see us so I am going to be so sad. The bad thing about this business is leaving your mate for months.

Our driver took Sam and Calvin to the airport. They began to cry. We were missing them because we will not see them for half a year. I couldn't take it but I knew I had to make the best out of it. Things really got to Jack. He couldn't see Calvin for months. His mind was going crazy. I told him that this is something that he has to get used to and that things will work out.

As the six-month tour was about to begin, Jack started to get sick. Stress was getting the best of him. It was hard for me to talk him through it. All I could do was call Calvin. He was the only one who could get through to Jack. I tried but it didn't work.

After Calvin finished talking with Jack, he was feeling better. Two weeks before the tour, Jack was in the studio day in and day out. He didn't get any sleep. My poor body was so weak. I didn't know if I was coming or going. I thought I was the singer for a moment. My throat was soar. My vocals were almost gone, and my body was through. I had to realize that I wasn't the singer. I am the assistant. It is tour time. I was happy. We love traveling to different states.

The two of us was so horny. We wanted to fuck, but couldn't because there were so many people on the bus. I had to find a way. My dick wanted some good ass. Our tour bus broke down. We had to stay at a hotel for a night. Everyone was so happy to be off of that extra small bus.

Lust, Lies & Love

When we checked into the hotel, Jack and I went straight into the room and lay on the bed. It felt so good to finally lie down. The both of us got up and took a hot shower. I was loving it. We got out of the shower and jumped into the bed. Jack wanted me to oil his body down. I got a bottle of baby oil, rubbed his body from head to toe and started rubbing his ass. Then I played around his asshole with my tongue. He couldn't take this tongue. I put the head of my dick in his tight asshole. I inserted it in slowly moving my body up and down while I kissed his neck. His body started to fold. I was fucking his body as if it was snow. The dick was so good. Jack was losing his mind.

After the six months of touring, we were back home with our soul mates. I thought Calvin and I weren't ever going to make it because we were gone for so long. It wasn't making things good between us. When Calvin and I got to the house, we had a very long talk. The tour brought the two of us closer together. We had a lot of time to think about life, us as a couple and where we wanted to be in life. I must admit that I was going crazy without my baby. He means the world to me. Calvin was moving up on the romantic side. He sent me on a shopping spree with my manager. The two of us had a blast.

Lust, Lies & Love

After the shopping spree, I went back to the house. To my surprise, Calvin had a mini band, a chef, and wine waiting when I arrived. I couldn't believe my eyes. My body froze up like a cube of ice. I was proud of him. He had been through a lot. This surprise cheered the both of us up. I was ready to make mad love. Calvin and I went into the bedroom while the band was playing and made crazy love. It was so different because he never made love to me. He put warm oil all over my body. He licked me from head to toe with cherries and started rubbing me down with feathers.

My mind was in another place. I couldn't help it. Calvin had my mind and heart so gone. We made sweet love the entire night. My body was loving it to the fullest. We were really enjoying ourselves. The band played so nicely. The music had me in another world. I went to sleep in Calvin's arms. He was holding me as if I was a baby. I felt so safe.

The chef had breakfast waiting for us when we woke up the next morning. The food was great. My man was looking amazing. Things were beginning to be in my favor. My career was going well. My relationship was working out for the best. It couldn't get any better.

I really miss the other guys, though. I wanted to call them over for dinner, but I was working on Calvin and me. We didn't need that extra weight on us. So that's why I didn't call them. They are very good people. We just didn't need to talk about us with everyone. I thought that was best. I love and care for Calvin even more because he was beginning to be there for me and our relationship. Calvin was my support and more. That's why I love him so. I took time off from work so I could build my relationship up and to get myself together. We wanted our lives to be built on a solid foundation.

My manager thought it would be a great idea. I could only take two months off due to the fact that we are about to start working on my first album. The six-month tour was a promo tour. I only took a month off. I was ready to start on the album. It was going to be a hit. Everyone was feeling the songs that I performed while on tour. The songs made people cry. The tour made me a stronger singer. Calvin came to the studio to see me. He couldn't take his eyes off of me. He had me nervous and shy. I can sing in front of thousands, but when it comes to singing in front of Calvin it wasn't easy. Some of the songs were really getting to me. I began to cry.

Lust, Lies & Love

The recording had to stop for that day. I couldn't stop crying. Everyone wanted to know what was wrong. I told them I was crying because I love Calvin. They thought it was so sweet. It was time to start working again. The album was in the making. Calvin resigned from his job. My eyes got big as hell because I wanted to know what was going on. He told me that he wanted to travel and be with me. My ears begin to ring. My heart was filled with love. I think he did the right thing.

A week later, the album was finished. It was time for another tour. We were more ready than ever. Calvin wasn't use to the road. This is his first time traveling from city to city within a couple days apart. He was really enjoying the extra small tour bus. He talked about it so much that you would think we were living in a five-star hotel. This tour meant the world to Calvin and me. He can really see how I work and the crazy things that I go through. He was very shocked about some of the things that were going on in the business. I told him that it is a lot of things that go on in this world that he doesn't know about. Through it all, he enjoyed the tour. Life for us was very lovely.

When the tour was over, things got even better. Calvin quit his job and joined me. I was happy because I knew things were about to go in the right direction. He will make a wonderful manager. That was what I needed. I missed Calvin and loved him so much. I couldn't stop things about how he used to dick me down. He joined the team two weeks later. It was the happiest day of my life. My baby was finally aboard. I was happy to see them working together. The management team took Calvin out for dinner to celebrate. We had a blast.

After we returned to the hotel, Calvin and Jack came into the room. We all sat down and watched television. I got up to take a shower. As I was taking my clothes off, Jack came into the bathroom. He needed some tissue. He got on his soft knees and started sucking my dick. My dick was musty and sticky from the heat. I didn't stop him because I wanted a good fuck. He went down to my balls and started sucking on them too. He had my eyes rolling into the back of my head. When he got up from licking and sucking, I bent him over the bathtub and started fucking him slow. I let Jack slob all on this big black musty dick. I had that bitch choking on this dick. I loved every minute of it.

After jack finished sucking my dick, I laid him on the floor. I put his legs behind his head and started eating his ass out. My dick was on rock hard. I couldn't get my dick to go down for anything. The more I ate his ass, the more my dick got harder. I was ready to fuck. I started licking him from head to toe. I stopped at his dick and commenced to sucking on the head of it with my tongue deep throating it. Jack was going crazy. Then I put whipped cream all over his body. I licked the cream from between his ass. The juice was flowing so good. The taste was so sweet. Jack had that good. My mind was about gone. I made love to him. It was so amazing.

Calvin came into the bedroom because it was taking Jack too long to come out. When he came into the bathroom, he saw Jack and me lying on the floor naked. He didn't get mad because he wanted some dick. He got on top of me and started sucking my dick. My body was so weak. That bitch's mouth was so wet and warm. My dick got hard so fast. I fucked the hell out of Calvin. His ass was so sore so he told me to take it slow. I kept fucking that bitch as if he was a dog. I didn't care about Calvin and Jack when I was fucking them because I had a man.

After we finished fucking, the three of us went to the studio. I was so tired. I could barely stand up or walk. Jack had to sit down in order to record. Jack sounds so good in the studio. I enjoyed every song, but I couldn't seem to keep myself awake. I left the recording studio and went to the bathroom. I needed to wake up and get myself together.

As I was putting water on my face, here comes Calvin walking into the bathroom talking about he needs to use it. Before I could walk out, Calvin threw me back in and started pulling my pants down. I was standing in the bathroom with a wet, sweaty musty ass dick. Sweat was dripping all in his mouth. He was catching all of it with his thick tongue. I didn't fuck Calvin. I only jacked my dick. When I was about to cum, I told him to open his mouth so I could cum all in his mouth and on his face. That punk was so nasty and weird. Those guys were so amazing.

It's now time to leave the studio and head back home. I couldn't wait to get home because I was ready to see Mike and Fred. I heard they were doing well. Plus, we haven't seen them in a while.

We arrived at our home sweet home. I called Mike and Fred because I really wanted to see them. The two of them came over two hours later and had dinner. I was feeling mad love in that moment. We were catching up on the good times. I told them about what happened at the studio. They began to laugh. Jack and Calvin were known for being easy in the bedroom. Life was so amazing for Mike and Fred. Matt's family was crazy, but nice at the same time. We talked about his life in Italy and the other guys. Matt and Fred were talking so much, and I was ready to fuck.

I asked Fred to help me take my clothes basket in the back bedroom. He said ok. I let Fred take the basket. I was getting ready to fuck. I called Mike into the bedroom. He got some good head and ass. I was ready to bust a couple of nuts. They both got undressed and started playing with their dicks. I was about to melt. My dick was getting hard. My mouth was getting wet. I knew the both of them had some good shit to serve. I was ready to fuck. My mind was going out of control. I was horny as hell; my dick was calling for some ass.

I began to eat Mike out. His insides tasted like soul food. His ass had my tongue stiff and my mouth wet. The taste had me insane. Mike's ass was better than the badest bitch. He had me where I couldn't move.

After all the fucking was over, we all took a shower. I called the guys. I wanted to hang out with everyone. We all went to a bar. That's where we met this guy by the name of Chad. He was okay but didn't fit in our circle. He was so stuck on himself. I knew it had to change. We all danced and laughed with Chad. He was looking as if we were boring him. I asked him to come outside. I wanted to know what was wrong. He said nothing, but I knew the bitch was horny. Every time I looked at him, my dick was getting harder and harder. Controlling it as so hard as it was seemed to be a problem. All I wanted to do was fuck. I knew he was willing. His body was looking fresh. His eyes were looking wonderful. His ass was looking tasteful. The club was calling our names. We went back inside the club and got a couple of drinks. I was willing to buy Chad as many drinks as he wanted. I wanted him to get wasted so I could fuck the hell out of him.

As we were leaving the club, Chad asked me if he could come to the house and hang out. I said sure because I knew it was about to be on. The guys changed their minds about staying the night. Sam was out of town. Things were about to get really lovely.

When Chad and I entered the house, I told him to take a seat. I fixed him a glass of wine. We watched television and drank two bottles of white wine. He could barely keep his eyes opened. He began to take his clothes off. I was happy as hell because I knew I was about to fuck. He laid on the bed naked. My dick was sticking up army strong. I rolled him over onto his stomach and started to massage him. His skin was so soft. I got a bottle of chocolate syrup and began pouring it from his neck down to his toes. I worked my tongue down his ass. I open up his booty cheeks and play with his whole asshole with my tongue. I had him moaning. My tongue was so powerful. Chad was shaking like a newborn baby. I turned him over onto his back and started to suck his toes. I worked my way to his dick and began to ride his dick like a psycho. I was losing my mind on his big black dick. The sex was so amazing.

After we were done, the two of us went to take a shower. I was so tired and out of it. The only thing I wanted to do was to go to sleep. Not long after the shower, the two of us went straight to sleep. That was the best sleep and sex ever. Chad had me going crazy.

The next day, we all got up and went back to the studio. Jack wanted Chad to hear him sing. As Jack begins to sing his heart out, Chad was in a daze. He couldn't believe Jack could sing because he didn't look like the type that could. Everyone was so proud of Jack.

Lust, Lies & Love

We later became friends with Chad. He was a very cool person. They guys wanted to go back on another trip, they wanted to show Chad how to party. I thought it was crazy because we just got back from Italy. I wanted to go to New Mexico. Mike and Fred can't make it because of work. Sam and I really didn't want to go. The seven of us went on the trip. I felt bad for Chad. He was the only one without a mate. I talked with him about it. He told me he was good with it and that he came to have a blast.

When we arrived in New Mexico, everyone was tired. From what we could see, the city was amazing. The hotels, the shops, and the city were wonderful. Our hotel was the best. Since Chad didn't have a master, Sam and I let him stay with us. He was so funny. We didn't go out that night. A couple of us thought it would be a good idea to stay in and get some rest. That put a smile on my face. Sam had been gone for a while. I knew my baby wanted some dick and ass.

I pulled Chad to the side because I wanted him to put those soft lips on Sam's dick. He was willing, ready and about to jump out of his clothes. I was ready to see Sam fuck Chad. Sam hasn't had sex in six weeks. I can only imagine. Chad lowered himself to his knees, opened his mouth and let Sam fuck his mouth crazy. My baby, Sam, has too much energy. He was fucking Chad like a crazy dog. Chad's asshole was red and sore. He was begging Sam to stop, but Sam wasn't hearing that. The ass was good so he was going to fuck Chad until his body gave out.

I felt sorry for Chad. He was trying to get away, but Sam just started fucking him harder. I stepped in and got Sam off of Chad. He was killing the poor guy. I spread Chad's legs open and began eating him out. He couldn't take it because Sam had fucked him so hard and stupid. I started kissing his asshole instead. His eyes begin to roll into the back of his head.

Later, I started licking his thighs, rubbing on his body and kissing his ears. Chad couldn't do anything but moan softly. As he began to moan and lay there, Sam came over and put my dick in his mouth. It was so warm and wet. He was sucking on the head of my big dick. It felt so good. I took my dick out of his mouth because I wanted him to continue fucking Chad like crazy. Sam put his dick into Chad. His body folded. That bitch started yelling. Sam started fucking him like a clown. I loved seeing the pain on Chad's face.

Lust, Lies & Love

Before Sam was finished fucking Chad, all of the other guys had come into our room and watched Sam fuck Chad. They laughed at Chad because he couldn't take dick. It was so funny to them. We had a fucking party going on. Chad's asshole wasn't tight anymore. Sam opened that fresh ass up.

After they finished fucking, Chad looked up as the guys were looking directly into his face. He couldn't do anything, but put his head down. I had to let him know that it was okay. This is how we party. Take a couple of dick for the team I told him. Out of all the guys and our new friend, Chad, only one person had some really good ass. That was Chad. I can look at his ass and start cumming. He had the best dick and ass here.

After we showered, it was time to hit up the bars and a couple of sex parties. I was ready to get drunk and fuck. I had to make the best out of this. This was our last trip together. We all went into the bar to have a few drinks and to get drunk. We didn't stay long because we were ready to hit up the sex parties. When we walked into the first party, I saw ass, fresh dicks, and dick sucking. My mouth couldn't close for anything. My heart was pounding like crazy. My dick was ready. I couldn't be controlled. They guys were looking amazing, but I was ready to fuck. I started walking around the party because I was trying to get to know people. I met this couple who never had a threesome and wanted to have one. You know I was ready for that. It wasn't my first time. I was going to fuck the hell out of them. The three of us went into his private room where they had everything you wanted inside.

We started off by talking. They wanted to know me a little more. I told them. We talked about everything each other wanted to hear. An hour into the conversation the other guys joined in but didn't stay long. They were trying to meet and greet some new guys. I was so happy when the other guys left our room. I was ready to do grown folks things. I knew they were also ready. The room was big enough to do whatever. I didn't ask the couple their names because that wasn't important. The both of them started taking off their clothes. They bent over and started playing in their asses. My dick was harder than a brick. I tied their hands to their ankles while they were bent over. I started fucking one by one.

The first guy's ass was so good. I was cumming back to back in his ass. Cum was running all down his ass. I took my dick out of his ass to put it in his mouth. That bitch was sucking and licking my balls. My dick was dirty. My balls smelled like old pussy. Dude was nasty, but I wasn't going to stop him. I wanted a good nut. My dick went too far down his throat because he started to throw up. I wasn't mad at dude for any reason. He licked the throw up off of my dick and told me that he enjoyed it all.

Now it's time for his better half to be fucked. I took my time and fucked him. He wasn't use to a big black dick. I Put him on the couch and ate him out. I made sweet love to him. I was easing my dick in and out of his tight asshole. His body began to get tighter and tighter. He was squeezing my neck with his legs. I couldn't move so I began to lick on his thighs. Then he let loose.

Later, I worked my way up to his balls and dick. I begin using this powerful tongue. Ole' dude didn't know what to do because he wasn't use to it. I was beating his dick with my tongue slapping it against my face. The punk was going crazy. While he lay on the bed horny as fuck, I got on top of him and started riding the head of his dick. He couldn't take it at all. Five minutes later the bitch started to cum everywhere. I made his better half lick it off and take all of it down his throat. He took it down like a pro. Those were two of the nastiest guys I have ever met, but I enjoyed them because whatever goes. Their freak game as an A plus. I couldn't take that from them.

We all went back into the main room where everyone was and started to chat. The guys were having a blast. Sucking and fucking were all in the open. I watched some other guys fuck Calvin and Matt like dogs. Those guys had them doing everything under the sun. They were passing Calvin and Matt around like they were cheap toys. I enjoyed seeing Calvin and Matt get their backs fucked out.

When everything was over and done, we didn't go to the second sex party. Everyone was tired and sleepy. So I thought that maybe we should go and get some rest. I really wanted to attend the second sex party, but the guys weren't feeling it.

The next morning we all went to Calvin's friend's house. He lived in New Mexico. I was ready for this. I heard he was sexy and very freaky. I love my sexy, tall and loving freaks. Calvin's friend's name is Mark. He was a doctor.

Lust, Lies & Love

When we arrived at Mark's house, he greeted us with love and care. His house was so huge. His yard was amazing. Calvin was so happy to see Mark. The both of them made me think they use to fuck each other by the way they were acting. If they haven't fucked before, I already knew I was going to make it happen. Mark had dinner prepared along with some tasty wine. I love a man that can cook. Calvin wanted everyone to go into the guest dining area to eat dinner. The area was wonderful. I notice that Mark was changing clothes in the kitchen.

A couple of minutes later, he was in the middle of the dinner table naked with food on him. His chef was placing the food on him. Everyone was taking food off of him and putting it on their plates. My horny-self had to take the food off of his dick and eat it. Mark's dick was so big. It took me by surprise and had my mouth on the floor. The guys were in shock. Mark's dick was on hard. I started to play with it. Everyone was looking at me as if I was crazy. So I took it and put it in my mouth. I went to work on that big dick. My face and mouth were tired, but I kept on sucking because I was ready for him to fuck me silly.

Lust, Lies & Love

As I was sucking Mark's big black dick, he laid me on the dinner table, opened my legs and started jacking his dick all over me. I began to shake like a crack head. As his dick got harder, he put his big dick in me. My body began to fold and got stiff. He was fucking me silly. I could barely take the dick because it was so huge and thick. My insides were loose as ever. What a big dick.

Not soon after, Mark threw me on the floor and told me to get on my knees because he wanted to hit it from the back. I was scared as fuck of a dick that big inside of me. He started hitting it from the back. I felt his dick in my chest. I thought I was going to pass out. I couldn't handle it. I wanted to run, but I knew that wasn't a good idea. He would've held me down and fucked the hell out of me. Mark's dick had my body taking in every language. I wanted to ride his dick, but I was scared. I thought about it and told myself that I better ride that dick for the team. That's what I did.

When I finished riding that dick, my ass was sore and in so much pain, but I rode it good. My ass had Mark's dick cumming like a waterfall. Every time he cum, his big dick got harder. Mark made me feel loved and sexy. We didn't have to leave Mark's house because everything we wanted or needed was there. I was thinking about hooking Chad and Mark up together. I had to think about it very hard. Mark got some good dick. I didn't want to share it with the other guys. His dick made me smile when I didn't want to smile. That's what you call some good. I tried to be a good boy while in New Mexico. I knew Sam was going to be there. He didn't care about me having sex with other men as long as I give him some dick at the end of the night. I wanted Sam to watch Mark and I have sex, but he wasn't around. I am a very freaky person.

After the sex was over, the eight of us went to soothe our bodies in the heated pool. Everyone was in the nude and looking wonderful. My mind was in the zone of sex. Sam begins to looks at me with the puppy look. He already knew I was going to have sex with whomever. I always had sex with Sam after I have freaked someone else. I had to save the worst for last or should I say the best for last.

Everyone's vibe was going well. Mark's chef brought out some fruit and red wine. The fruit was amazing, but the wine was getting me drunk. I began to get horny. I was ready to fuck some tight, sweet, juicy and loving asshole. No one wanted to make a move so I proposed that we play fuck ball which is like volleyball. IF you don't hit the ball across the net, you get fucked. I never hit the ball across the net because I was ready to get fucked or fuck someone else. They didn't want to stop playing the game, but I was ready. I worked my way over to Calvin and Chad. These two stayed ready for any and everything.

CHAPTER 6

As I got close to the both of them, I began to remove the balls from the pool and started touching on them. Calvin was moaning as if I was fucking him. I knew that ass was going to be good. Chad's asshole was so wet. I couldn't wait to play in it. When I looked over, I saw Sam looking at me. I told Calvin to go to the edge of the pool and bend over. His ass was so big. That hole was looking right. I approached Calvin. He opens that ass up and I start eating. His ass tastes like strawberry cream cheese. I didn't want to stop. It was so good and tasty.

I put Calvin in the doggie style and fucked the shit out of him. He was telling me to stop going in so deep, but that's how I like it. When he told me to stop going in so deep, I slapped him across the ass and told him that this is my ass and that I fuck it how I want to. Calvin was throwing that good ass back. The faster he threw it back at me, the deeper I went in. His ass was hurting like hell. I rough fucked him for about an hour. He stopped crying like a baby and started taking it like a pro. I was so proud of him. I knew it was time to fuck his brains out. I fucked him until his body couldn't focus. He stopped moving and talking, but I didn't stop because that ass was mine for that moment.

After we finished having sex, Chad came over and began eating Calvin's asshole softly. He was licking it up and down with his tongue rubbing his lips across his ass making him feel like the man of the house. Calvin began to come back to his senses. He started playing in his ass while Chad was eating him out. My dick was getting hard as fuck. I had to join in because it was looking so good.

As Chad was eating Calvin's fine ass out, I put my dick inside of Chad while he put his dick into Calvin. We were having a fucking party. Everyone was looking. Sam was looking like he wanted to join in the party. Even though Sam was my boyfriend, I called all of the guys over to the edge of the pool. I knew they all wanted to fuck. I wanted them to fuck Sam all at one time because he acts like he was going to die if he didn't get any dick.

They were ready. I knew Sam was going to say yes because he wanted to make me happy. They guys were having sex with Sam two at a time. He had a dick in his ass and mouth. I was sitting back in the chair enjoying the whole fuck show. I was loving it because Sam was crying. I already knew he couldn't take dick. Sam was moaning and crying so loudly. All I could do is laugh and shake my head. Jack was fucking the hell out of Sam. He had him in every position that he could think of.

Things were heating up really well for the guys. Sam didn't like when the guys put his legs behind his head. He couldn't take it. I told them to put his legs behind his head and fuck the shit out of him. That's what he needed. That's what I wanted to see. Every time one of the guys took their dicks of Sam's ass, I could see his hole throbbing. It was looking nice, but loose. They were fucking him like he was a nobody.

When they were done with Sam and his lovely body, he got up and went to the bathroom. Sam could barely make it. His body was in so much pain. I had to go inside of Mark's house and run him a nice and hot bubble bath. My baby was messed up. He was hurting so badly. I helped to put Sam into the hot bubble bath which he loved. The water began to touch his body. He moaned softly. Sam's body had me horny and in the mood. I knew he couldn't take any more dick, but I had to get me some of that good ass. I didn't fuck him for that long. I knew he couldn't take it. His body wouldn't let him operate the way he wanted.

The next day, Mark had a limo waiting for everyone. We all took a tour around New Mexico which was nice and amazing. The cost was a lot cheaper. I see why Mark didn't want to come back Georgia. New Mexico was lovely and treated Mark with a lot of respect and love. He was well known around the city. Every time he came to Atlanta, he always went out to the club with us. So we thought maybe it would be a good idea if we go out with him.

Whenever we told Mark we were going out with him, he couldn't believe it because we were so stuck on our clubs. Mark wanted everyone to wear blue jeans and a cowboy hat. We all thought it was a great idea. As we were on our way to the club, I heard little sounds in the back of the truck. When I turned around and looked, Jack was sucking the hell out of

Calvin's dick. Calvin was moaning as if he was having a baby. I was wishing that was me in the back seat. I wanted my dick sucked, and Sam was acting stupid.

As we pulled up to the club, Jack came all over Calvin's face. Everyone begins to laugh and calls Calvin white face. We had to stay in the truck for ten extra minutes. Calvin had to clean up his face. After cleaning, it was time to party. The line was long as fuck, but we didn't care because we wanted to party. We got into the club and it was banging. Men were walking around with their dicks hanging out of G-strings. I was on cloud nine. I couldn't believe my eyes.

It was so many freaks in the club. People were walking around in the nude with everything flying from left to right. This one guy walked by me and his dick was big a fuck. His ass was firm. He was sexy as hell. I had to find him before the club was over. They guys and I went to the bar. We all had three shots of patron a piece. I was beginning to feel the shots. I went on the dance floor and began to dance. I was so feeling myself. Those shots and the dance floor had me in another world. That was my night. The guys and I started dancing together. It was so funny because everyone was drunk and couldn't stand up straight. Mark thought it was time for everyone to leave.

As we were leaving the club, the guy that walked by me in the club was parked behind us so I went over to his car and started to talk to him. We had a small conversation. He wanted me to go back to his place, but I had to make sure that it was okay with Sam. He said yes, but to not get into any trouble. The guys looked at Sam like he was crazy. It didn't matter because Sam already knew what was up. The guy and I drove off to his place. His name is Paul. He is from New York, but he is in New Mexico visiting friends.

When we arrived at Paul's penthouse, I felt in love with it. It was amazing. He opens my door. He takes me into the guest room and tells me to wait for fifteen minutes. That's what I did. After those minutes were up, Paul comes into the bedroom, places a blindfold over my eyes and walks me into his master suite. When we got into the suite of all suites, he takes the blindfold off. I was in shock. He has rose petals all over the bed. A bottle of time is resting in the center. The bathtub is filled with roses and candles. He takes my breath away. Paul undresses me as if I am a baby. He puts me into the bath tub and makes me feel like a real man. He goes to the bottom of the bathtub, starts crawling to me, and stops at my dick. He starts to suck the hell out of it. He puts my legs into the air. He sucks my thighs with lips and starts licking my body up and down. My body needs that good loving. He is really putting it on me.

The next morning, Sam is calling my phone like crazy. I let him call for about an hour because I didn't want to talk. When I did call him, he was so happy to hear from me. I was so worn out, though. I went back to Mark's house. Sam and the guys were waiting for me. It is time for us to leave New Mexico. New Mexico treated us with love and care. What a trip we had. I didn't want to go back home, but I knew we all had business to take care of.

I had to call Mike and Fred because this trip was the best ever. Everyone had a blast. Mike came to the house a couple of hours later. Fred couldn't make it. I told Mike everything that went down. He was so in shock because he couldn't believe what some of the people had done. He felt bad about not going, but we all understood.

When Mike left the house, my phone starts ringing. It's Chad. I couldn't believe he called me because I thought it was just a sex thing. I think he wanted more. Chad had me smiling from ear to ear. He wanted to come over for a little conversation, but Sam was home. I told him to come in an hour when Sam will be at work. He called back an hour later. I told him to come over and be ready to have sex. He said okay and that he had something to tell me. I was looking like what is it?

He told me that he loved me. My mouth dropped to the floor. I didn't know what to say or do because I thought it was only a sex thing. He wanted to know how I felt about it. The only thing I could say was wow. Every time I tried to say something to him, my words wouldn't come out at all.

I went into the living area. Chad followed me. I had to get my mind back together. After getting myself together for the good news, I went into the kitchen and got some grapes and whipped cream.

As I was going back to the living area, I notice Chad getting undressed. I finish helping him undress. I throw him on the couch. I am ready to fuck. I put whipped cream and grapes all over his body licking the cream off every inch of his body. He starts teabagging the hell out of me. Those balls were all the way down my throat. The grapes were looking so good. I thought maybe I should put a couple in my mouth and start fucking the inside with grapes in it. I choke like a bitch, but I took it like a pro.

After he fucked my mouth so good, he takes his dick and sticks it in my tight asshole. He made real love to me. I was falling in love with him. Chad meant so much to me because he was sweet, caring and loving. I wanted to make him mine. I love the way he puts me on his knees. I start off by sucking the head of the dick. Then I deep throat his dick. He made love to me and fucked me nasty. That's how I liked to be fucked. I didn't want Chad to leave, but he had to because Sam was on his way home from work. He gave me a kiss and told me he loved me. My heart melted with happiness.

Sam just arrived home and wanted to go over to Jack's and Calvin's house for dinner. I said okay. We went over to their home. I really wasn't talking to Sam on our way there because Chad was on my mind so deep. Sam asked me if I talked to any of the guys today. I said yes, Chad. He had that he liked Chad a lot because he is such nice guy. Every time he said Chad's name my body begins to shake with love and joy. That's how much control Chad had on me and my body.

We finally arrive at our destination. I can smell the food on the outside. It was a smell you will never forget. We walked into the house. The two of them greeted us with love. These two guys are the best. The good was so amazing. The wine was lovely. Their relationship was going well for the moment. Jack stopped hanging with some of the people in the circle. I couldn't blame him. They will try to ruin a relationship.

Sam and I always kept it real. That's why people loved us so much. Jack and Sam decided to take Calvin and I shopping. I really needed that spree. Sam told me to shop until I drop. I shopped and dropped in the store. Jack laughed at me until tears started to flow down his face. When I got off the floor, Jack, Calvin, and Sam had big smiles on their faces. I was laughing at myself. I wonder how I passed out, but then I thought about it. Sam told me to shop until I drop, and I dropped.

After we left the mall and after making of fool of myself, we all went to dinner. Jack and Sam treated us with love the entire day. I was enjoying every moment because it's been a long time since we have done anything like this. Calvin and Jack wanted to come back to our place and chill. We were up for that since we have been hanging out all day.

When we got to the house and got settled, Sam put in a movie and got everyone a bottle of wine. He was trying to sex me because he already knew that wine makes me drunk. I love the idea, though. The other guys were sipping on their wine. I was drinking mine. There was no need for playing with it. After the fourth glass of wine, I was drunk as hell. I started to sweat. I was horny and ready to sex someone. Sam knew I was drunk and in heat. I turned my head towards Sam. He was talking to Calvin and Jack very softly. I knew they were planning something.

I was ready for whatever. My head began to spin and spin. I was becoming drunker than ever. I was ready for some good dick. I blanked out for a couple of minutes. When I came back to myself, and I mean myself, Jack was standing in the front of me. Calvin was in the back. I got up on my knees. I let Jack put his dick in my mouth and let Calvin out his dick in my ass. Sam was enjoying the soon to be show. The two of them had me moving like a rabbit on crack. I didn't know that I could ride dick so well. I bounced on Jack's dick about three times. He was ready to cum. That's what you call that good good.

Calvin was sexing the hell out of my mouth. I felt dick and balls all in my mouth. I didn't want him to take it out. Having a mouth full of dick and balls is what I love. Sam came over and put me in a headstand. My legs were spread like a field goal. He got on top of a ladder and dove into my ass. The only thing I could day was damn daddy fuck me good.

Sam made up for the old and new. He had me where I couldn't walk straight. His dick was so powerful and amazing. The three of them stood up with their dicks hanging low. I went up to each one of them and started sucking their sticky, sweaty old balls. This mouth of mine smelled like old pussy, but I had to get my suck on.

Sam asked me would I eat the three of their assholes. I told them to bend over and to spread open those cheeks. When they spread open, I went down the line and ate them out. It was the best I ever had. I tongue fucked all of them. They began to shake, rattle and roll. I told Sam to bend down and ride my face with that sexy ass of him. This tongue was so good to my baby. He was riding out of control. I was loving it.

Lust, Lies & Love

After riding and eating, I fucked Sam's mind sideways. That bitch ass was so tight and yummy. I will eat Sam out any time of the day or night. We were having a sex feast. I didn't want it to end. I wish Chad could have gotten some of this good ass or dick. Dude fuck so good and sweet. Every time someone says Chad's name I cum all over myself. He had that affect on me.

After we finished having sex, Jack and Sam went into the kitchen and made breakfast. We were both hungry. Jack and Sam called us in the dining area because it was time to eat. They had our food already prepared. I thought I was in another world. My baby was going bug and sweet things.

After we had breakfast and a little talk time, we went to Chad's place. My day was going even better. Chad wanted to talk to everyone about his new business. I hope he does well because we all went through some hard times with our friends who were in this business. Everyone was very proud of him because this is something he always talked about. I knew the guys were going to plan a party for Chad. I wanted to plan for Chad and me to have a one on one party just the two of us making love and loving on each other. That would nice for the both of us. I thought the guys were going to plan the party for next weekend, but they planned to have it this very night. They didn't give me time to get my ideas together. Everyone went to the stores to find decors and gifts for Chad. I didn't buy a gift because I was the gift that he wants.

After we left the stores, we all went back to Chad's place and made it cute for his birthday. I invited Tom and Matt because we haven't talked to them in so long. I wanted to enjoy the both of them. We had a lot to catch up on. Chad's party was going to be the one to remember. We had the people, the food, the drinks, and the A-list all there. This was going to be a party to remember.

Tom and Matt came back to our place to get dressed. As we were getting dressed for the party, Chad walked into the room and started to cry. He couldn't believe what we did. I asked Sam and Jack to take Chad back to his place. He needed to get ready for the party. I was happy that Tom and Matt came to New Mexico on our last night. Everyone began to get ready for Chad's party. They were ready to take him back. Everyone had big gifts for Chad at the house. I was his gift. I knew he was ready to fuck it. I wanted to be extra cute for his party. The guys and I went to the rental company to get Chad a limo for the night.

As we started to get dressed for the party, Tom and Matt came into the room. I was so happy to see them. The three of us hugged each other. My body got weak because I was so ready to freak the both of them, but I didn't want to be late for the party. I was Chad's gift so I have to be the show stopper and late.

When Tom and Matt changed their clothes, I saw them naked. My dick got hard as fuck. Matt's ass was looking right. Tom's dick was big as hell. I was ready to fuck and suck some dick. My body couldn't take it anymore so I took off my clothing and played with my dick. The throbbing was killing me. My body was ready. I pulled the both of them over to me. I lowered myself to my knees and started sucking their dicks. My mouth was full as fuck. I tried to put their balls in my mouth as well. The dicks were good as fuck.

I took their dicks out of my mouth to let it get some rest. I let the both of them fuck the shit out of me. They had my ass hurting so badly, but I took the dick. Tom had sweat dripping from his dick. I lick it all up with my tongue. He let me suck that dick dry. Matt was the freak of them all. He fucked me on top of the washer and had me where I couldn't move. My ass was up in the air. He was fucking me stank. The dick felt so good.

After such amazing sex, the three of us had to take a shower and get ready for the party. I thought we had to call a can in order to get where we were going, but Tom had already called the limo service. My body couldn't wait to get in and have a seat. My legs were hurting. My mouth was tired. My ass was stiff as ever. I was messed up because I could barely move. The fucking party is what I love the most. It was time to party and I mean party. Tom and Matt had their gifts ready, but you know how I do. I was the gift and more.

When the three of us walked inside the building, everyone was having a blast. People were drinking, dancing, and having fun. Sam and the other guys were already at the party. Things were going very well. I needed a drink to start my night off. A sex on the beach was going to do it for me.

Chad approached me while I drinking and trying to get my groove on. He came up behind me and gave me a hug. It felt so lovely because I was feeling me some him. He put his dick on my ass and whispered in my ear that I was his gift, his heart and that he wanted me to be the man in his life. I paused with love and couldn't say anything, but I love you. When Chad left me on the dance floor, Matt and Tom started to dance with me. We were dancing in circles forever and ever. The night was going by spectacularly. Chad's choice of outfit was the best. I was loving it to the fullest. We were feeling ourselves. Chad had gifts and friends out of the ass at this party. All of the guys had a blast.

When the party was over, we all went back to Chad's place because the party wasn't over. It was our last night in New Mexico. We were going to party and fuck the night away. Sam and Jack began to make drinks and food for everyone. I was beginning to get wasted and horny. Everyone had the fuck look in their eyes. I was ready to make things happen. The guys were looking sweet and ready to eat. Ass is what I was ready to eat and dick. I was ready to suck. Everyone wanted to talk and laugh all night, but I wasn't going for it. My dick and mouth were ready to feel something warm. The long I waited, the more my dick got harder.

I call Sam and Jack on their phones because they were in the kitchen preparing food. When they called me back, I told them I wanted the two of them to come into the bathroom and fuck me crazy. Sam thought something was wrong. I told them I was ready to fuck. The both of them had big smiles on their faces. They knew what was about to go down.

Sam starts taking my clothes off. He lays me on the floor and spreads my legs apart. Jack comes up and eats and licks my ass so well. He was getting it good and wet for Sam. When Jack was done eating, Sam put his big black dick inside of me. The dick took my breath away. He had me feeling so nice. My mind was in a zone.

Sam was making me feel like a man by rubbing my body and talking softly in my ear. He was looking seductively in my eyes. Sam was so amazing and sweet to my heart. Jack finished me off with a bang. I rode his dick so good. Jack fucked me into the mid-morning of the hour. That was the sweetest sex I ever had. Jack had my fucking mind messed up. If I wanted to think on my own I couldn't. His dick had my mind crazy and silly.

After the sex was over, we all went back to the kitchen for drinks and dinner. We were hungry as hell. The fucking and sucking those big dicks had me tired as hell. I had to act like nothing happened. It was time for a couple of spades games. I never could play, but I was ready to see the guys have a blast. Since I wasn't playing, I thought maybe I would sit in front of everyone naked. I knew no one would be able to keep their eyes on the table. Every time someone won a game, I pulled off a piece of clothing to shake some things up.

My shirt was the first piece that came off. Sam wanted to know what I was doing. He was ready for my clothes to come off. It was taking so long for the game to be over. My clothes just started coming off piece by piece. This bod was hot and ready to make music. The kind of music when you are ready to fuck. All of the guys were ready to bang the hell out of me. I was willing and ready because I knew the guys were ready to fuck.

Since this was the last night in New Mexico, I had to let all of the guys sex me because I had to take it for the team. They sexed the freak out of me. Matt and Tom was so happy they came to New Mexico. If they have stayed home, they would have missed the amazing party. We all enjoyed New Mexico, but now it is time to return home. We didn't want to leave, but we knew we had to go back home. New Mexico treated us with love, care, and happiness.

Lust, Lies & Love

Now we are getting on the plane heading back to home sweet home. Everyone was going their different ways. I began to cry and cry. Things were going to be different once again. I really hated that because we are not going to see each other for a while. I really enjoyed the guys in New Mexico. What a blast we had. We got drunk, had food, fucked each other and had an amazing time.

After the trip, Sam and I moved from Atlanta, Georgia and headed to the big apple. Things were looking good for the both of us. Sam got a new job. My career was booming. Life couldn't get any better. The guys didn't know we moved to New York. We told everyone a month later. We wanted to get settled and get to know the city. The two of us were so happy to be here. Sam was over a management company. Things were looking good for us. Our friends moved from New York back to Georgia.

We decided to meet new people and find different things to do. The people were friendly and amazing to us. Sam's job required him to work seven days a week. I didn't like that one bit. I can't complain because we needed the extra cash. The cost of living was higher here than in Georgia plus we enjoyed living the good life. Things are really working out for Sam and I. My business is growing.

It's going on our second month in New York. I thought it would be a good idea to call and invite some of the guys over. Calvin was the only one that came to visit. Everyone else came two days later because they had to work. We couldn't wait to party like the stars we are. Our home was big enough to accommodate everyone. Sam was treating me like a royal king. Sam greeted everyone with love and care when they arrived at our home. I was so happy to see everyone. It has been a long time since we have seen everyone. We wanted to treat them with love. Sam and I invited this guy named Kevin over.

We met him in downtown New York and wanted the guys to meet him. Kevin was a sexy, tall, breath-taking young man. He seems like a very nice guy. I thought that I would invite him over to chat with the guys. Sam called one of his friends up who was a chef. His good was so amazing and tasteful. When the chef came to the house to prepare the food, I called Kevin over for dinner. When He walked into the house, the guys were looking strangely at him because they didn't know him. He came in with a smile on his face and said hello to everyone. The guys waved their hands, turned their heads and resumed talking amongst themselves. I couldn't believe it because my group of friends is very nice and respectful. I think they were acting like that because Kevin was the new guy. They knew I was going to fuck him first.

The chef came into the living area and told everyone that dinner was ready. Hearing those words made me happy because the vibe I was feeling from the guys was not good. I wanted everyone to get along. I stood and made a toast to everyone hoping that they would get along just fine. We ate and drank. Hours went by. My body was feeling amazing and special. Sam wanted to play a game that was called fuck me. I was ready because Kevin looked like he had a big dick and some good ass.

When it was time to play the game, I was the first one with my hand out ready to play. Sam passed out the cards. I was getting happy by the minute. We played the game and I couldn't keep my eyes off of Kevin. He was looking sweet and sexy. My mouth wanted to suck him up. A big dick needed to be in my mouth and ass. Matt and Jack went into the kitchen and started to make drinks. I was hoping the two of them make the drinks extra strong so that everyone would get super wasted. Some of the guys started taking their clothes off. The drinks had them hot and heated. I told Kevin I wasn't feeling well and will he follow me to the bathroom. I knew he was going to play the fuck me game. My ass was wet. My mouth was watery. I couldn't wait for Kevin to fuck the hell out of my tight ass. I haven't had any good dick since the trip. Sam was decent, but I needed better.

When Kevin and I walked into the bathroom, I told him that I feel really wet. I wanted him to come with me because I was ready to fuck. Kevin was talking about the guys and the dinner. I pull up his shirt. I kiss on his chest. I work my way down to his stomach and lick on his dick. His dick was big as hell. He pushes my head all the way down as I lick his dick. The whole dick was in my throat. Slob was running all down my chin. I couldn't catch my breath. I was loving it.

He puts me on the bathroom sink. He folds my legs back and begins to fuck me. His big dick had me going crazy. He was hitting that spot. I was Cumming back to back. My hands were tied up. He was having his way with me. He was fucking the hell out of me. He had my ass hurting. I couldn't move if I wanted to. My legs were stiff. My body was crying for help.

After Kevin was finished with me, I got his dick and put it in my mouth. It seemed like his dick was getting bigger in my mouth. I didn't know what to do but to keep his dick in my mouth and suck, suck, suck. My jaws were tired, but I didn't let it phase me. I kept sucking like the pro I am. I had Kevin shaking and yelling for me to stop.

After I finished sucking his dick, he got up and walked really slow. I stopped him before he opened the door. My ass was still in heat. I wanted him to eat me out. Kevin told me to bend over and let him fuck my ass with his tongue. His tongue was so wet and long. My ass was loving that strong feeling. I was shaking like a baby monkey. He fucked me with so good with his tongue and with his powerful dick. I didn't know my own name when he was done with me. We took a shower afterward. We couldn't stay in the bathroom too much longer. We didn't want the guys to wonder what was taking us so long to come out.

When we came out and went into the living area, everyone looked at us funny. I was so shame-faced. I had to play it off. I asked everyone who wanted to go clubbing. No one replied to my question. Sam got up and said this. Since Kevin and my baby had a fuck fest in the bathroom, everyone should take off their clothes and fuck each other. Sam was trying to make me mad, but I didn't get mad. I wanted to freak Calvin anyway so I played along. He gave me the business too. My body felt so much better. Matt stood in front of me with his dick on hard. The shit smelled like old meat and fresh blood. His dick was stank. I made him get away from me. The smell was killing me. Sam came over because he thought I was going to give him some ass.

When he tried to touch me with his soft hands, I walked away. He told me that I should give it to him or he would take it. I laughed and said that if he wants it then he should take it. That's what he did. I didn't try to fight him. I had something for him. Sam told me to bend over so he could fuck me stupid. I did what he asked of me. He starts to freak me on the living room floor. I started to fake moan. He thought he was going the damn thing, but I had something in store for him. The harder he fucked me the more I had to shit. When he lost his mind in my soft, gentle, amazing ass, I shitted on his big black dick. Then I laughed. He wanted this ass and I gave it to him. Sam was mad as hell because he knew I did it on purpose. I wanted Kevin to fuck this ass again. He was the only one that could make me speak in Spanish while having sex.

Sam made me go into the bathroom and take a shower. Before I took a shower, I called Sam into the bathroom because the bath tub wasn't acting right. He called Charlie, his brother, over to fix it. When he came over to fix the tub, I stayed in with him so that everything goes as planned. As Charlie got more into his work, I started to take my clothes off. I couldn't control myself. I stopped Charlie from working. I got in the tub and let him freak me crazy. His lips were soft His hands felt like a feather.

His body was lovely. His dick was huge and pretty. I downed that dick so good. He put my legs in a bow and my hands under my back. He taped my mouth. He fucked me so good making me feel sexy and human. He entered me slowly and gently. Then he took the tape off of my mouth to put his dick down my throat. He fucked my mouth. I had to take his dick out of my mouth because I was ready to ride his dick. He laid down on the bathroom floor so I could ride him like a cowboy. My ass was so wet. He could barely take it. I was on these tip toes bouncing up and down slowly giving him this good ass. He was Cumming out of control. He fucked better than his brother. I let him cum all down my throat. The sex was so amazing. I had to suck on the head of his dick because it was looking so scrumptious. I couldn't let him go without tasting it. The feeling in my mouth had me going insane. He wore my ass out.

After Charlie finished both of his jobs for the night, I went into the living area to finish watching the freak fest. Everyone was looking tired as hell. I thought it was sweet because the guys were really enjoying themselves.

Sam and Mark went into the kitchen and concocted this weird snack. The taste was okay for me, but I don't think that the other guys liked it much. Sam never found out about Charlie and me. His dick was no comparison to his brother's. He fucked like a real man and not like a little boy. Kevin thought it would be a great idea if everyone would go out on the town and have a blast. We all went to this bar and grill. The place was nice and quaint. It was different from what I am used to, but the drinks were the same. We all walked into the club with a smile on our faces.

Lust, Lies & Love

Some of the people inside of the club didn't have on any clothing. I thought we were at a bar and grill, but Sam tricked us. Instead, it was a strip club. My eyes got so big when I saw ass and dick everywhere. Sam paid for me to get a lap dance. In lieu of a lap dance, I got a dick in my mouth. Sam didn't say anything. He only looked with a smile on his face knowing he was going to get some good ass whenever we left the club. We all took shots and danced the night away. The night went very peaceful at the club. I couldn't wait to make it home and sleep the day away... All of the guys were tired from fucking, drinking, and dancing.

When we woke up the next morning, some of the guys thought we should take a whole day and enjoy downtown. We haven't really been out. It was so hard trying to catch a cab. We finally got one, though. We did a lot of shopping and walking. Our legs were killing us so badly. It was worth it because we were together.

Later that night, we had dinner at this down home cooking restaurant. They had the best food in town. We met so many people that were from all over the world. The guys were having a blast. After dinner was over, we went out on the town to dance and party. The guys stayed with us for a week and became party animals. This became a problem because Sam and I had to work and tried to keep up with them all at the same time. Through it all, every moment was worth it. I wasn't ready for them to leave, but I knew they had things to take care of back at home. We had one more night to enjoy the guys.

We took them to a couple of strip clubs. I wanted them to have a night to remember. The strippers have big dicks for days and ass for weeks. Sam was so ready for me to get a lap dance, but I wanted a lap fuck. My eyes can only take so much. I was ready to freak something. The club was packed wall to wall with people. They guys were going crazy. People were on the stage sucking dick and getting freaked. I wanted to be one of those people.

I was ready to suck and get freaked by a big dick. The club was so amazing. I went to the bar a got a couple of drinks. I needed to get loose. I had about four drinks while at the bar. I was feeling myself now. The guys came over to the bar to get me. They were ready to party and let loose as a goose.

Lust, Lies & Love

By the time we started dancing and getting loose, I was wasted and horny as hell. I started dancing with everyone. Things started to get crazy for us. Guys were walking around naked. My circle of friends was looking with their mouths opened. Their mates weren't happy with it, but I told him we came to the party. Whatever goes down, go down.

We walked pass the stage and noticed some of the guys looking at us with smiles on their faces. I stopped at the stage, pulled one of the strippers down and played with him. Sam didn't care. He knew we came to have a great time. The stripper took me into this private room and freaked me silly. I took his underwear off with my teeth. I lowered myself to my knees and sucked the head of his dick. It was so sweet and big. He freaked my mouth gently and slowly. Sweat was falling from everywhere.

He put me on the floor and danced over me. He dropped down and started licking me from head to toe. I was shaking so lovely and firmly. The stripper pushed my legs back and started eating my asshole out. Simultaneously, he was jacking my dick. This body of mine was weak.

After he took his tongue out of my ass, I draw my legs back so he could slowly slide his dick into me. I felt every inch of his length inside of me. He was so big. My tight ass was loving it. He moved up and down slowly before pounding my ass. His dick was powerful as hell. He came four times inside of me.

When we finished having wonderful sex, I went back into the club so I could check on the guys. They were having a blast without me. The stripper freaked the hell out of me. Sam came up to me and asked how it was with the stripper. I told him that it was everything that I imagined. He looked at me with a smirk on his face and said that he was glad I enjoyed myself because it sure as hell cost a lot. I thanked my baby so much. I really needed sex from the stripper. Everyone was ready to go back to our place. It was the guys' last night with us. We were going to party and freak the rest of the night away.

When we arrived at my place, Chad and Sam make drinks and more drinks. We all wanted to get wasted. Sam made sure everyone got wasted. He was ready to freak all of the guys and me. I took my clothes off so fast, but the guys were moving slow as fuck. I couldn't have my baby waiting on some ass and dick.

When Sam was ready to give it to me, he wanted to sex me in front of everyone. I told him I was okay with it. He called all of the guys into the living area and told them what he wanted to do. They were all up for it. They were horny and wanted to see some hot action. I went into the guest room and got undressed. It didn't take me long to come out of my clothes. I was ready to put on a wonderful show.

When I talked into the living area where everyone was, Sam was already naked and ready to freak me. Everyone was sitting down watching intensely. We were about to put on a show. Sam started off by rubbing me down with baby oil. I danced for him. Then he lies on his back and I straddle him. I ride the head of his dick. It was big and pretty. He pulled me down, held my hips and fucked the hell out of me.

My ass was hurting like a monkey's ass. I was taking that entire dick. He pushed me off of him and threw me to my knees. He freaked me doggie style. I felt all ten inches inside of me. My body folded. I couldn't control myself. Next, he stood me up and put one of my legs on the air. He freaked me sideways. The dick was feeling so good. He bussed in me like a waterfall.

Lust, Lies & Love

After he did me upright, he lowered me to the floor to my back and made love to me. He kisses me from head to toe working his way up my body with his tongue stopping at my dick. He sucked me off so expertly. My baby had a good head game. He was making me crawl up the wall. I could only lay there and let him have his way with me. He freaked me in a way that I have never been freaked before. The guys were sucking and fucking the hell out of each other.

As I watched them get their freak on, my ass was getting so wet. I didn't join in because Sam wore me out. This body of mine couldn't take any more dick. I wanted to lie down and go to sleep. I couldn't because the guys were having a party in the living room. Sam was ready for their little party to be over. Someone's ass was so stank. All of their dicks smelled musty and raw. I don't enjoy stank ass or dick because I like putting my mouth on those two places. This mouth of mine always keeps a big clean dick in it. Time is passing by. They are still having their sex party so I sat on the couch next to Sam with his dick in my mouth. His dick was jumping up and down. I bent over and kept it under control in my warm mouth. My baby was loving it.

Lust, Lies & Love

A couple of minutes later, the guys were finished having their sex party. They looked tired and sleepy. New York was so good to the guys. Now it was time for them to go home. Sadness came over us. We didn't want them to leave.

Before they got ready to leave, we all went out for dinner and a couple of drinks. We were the life of the party. The diner closed early so we went back to our place and went to sleep.

The next morning, Sam got up early to prepare breakfast for everyone. I started to cry because I was already missing the guys. They came over to give us a hug and to tell us not to cry. They told us that they were coming back to visit very soon. I really had a blast with the guys. I tried to not cry, but that attempt failed. Tears started to flow. They mean so much to me. Now it's time for Sam and me to go back to our old ways which is working and chilling on the town and meeting new people.

Six months into being in New York, I started traveling with my business. I needed to get away for a while. Sam was fine with it. Business was picking up for him also. He didn't want me to be gone for so long. Since I was missing the guys, I traveled to Atlanta to pay them a little visit for a couple of months. The guys didn't know I was coming. I wanted to surprise them. They were so happy to see me. Matt and Mark wanted to know why I was here. I told that that I missed them and that I needed to do some work here. They thought it was a great idea. I knew it was about to be on. I called Sam to tell him that I was staying in Atlanta for three months. He wasn't pleased at all, but I had to do what was best for me and my business. Sam really didn't want me staying that long because he knew Chad had something for me. I tried to come to a compromise with Sam about my staying in Atlanta. He wanted me to come back home and do business in both states. I didn't agree with that.

After we got off the phone, I told the guys what we talked about. They told me to what is best for me. I stayed in Atlanta. Chad came to the house two days later. He was on a business trip in Spain. We were so happy to see each other. When I needed someone to talk to and love me, Chad was always there for me. I wanted to thank him for that. It was time for us to party and have a blast. The guys were ready to take me out on the town. Chad couldn't make it because he had a lot of business work to finish. My heart was hurt and sad. I wanted to spend some time with my sweetheart.

After the club, I knew things were going to be on the popping. Chad picked me up. We all went to his place for some fun. It took the limo an hour to pick us up. People started taking their clothes off and wanted somewhere to lay their heads.

When the driver called the house, everyone started getting ready. The company gave our money back along with a free ride. On our way to the downtown bar, we were taking shots and having a blast. We pulled up to the club in style. People were walking up to the limo as if we were celebrities. That was the highlight of the night.

As we were walking into the club, I heard a voice calling my name over and over. When I turned around, it was Chad. My heart skipped a beat. My sweetheart was able to make it after all. The club was nice. People were walking around half naked. The guys had big asses. The owner was fine as fuck. The music was right. Everyone was looking good. Chad offered to get me a drink. That is so sweet of him. I didn't dance or drink with the guys. Chad wanted to spend some time with me. The both of us had two drinks a piece. He wanted us to leave. I needed that alone time with him.

When we left, he wanted to go back to his place for some good, hot and steamy sex. Rose petals trailed the pathway through the house to the bed. Candles lined the wall and lit up the room. A bottle of wine was chilling on the bedside table. My sweetheart knows how to please me with gifts and more. I went into the bathroom where there was candles and wine all around. The bubble bath was hot. We made real love while in the bath. I stood up, put my hands on the wall, and bent over to let Chad eat me out. His lips felt so amazing and smooth. I could barely stand because his lips and tongue were feeling so lovely. He had my asshole jumping like a frog.

Chad helped me out of the bathtub and carried me into the bedroom. Things were getting so romantic. Candles, wine, rose petals and strawberries were everywhere. Chad laid me onto the bed, fed me strawberries and gave me a glass of white wine. I was falling in love with Chad. He put strawberries and rose petals all over me. He eats strawberries off of me with his juicy soft lips. My legs couldn't stay still. He was making mad love to me. He loved me right to sleep, and I loved it.

Lust, Lies & Love

The guys called me the next morning because they wanted to know how my night went. A couple of them were shocked and upset because Sam and I were still in a relationship. I didn't care what they thought of us. Chad was in love with me. I am falling for him and only him.

My business was going so well in Atlanta. I didn't want to move back to New York. Jack called me on the phone. He wanted to know what was really going on with me. I told him that we should go out to dinner and have a long talk. He was up for it. He came and picked me up later that afternoon. The dinner was nice, but the look on Jack's face was scary. Telling Jack about Chad was very hard because Sam and Jack were best friends. I didn't know how to tell him about us.

As dinner began, I thought I should tell Jack about Chad and me. As I was telling Jack about us, tears started to flow down his face. My heart felt like a broken heart. Jack cared about Sam a lot. I was treating him like dirt without him knowing.

After the dinner was over, I called Sam because he really needed to know what was going on. It was time for me to leave Atlanta for a couple of days. He wanted me to come back home for a couple of days. That's what I gave him. Sam wanted to know why. Like I told him, baby you are always gone on business trips. I need someone to love me. He looked at me crazy as hell. The truth is what I told him. He wasn't there for me anymore.

Jack and Sam began to talk. He thought we needed some space. Sam wanted to know if I still loved him. Of course I like him. Love doesn't live here anymore. Tears were everywhere. Dealing with it wasn't good. The crying was working my nerves. Jack left to go back home. I tried to cheer up Sam. We haven't had sex in a couple of months. So I went into the bathroom, took a hot shower and let Sam fuck me dizzy. He put his dick so far down my throat. I couldn't move my tongue or my neck. Sam was freaking me so well. He had my asshole and stomach hurting. I don't know what got into Sam, but he started fucking me like he didn't know me.

After we were finished, Sam told me to go and take a shower because he wasn't finished with me yet. He wanted to punish me and my body. I laughed at him for saying what he said. He turned the shower on and put me in it.

After I got out of the shower and started having sex, laughing was the last thing I did.

Lust, Lies & Love

He fucked me hard as fuck. His big dick had me about to cry. I thought about Chad as I was taking Sam's dick. I was riding and sucking it stupid. He didn't know what to do. His dick was yelling for this good ass. The simple bitch went to sleep after he got this good... good...

Ten minutes later, Chad was calling. I didn't want to answer because Sam was beside me, but I had to. My sweetheart was missing me. We talked about thirty minutes. Hanging up the phone on Chad wasn't easy because he is my baby. I thought Sam was sleep to the world, but he wasn't. He woke up and said I see you are in love with Chad.

My mouth didn't open at all. Sam told me since I couldn't open my mouth that he could help me by putting his big dick all the way down my throat. He was choking me with his dick and balls. He was trying to teach me a lesson, but I was used to it. He was killing my throat. I was ready to return to Atlanta. The guys wanted me to stay longer, but I had to get back to Chad. He was missing me a lot. I stayed with Sam for about four days. He fucked the hell out of my ass every day. I had to leave and give Chad some of this good.

Lust, Lies & Love

Sam took me to the airport. Whenever I got out of the car, he said that he loved me and for me to be safe. My head turned so fast. I looked the other way. I thought it was funny. Sam was losing his everlasting mind. I couldn't wait to get on the plane. I was missing my Chad so much.

When we arrived at the airport in Atlanta, Chad was there to pick me up. My face was glowing like a light bulb. My baby was looking sexy, lovely and sweet. I missed him so much because I am in love with him.

On our way to the house, Chad told me how much he loved and cared about me. I started to cry because my baby was pouring out his feelings to me. I never saw it before. Life was getting better for Chad and me. He took me shopping and out to eat. The veins in my dick wanted to pop out. My baby was being extra nice to me. I liked him even more and enjoying him. Something was funny about Chad. He was being a little too nice. Perhaps, he was changing for the better and wanted things to work out with us. That's what I was hoping.

After we got back from shopping and dinner, we walked into the house. The romance was in the air, I was feeling it so much. Chad and I took everything slow that night. People thought I was crazy for leaving Sam. I didn't leave him. I was trying to get myself together. The guys thought otherwise. The truth was the truth. They couldn't take it. Sam called me because my business in New York needed me. That's not what I wanted to hear. Telling Chad was going to be hard, but I had to do it. He walked outside where I was. He heard me yelling and crying while I was on the phone with Sam. He thought I was going crazy until I told him what was going on. The thought of me going back to New York was killing me. Chad wasn't happy. Dick never wanted you to leave when the ass is good, but I had to do what was best for my business. Things were getting out of control and it was time for me to step back in and take over.

Chad and I talked the whole night before I left. He lets me know how he feels about me and our relationship. The words shocked and surprised me. My baby began to talk with pride, joy and love. I didn't want to leave him, but I needed to. Those two days with him were killing me because it wasn't enough time to love and cherish him. Instead of us talking the whole night, we could have been freaking the night away. My ass was wetter than the ocean. My dick was harder than a rock. I wanted that big dick all in me. I wanted to make it touch my stomach and lungs. I was going to miss Chad because he was my world, strength, and love.

When we woke up the next morning, it was time for me to leave Atlanta. Before I left, Chad wanted to take me out for breakfast. I thought that was so sweet of him. My mind was in another zone while going to breakfast. He was telling me how he loved and cared for me. My body, soul and mind were in another world. Leaving Chad was going to be the hardest thing I have ever done.

When we got to the breakfast diner, Chad opened my door and let me out. Things were sad for me. We walked into the diner and it was so nice. The food was great. The waiter was amazing. My baby was looking sexy as ever.

After breakfast, it was time for me to leave Atlanta and fly back New York. Chad started crying on our way to the airport. I felt bad for him. I know I mean the world and all to him. Before I got onto the plane, tears couldn't stop rolling down my face. I gave Chad a hug. Then he left the airport. My life was going to be a mess without him.

Lust, Lies & Love

I called Sam to let him know I was on my way back home. He sounded so happy. I don't know why because I wasn't ready to see him. Our lives were the same. I didn't want to make things work.

The place was feeling so good. I slept the entire time because I was missing me some Chad. He was the best thing I ever had. When I arrive at the airport, Sam was there to pick me up. He had a big smile on his face with nothing but teeth showing. I wanted to run, but I kept my cool. He started kissing and loving on me. He made my skin crawl. That was the worst kiss I have ever had. He wanted to take me out to eat, but I wasn't feeling it. Chad was on my mind like crazy.

Jack called to make sure I made it back safely. He made my day when he called. I really needed to talk to him about Sam and me. Jack was Sam's best friend. I knew he was the best to talk with. As Jack and I began to talk, Sam walked into the living area and asked me who I was talking to. I looked at him crazy and said, Jack. He walked out with a happy look on his face. Jack thought that he should fly to New York. He wanted to have a sit-down talk with me. Yes, yes, yes, was all I could say. I needed some good sex. Jack has that mean good ass and dick.

After our phone call, Sam asked me what Jack was talking about. I told him nothing and that he was on his way to visit us. Sam's face started to glow. The both of us were happy to see Jack. Sam wanted to pick Jack up from the airport. Instead, I went to pick him up. This dick was about to be sucked so good. This ass was going to be eaten out as well.

I arrived at the airport ten minutes after Jack made it. I had to make it up to him because I was a couple of minutes later. When I saw my freaky friend, he ran into my arms with joy. Seeing him was the best thing ever. We went to a friend's house. I wanted to spend some time with Jack. He was once my little heart. Sam called me to tell me that he had to go out of town for business. That was the best news I could hear at the moment. Sam was leaving for two months. I was going to be freaking Jack. When I told Jack the good news, his face started to glow with love. He was ready to get inside this fat ass.

I started to fake cry on the phone. I told Sam that I really cared and loved him. He started to break down and didn't want to attend his business trip. We couldn't have him staying.

Lust, Lies & Love

We talked him into going because I needed the extra money. Sam and I talked about an hour. I couldn't keep Jack waiting so we left Jack's friend's house and went to my house.

Paul, who is a friend of Sam, called me. He was in town. I asked him to go over to my place to get things ready for us. He didn't want to do it because of Sam. I bribed him with a great sum of money and he happily obliged. The bed and bathroom looked amazing. Paul strategically placed rose petals all over the floor and placed candles everywhere. Love filled the air. Jack was still outside talking to Paul. Getting his body clean and fresh is a must. He hasn't had any of this good ass in months.

When Jack and Paul walked into the bedroom, I was lying on the bed covered with strawberries and cream. Paul's mouth dropped. His eyes got bigger. His dick was sticking straight up. Jack started laughing. I have never freaked Paul and have never thought about it. When he took his clothes off, I saw his huge pretty dick. I knew we were going to make things happen.

Paul walked over to me and told me to open my mouth. He put his dick inside. His dick was huge as fuck. I started to deep throat that dick like it was nothing. My mouth kept it wet. After he took his dick out of my mouth, Jack pulled my ass cheeks apart and let Paul fuck the hell out of my tight ass. The pain was so out of control that I couldn't take it. Every time I yelled or moaned, Paul fucked me harder. His dick was freaking my insides. When he took his dick out of my ass, I thought everything was over, but it wasn't. The both of them put their dicks in my ass at the same time. I was crying and shaking. They didn't stop because they said I should be able to take it.

Paul's dick was the biggest. I felt his balls and all. It felt like the bottom of my ass had fallen out. They were making me pay for the way I was treating Sam. Perhaps, I need to treat him that way all the time because they gave me the dick good. Paul got up and asked me how I felt now. He also said that he knew my asshole is sore as hell. There was nothing I could say. I could only lay there.

Paul had to leave for work. Jack cuddled with me. He made me feel like a real king. He fucked me good, loved on me and took me back in time. Those two dicks were the best ever. After Jack went back home, I called Chad because I was missing him. He wanted to fly to New York for a couple of days. I thought that was a great idea. He was going to get a hotel for a week, but I asked him to stay with me instead. We have two guest rooms for company whenever they come over. Our housekeeper was getting one ready for Chad.

As I thought about it, I had a change of mind. Chad was going to sleep in our bed. We were going to be fucking and sucking the whole week. Maybe I would sleep on the couch the last night, but before then I will be in the bed with Chad the rest of the days. I knew it was wrong, but who gives a fuck. My baby wanted to be with me.

The first night Chad was at the house, we made some powerful love. His hands felt like feathers. His body felt like snow. Chad took over my mind, body, and soul.

Six o'clock the next morning, my business called me. They needed me to come to the shop because something happened. I wondered what could be going on. Chad was asking all kind of questions. We left to see what was going on.

When we got there, everything was already worked out. I felt so much better afterward. Chad took me out to eat and shopping. He wanted to get my mind off of everything. We didn't stay in New York the whole week. Chad had to take care of some business. I left my co-business partner in charge.

We arrived in Atlanta. Mike was at the airport to pick us up. He had an angry look on his face. He didn't say anything when we got into the car. Mike was angry because I was with Chad and that I would not fuck him anymore. He dropped Chad off at his place. He and I went to our secret spot. He started to talk and cry. Tears came all over me. I took my dick, got it on hard and let Mike suck away. I was missing that wet mouth. He had my eyes wide opened and crossed. That tired bitch was giving it to me with no problem.

After he finished sucking on this dick, we went to meet the guys. My mind was happy to see the guys, but they weren't happy to see me. They heard about Chad and me. Trying to talk to them was not easy. The more I tried to talk to them, the louder they got. I was over talked. I was feeling like shit because they had a reason to be mad at me. I had to call Sam because we needed to talk. One of the guys had already told him everything, but he wasn't mad. He knew I was a freak and that I fuck friends. Sam was stupid for staying by my side. I cheated and everything on him. He still loved me. He is such as fool. I had to leave the guys early.

Chad took me to the airport. I was loving it. Sam talked to me the entire flight. I wanted to throw up. I took a can to the house. He wanted to come and pick me up, but I wasn't having it.

When I got to the house where Sam was, he wanted to have sex and talk later. I called up an old friend that lived in New York and told him to come over. When he came over, I asked him to fuck Sam in front of me. They both agreed to do it. I knew Sam couldn't take Tim's dick. He wanted some dick. I found him some. I started laughing when Tim started fucking Sam upside down. Sam was crying and shaking like a rat. I told Tim to fuck the shit out of Sam.

Since Sam is so crazy about sex and love, Tim fucked him so hard and crazy. I wonder if he still wants to have sex. I am not giving it to him unless it is with my lover, Chad. He is the one who makes me feel sexy.

After Tim fucked Sam crazy, Sam tried to get out of the bed, but he couldn't. Time put it on him. I looked at Sam and asked him if he wanted anymore dick since Tim fucked the shit out of him. He told me no. I laughed. In my mind, I was saying you crazy bitch. Tim was ready to leave. I drew Sam a bath. I made sure it was extra hot. I wanted that slow bitch to feel the heat.

Since Tim did me a favor, I took him home and sucked his dick. I had to stop. Sam's ass was stank as hell. He had Tim's dick smelling like old pussy. I made it up to Time because Sam did him wrong.

After I dropped him off at his place, my car wanted to act crazy. Tim came out of his house to fix my car. As I was about to let the hood down, Tim pulled my pants down, bent me over and fucked me slow. His dick was feeling so good. I love the way it went in and out.

Five minutes after fucking my asshole so good, he took out his tongue, spread my cheeks and tongue fucked me. My body was in love again. Tim was better than Chad, but I didn't let him know.

When I walked into the house, Sam asked me what took so long and I told him. The car was acting up and that Tim fixed it. I let him fuck me good for doing me a favor. He didn't say anything, but he loved me. I could care less. Sam wanted me to sleep with him, but I slept on the floor. I slept just fine. I didn't have to look in stupid's face or smell his stank mouth. I woke Sam up early that morning and went back to Atlanta. Chad was ready for me to come back. Life was trying to get boring for me.

I called everyone up and asked how they would feel if I have another sex party. They were up for it. I was happy because this will be Chad's first time attending one. I was going to be the life of the party. Jack called Sam and told him about the party. Sam wasn't happy, but he was coming. It took me three days to plan the party. Now it is party time. I am wearing nothing.

When I arrived at the party, people were having sex, doing drugs and drinking. I was ready for the sex and drinks. Chad met San for the first time. Neither one of them liked each other, but they didn't show it. I could tell. Chad wanted to fuck me in front of Sam. I said no because that is disrespectful. Chad wasn't cool with me tell him no. He was looking sad. I had to cheer my baby up. He and I started kissing, touching and loving on each other, one thing leads to another. We were having sex in front of Sam and everyone else. Sam stood there and looked surprised.

Ten minutes into our having sex, Sam thought he would join the fun. Chad loved every minute of it. His dick was getting sucked from left and right. That dick stayed wet. I was glad Sam took it for the team. My ass was ready for some hard dick. I bent over and started shaking this fat ass. I had to get Chad's dick extra hard in order for it to go in my mouth. When it came to Chad and me to have sex, we made love instead. Sam wasn't a fan of that because he knew I was enjoying it and never really enjoyed it with him. Chad as having his way. My baby was making me feel special.

The guys couldn't believe what was going on. Sam was upset, but he got over it. He didn't make me feel special anymore. It was time for me to be love. Chad pulled me away from everyone and took me to the bar. We had a couple of drinks together. I enjoyed our time together. People were looking at us crazy, but it didn't matter. There were things at the party that I never have seen before. Some of it freaked me out. That was a sex party to remember. The guys really enjoyed themselves. This was my second party, and I had to make it a blast. The drinks, sucking and the fucking was the best.

Lust, Lies & Love

After the party, I went back to Chad's place. He had something special to give to me. I couldn't wait to get it. I knew it was going to be big and good. I was hoping it was some good dick. He knew I couldn't get enough. Anytime he says you want some to me, it is already in my mouth. My baby kept me happily filled with love. He asked me was Sam staying around. The only thing I could say is that he still loved me. He always thought Sam was crazy because of the things I have done to him and he still stayed by my side. I told Chad to his face that Sam once meant the world to me, but now he doesn't. I also told him to not talk about him as if he is a bad person. Chad agreed which made me happy.

Moving back to New York with Sam was going to be the best for me. My number one business was there, and my people need me. Chad and I called it off for a while, but not for long. I had to work on my relationship with Sam. He wanted things to work, but I was so confused.

Since Paul was a good friend to us, he moved in with us for a few weeks. Those three weeks are going to be my best weeks ever. Freaking Paul, eating ass and sucking dick are what I do. I couldn't wait to have some fun.

Lust, Lies & Love

I stayed home from work for a couple of days. My head was killing me so badly. Sam went to work. Paul stayed to take care of me. He made me some soup which I appreciated.

Two hours later, I began to feel a lot better. My Dick was sticking up and I was ready to fuck. Paul was looking sweet and ready for me to eat. His ass looked tasty, fresh and worth eating. Sam came home from work earlier than I expected. I was mad as hell. My body was hoping to get some of that good dick and eat some wet ass. Paul started preparing dinner as Sam was resting. The menu was looking good. Paul wanted me to sample the good as he cooked the different items. The food was very tasteful and amazing. I went into the bedroom and got Sam for dinner.

When we got to the dinner table, Paul had everything out and ready. Sam enjoyed the meal a lot because he hasn't had a home-cooked meal in so long. Paul was the best. Sam started to feel sick. His head was hurting very badly. I have him some medicine that knew was going to put him to sleep.

Thirty minutes later, he was sleeping like a baby. Paul took as shower and went into the guest room and laid down. I got him up because I wanted him to lay with me. I made

Lust, Lies & Love

sure I dragged Sam up and brought Paul into our bedroom. We talked for a couple of minutes. After the talking, we got our freak on. Sam was asleep and didn't know what was going on. Paul was fucking me so good. He started to dick me down so good. He started beating down my asshole and had me yelling loud as fuck. That dick was amazing. I was turning around on his dick while it was still in my ass. I am a bad bitch. Paul was Cumming out of control. I was catching every drop in my mouth. I would do anything for a man with a big dick. He had done and I didn't whatever it took in order to please him. Sam didn't wake up while Paul and I were making love.

When he woke up the next morning, I have him a big kiss on the lips. Paul started laughing because he knew I had sucked his dick good with those same lips. Loving Sam wasn't easy for me. I wasn't in love with him anymore, but I had to play the role of being his lover.

Within the three weeks that Paul was with us, I began to fall in love with him. He knew how I wanted and liked it. He was a very special man to Sam and me. Things were getting crazy and weird. I was loving two wonderful men. The both of them meant the world to me. Every time I thought about the two of them, my mind was in a better place.

Paul had to leave one day early. Before he left to go back home, we wanted to take him out on the town. Paul thought it would be a great idea to stay at the house. He wanted to watch a movie and have dinner. We compromised and watched movies and had dinner. This is what Sam enjoyed doing anyway.

When we started looking at the movie and eating, Chad crossed my mind. I couldn't stop thinking about him all of a sudden. He was the love of my life. We were missing one thing. That was the wine. Without wine, my night wasn't t going to go so well. Paul went to the store and got me a bottle of my favorite wine. I wanted to get on my knees and start sucking the hell out of his dick. My baby knows what I like.

The dinner, movie, and the wine went well. After dinner, it was time for Paul to return home. Sam and I really enjoyed him and the things he did for us. Talking Paul back to the airport was very heartbreaking. He was so sweet and kind to me. I stayed with Sam for two extra days. It was time for me to go back to Atlanta. I was missing my Chad. He was the best thing that ever happened to me. Sam didn't want me to leave New York, but I had to.

The guys, Chad, and my business were missing me so much. Atlanta treated me with love and care. New York didn't mean me well. When I got back to Atlanta and Chad, things were getting where I wanted them to be. I called everyone up because it was time to party. They were all happy to see me back. Jack wanted to take everyone out for dinner. I had a why moment. I had a twisted look on my face. I didn't want to talk about my trip.

When we all got to the diner to eat, Jack wanted to know how things went. I smiled and said lovely. I wouldn't have had it any other way. He began to smile and said wow that's great. In the back of his crazy mind, I knew he was saying to himself that it was a lie.

The dinner went okay, but it could have been a lot better. Chad didn't show up because some of the guys didn't care for him. Since my baby didn't come to dinner, I had to make it up to him. I went to his apartment. He was lying in bed naked. His body was looking great. His dick was big as hell. I ran and gave him a big hug. I needed to shower before he fucked me good.

Lust, Lies & Love

As I was getting into the shower, Chad was behind me with his dick on hard pressed against my backside. A big smile was on my pretty face. The water was warm on my body. I was ready. Chad bent me over and started to eat my ass. His tongue felt hella good. I wanted to stop him, but I couldn't. The feeling was amazing. Not long after that, he stopped.

I had to finish my shower so Chad went back into the bedroom. When I was done, I let Chad lotion me down. His hands were doing the job. After he rubbed me down good, he spread my legs open, kissed my thighs and used the wonderful tongue on me. He was working my body with love. I push him over so I had better access to his dick. I suck on his dick and play with the head. It was tasteful and good. He makes mad love to me. He was getting the best of my love. It was so good that I wanted to fall asleep. I wanted more sex, though. Chad was ready for more loving. I was willing to give it. I got into the bow position and let him put his dick in me slowly. The feeling was so good. My baby was getting a good workout.

When we finished making love, Chad expressed his love to me. I was stuck in between the two. While thinking who I should be with, Sam called and wanted to talk. He wanted me to know that he still loves me and that he is always going to be there for me. I wanted to cry. Sam has been nothing, but good to me. Even thought I cheated on Sam with his friends, best friend, and brother, he was still there for me. I don't want to leave him, but I needed to. Our conversation went well, but I was ready to move on. The love wasn't like it once was.

When I hung up, tears streamed down my face. I remembered the good and bad time we shared together. Sam wanted our relationship to work because he really cared for me. Chad told me to not worry about the past and to focus on the present. That was sweet of him to say, but he didn't understand how hard of a concept it was to grasp.

Paul wanted to meet up with my circle of friends. He heard a lot about the and wanted to meet them. It was going to be crazy. I called and told the guys. They were fine with it. I didn't know why he wanted to meet them. Something is telling me that Paul wanted to meet Chad in particular. That was something I didn't want to happen.

We all met up that night. Chad didn't attend because he didn't care for the guys. Paul took everyone out for dinner. He didn't stay long because he had somewhere to be. I was in a great mood. In order for me to be happy, I called Sam and told him that we were over for good. I could hear the phone drop to the floor. I felt bad. It was the happiest day of Chad's life. They guys were hurt. They couldn't believe what just happened. I broke up with Sam for me. People think I did it for Chad.

I went back to New York to get a couple of my things. Sam agreed to send the rest to me. I moved to Atlanta with my baby. Being with Chad was going to be great. He knew how to treat me. Same wanted to take over the business in New York. Chad wasn't having it because he was about to be the co-owner. When Sam heard about it, he called me with madness in his voice. He was yelling, fussing and using really foul language. He was so upset because Chad was taking over. Sam was very business-minded. We weren't together anymore so I wanted to no longer deal with him. I should have given it to Sam, but dealing with him wouldn't be easy. I will always care for him. At the moment, I love me some Chad. He is going to be my baby until the end.

Chad thought he would take me on a mini trip. He said that I was going through a lot. He wanted to ease my mind, soul and heart. I started crying. Their trip was going to help the both of us. To my surprise, we vacationed in China. I smiled the biggest smile, and my eyes lit up like Christmas. I was ready to give my baby some of this good ass. It was wet and ready to be fucked sick.

The hotel was amazing. We checked into the hotel, ordered room service and started to play around. Since I am the freaky one, I jumped on top of Chad and unzipped his pants. I started sucking his big black dick. My mouth got so wet and juicy. I deep-throated his dick so good. It wasn't good three minutes and he was Cumming. I have to give it to myself. I have a mean mouth game. I was going to call it wet wet because it was.

An hour later, I put this wet ass on Chad. He gave me the best sex every. We started off by licking whipped cream off of each other. Then he put me in the middle of the bed surrounded by roses. He poured wine on me and licked it all off. My body began to shake like crazy. The more I shook, the more I became crazy and out of it. I told him to take his time because this body belongs to him. He tied my legs and arms up. He put an apple in my mouth and sexed me all night.

Lust, Lies & Love

When he untied me, I went bunny rabbit on him. I started bouncing up and down on that dick so good. I felt dick and balls all in my ass, but I kept riding. I had to keep the boo happy.

There was towel beside me. I reached for it because I was making so much noise. People were next door. I didn't want them to hear me. Chad was dicking me down so good. My thighs felt so weird. My mind was really gone. His dick was like food, so good I can't let go. He will always be the love of my life.

My heart was missing Sam so much. He stayed on my mind. If I could change the way I treated him I would. He never hurt me or tried to down me. Sam was my world, but Chad and I are living the good life now. Things are going well for us. Chad loves me more and more.

The guys stopped talking to me because of Chad. They didn't like him. I was going crazy. I couldn't let my friends go because of a man. They all meant the world to me. No matter what they say, I will always care for Sam. Chad is my new pride and joy.

Chad and I moved from Atlanta to New Jersey. He wanted to get away from all of the drama. I was down for it. I didn't want to leave the guys, but they didn't want to see us happy. I had to do what was best for us. We were staying in Atlanta for three more months before the big move. The house in New Jersey wasn't ready. Those few months were killing us. The guys weren't treating Chad kindly. I was stressing. I couldn't wait until we could leave. It felt like the builders were taking all year. We were ready to start our lives together.

A month later, it was time for us to leave Atlanta and head to the garden state. Things were about to work out for the best. I started packing our things for the new move. I couldn't pack fast enough. Before we left Atlanta, I wanted to meet up with the guys. Chad thought it would be a great idea if we all went out for dinner. Everyone agreed to meet. The drama was on its way. I was ready for it this time.

Jack and I were the last two people to enter the diner. Heads turned as we walked in. I was ready for it all. Some of the guys started to talk amongst themselves. I thought that was so rude. Spending time with the guys and having a blast are the two things I wanted to do, but that didn't happen. Everyone was talking about Chad and me. I got up from the table and left. I kept my cool. Leaving Atlanta and going to New Jersey was the best thing I can do right now. I didn't have to deal with the drama from the guys. Chad and I were going to live our lives happily.

Jack and Calvin took us to the airport. They helped us take our bags out of the car. I started to cry thinking about the times we had together. I was going to miss Jack like hell. He was my friend, sex partner, and my homeboy. He is such as great guy. Now it is time for us to get on the place and head to Jersey. Chad smiled from ear to ear. MY baby was ready to leave and spend the rest of his life with me.

When we arrived in New Jersey, Chad looks scared. This was his first time moving out of the state of Georgia. I felt sorry for him. The limo took us to our new home. It was huge and lovely. Chad really surprised me. Our lives were about to start. Calvin and Jack called us days later to make sure that we were settled and to find out how things are going. Chad was running my New York business. I was over the Atlanta business. We were only in New Jersey for two weeks. The businesses were doing well. We didn't know anyone here, but Chad made friends easily. He was such a people person. That's what I loved about him.

Lust, Lies & Love

We were invited to a networking party. We were so happy to be invited because only the best were invited. Things were looking up for us. The teacher taught us so much about the business. That was what we needed.

After the party, we went out on the town for dinner. He treated me like royalty. MY baby gave me a dozen roses and a bottle of wine. I loved him so much.

The limo took us around town. It was a view you will never forget. We saw the highs and lows of the city. Through it all, we enjoyed it. When we got back to the house, Chad had everything laid out so nicely. I wanted to jump on that dick and ride. I wanted to show a little gratitude. We cuddled in front of the television and fell asleep.

When we woke up the next morning, I felt something hard, big and straight up inside of me. It was Chad's big dick. He had my ass stiff as hell. I couldn't do anything but back this ass up on him. He began to dive in and I was losing my mind. He fucked me doggie style for about an hour. This tight ass was hurting and crying for help. My knees were weak and sore, but I took it like a real man.

Lust, Lies & Love

After taking it from behind, I decided to ride that big dick. My body was in pain, but I wanted to satisfy my baby. My legs, knees, and ass were hurting. I headed straight to the shower after we were finished. I cried in the shower. Knowing my baby was there made me feel good.

I invited a couple of people over for a get-together. Chad hired a personal chef for the event. Altogether, there were about sixty people over. They were the most respectful people you could ever meet. There was no drama, looking crazy or rudeness. They are down-to-earth people. Chad wanted me to meet his friend, Alvin.

Alvin is a pediatrician. He came over to the house the next day. He is a very handsome guy. I wanted to eat him up. His body was amazing. His skin is flawless. He is tall as hell. I Knew he had a big, long dick by the way was walked up to the door. He was nice and respectful. I knew his circle of friends had to be the best. Having friends like Alvin couldn't get any better. The table set up was so amazing. We sent a limo to pick up Alvin from his home. He was so surprised.

When Alvin arrived at our place, we had everything laid out and ready. The look on his

Lust, Lies & Love

face was priceless. The chef fixed our food and we ate. Everything was wonderful. After we were done eating, we all went into the movie room to watch a couple of movies. Of course you know I had to have my wine. It was so good and tasteful.

During the movie, I noticed that Alvin kept looking at me. His eyes were speaking to me. A couple of minutes into the movie, he started licking his lips. He touched his dick and played with his tongue. I was getting horny as fuck.

Chad noticed what was going on, but didn't say anything. He was ready for a good threesome. I was going to give it to him too. The wine was making me feel myself. My dick was getting hard. My mouth was wet and ready to be fucked good. Chad had to turn the air down because it was getting hot. My clothes began to come off on their own. Alvin was looking like was I for real? Chad told me to stand in front of Alvin and dance. My body began to flow. My heart started singing. My mind was feeling it all. I put my all into Alvin's special dance. I went over to him and started to suck on his dick. It was big as hell. I loved the way his dick felt in my mouth. The rush was the best part. He knew how to work that dick. Alvin's face-fucked me so good. After he took his dick out of my mouth, Chad bent me over and put Alvin's dick inside of me and watched him fuck my ass sloppy. I was taking the dick with no problem.

Chad didn't join in because he wanted to see what Alvin was about. He loved what he saw. He was ready to fuck him, but Alvin has never been fucked in the ass. Chad promised to take it easy. When Chad started to put his dick into Alvin's tight ass, Alvin jumped into the air. Chad's dick was too big for his little asshole. I told Alvin to shut the fuck up and take the dick. He was crying and shaking like a hurt dog. Chad was getting upset. He started fucking the hell out of him. His ass was red and in pain.

After Chad finished fucking Alvin, his body wasn't good for nothing. That was a nice way to meet someone. Alvin was going to be our best friend.

Calvin called when I was running water in the bathtub for Alvin. He wanted to know have we met any new friends. I told him that we met one and that he is a very special friend. Calvin got silent for a few minutes. He knew where I was coming from. I didn't like that Calvin ended the phone call so quickly.

Lust, Lies & Love

I was happy that Alvin couldn't bathe himself. I gladly took over. His body was soft and sweet. Alvin told me that he loved being around us. We stayed in the bathroom for over an hour just talking. We talked about our lives and much more. Chad came into the bathroom to check on us. He thought something happened to Alvin. Everything was good with us. I really enjoyed our conversation. It was very stimulating.

Now it's time for me to resume working. I took a break for a month from everybody and everything. Chad wanted me to get my mind back on track. That's exactly what I did.

Someone called the shop and ordered five dozen roses. I was trying to figure out who it was because this was a first. When I looked at the call ID, it was Sam. My mouth dropped to the floor. I couldn't believe he ordered so many flowers. I took a mini lunch break. When I came back to the shop, five dozen roses were sitting on my desk. I looked at the white tag. Sure enough, it was from Sam.

Chad came to the shop and asked me who roses were these. I looked at him and told him that they were Kathy's and that it was her birthday. He was like wow her hubby must love her. To make me feel good, he told me that he loved me too. My heart was going through the motion all that day thinking about Sam. He still had a love for me and only me.

Kathy knew something was wrong with me. She offered to take me out to dinner. I began telling her how much I love Chad, but still had a love for Sam. She told me to follow my mind. Our dinner went very well. I didn't want to leave. My mind was at ease.

After we left our dinner date, I went home to get ready for my baby. He was going to freak me real good. My baby had a long day. I was going to ease his stress away.

Chad came into the house all upset. I didn't know why and he wouldn't tell me. The last time I tried to ask him, he told me to open my mouth and he shoved his dirty dick in my mouth. Chad asked me did I really want to know what was bothering him. I couldn't say anything. He was hurting my throat. Things were getting out of hand. He wasn't the same Chad. I knew he was going through. It was my fault for asking him all those questions.

After Chad took his dirty dick out of my mouth, he put it in my ass and laid down and went to sleep. Something wasn't right with my baby. He was changing for the worst. Since he was stressing, I sent him on a week's long vacation. I was going to be lonely.

I called and invited Sam over for the week. He was willing to come. Chad left the next day and Sam flew in two days later. I sent my limo driver to pick up Sam. He was so happy to see me. We were about to have a blast. He wanted to take me out for dinner and a movie. My heart filled up with love. I missed him so much. He didn't want to stay at our place. He had something a lot better planned. We stayed at a nice resort. My boo showed me a good time. We had dinner on the beach and watched the sunset. Then we made sweet love. He started kissing on me with strawberries in his mouth. He had my spine going every way. Then he opened my legs and starting eating my ass. He was holding me tight. He was making me fall in love with him all over again. I enjoyed his tongue and dick on and inside of me.

Someone woke up the next morning. I had sand in my ass and on my dick. I didn't care because I was with Sam. The guys called and I told them I was with Sam. They couldn't believe their ears. Everyone was so happy because that was what they wanted. Sam was treating me with much respect. I loved it.

Lust, Lies & Love

I took Sam out for breakfast. I ordered him the best. We talked about our relationship and where it went wrong. I admitted to him that I was in love with two men. I was wrong for it, but that is what my heart felt at the moment. He understood where I was coming from. When I told him about Chad and me, I felt bad because I left him for Chad. He wanted to know how Chad was treating me. I wanted to tell him everything was lovely, but I couldn't. I told him that Chad had been stressing and being very mean to me. That was enough about Chad and me. I told Sam that we needed to talk about us. He didn't do much talking.

The bar and drinks were calling our names. People were so drunk at the bar. We had six drinks a piece. I was wasted, horny and ready to fuck. Sam was moving his body so seductively on the dance floor. I knew the bed action was going to be amazing.

We left the bar and went back to the resort. It was time to give Sam some good ass. When we got back to the rest, he opened the door and fell on the couch. He went straight to sleep. My freaky ass unzipped his pants and started sucking his black dick. I stuck it in my ass. It was wet as hell. That woke him up. He started making love to me. He was taking my mind and heart away. We were meant for each other. I was going through some changes. I was dealing with Chad and thinking about Sam which wasn't an easy thing to do. The both of them meant a lot to me.

It was time for Sam to go home. Before he left, I gave him the time of his life. He loved it. I am going to miss the way he held and kissed me. I am also going to miss the way he treated me. Seeing Sam leave was hard and painful.

Chad came home a couple of hours after Sam left. I felt something, but happy wasn't it. I questioned myself for being with Chad. He didn't act happy to see me. When I tried to talk to him, he kept walking like he didn't hear me. My feelings were hurt. Something wasn't right with him. He left happy and came back upset. I couldn't help wonder if I was the cause of his unhappiness. I couldn't get through to him. He didn't want to talk about anything. My baby was acting crazy with me.

When he left the house, I packed some clothes and went back to Atlanta for a couple of days. Chad called me because I wasn't at the house. I explained to him how I felt about his not talking. He started to cry. He was going through.

Lust, Lies & Love

I went back home the next day. When I arrived, Chad was looking a hot mess. I called a party planner to help me throw Chad a striptease party. It was going to be grand. The planner invited fifty of Chad's closest friends. I was happy about that. The party was in a day. We had to make things happen. There were a lot of last minute things, but everything came together.

It's striptease party time and I'm ready. The strippers were there. I had a private show planned for Chad. He was speechless. The stripper pulled out his dick and slapped Chad in his face with it. Then he started grinding on him. My ass wanted that dick. The stripped started grinding his dick in Chad. My baby was grooving with him. People were looking at me crazy. I told the stripper to fuck him good. He needed that stress knocked out of him.

I decided to take the other stripper into my bedroom and pulled down his pants. I started eating and licking his asshole. His ass tasted so good, but the punk was yelling like a little bitch. I had to shut him up. His ass was so wet. The bitch bent over because he wanted me to fuck him standing up. I fucked that little bitch like he was a nobody. I had him crying, yelling and asking me to stop. He asked me would I please stop. I laughed and told him that he was a stripper and that I suppose to fuck him like he was nothing.

When I took my dick out of his wet asshole, shit started to fall out. His body fell to the floor. Things weren't good for him. His friends came to take him home.

After that happened to the young man, I went to sleep. Chad was fucking or being fucked. I went to sleep with Sam on my mind wishing the stripper was him.

Chad cheated on me with different guys. People were telling me, but I didn't believe them. I thought they were his co-workers until I walked into our bedroom one day and he was having a threesome. My lips dropped to the floor. I thought to myself what to do. Chad grabbed me and told me that if I loved him he would I would let his team fuck me. My feelings changed for Chad at the moment. He threw me on the bed and let them tie me up and fuck me until I blanked out. They were fucking me rough and hard. Chad told them to cum in my ass and mouth. I was surprised at him.

After they got the best of me, Chad fucked me, but I blanked out. When I woke up, it was two different guys playing in my ass. They were all friends of Chad. He had me sucking and fucking his friends all of the time. My ass was no good. My body was hurt and torn. I became Chad's fuck slave. He started beating me. He let his friends sex me whenever I made him mad.

After they fucked me crazy, Chad always said he was sorry. I believed him every time. I lost my mind on Chad. I tied him up while he was sleep. I fucked the shit out of him. I stuck a broom in his ass and kicked the hell out of him. I wanted to take his life. The bitch was doing me wrong, but I stayed with him. Leaving Sam was a mistake.

Chad and I left for New York for a business trip. I was hoping they asked me to stay. While in the West Keys which I loved a lot, I was supposed to meet up with John. He was on a business trip with me. Chad went to Texas for his meeting.

John called me later that night. He wanted to go out for dinner. I went out with him. He was nice, sweet and very loyal. He loved Mexican food. We laughed and had drinks. We talked about us. We had so much in common. He was a good man and a freak. That was what I wanted to hear.

Lust, Lies & Love

John started to get sleepy. This dick of mine was going to wake him up. I asked him did he want to go to my place. He agreed to come. He laid on my bed and closed his eyes. I wasn't about to let him go to sleep. If he lies down on my bed, then something is going to happen.

Things went easy for him. I only deep ass-fucked him. He was moving everywhere. My dick was hitting all of his sex spots. He was going crazy as fuck. I kept bouncing up and down in that ass. My balls were hitting my thighs. I felt his stomach and all. I was working his ass so good. The punk couldn't take it. I was banging his walls and more out.

After I came in his ass over and over, I finally let him up. His legs were about to buckle. I felt sorry for him, but he made me feel stupid after we fucked. He didn't say anything to me. I took him to the bathroom and put him in the shower. Then I fucked him again. I shout to him as I am pounding him, "When I am sexing you, let me know how it is."

The bitch could barely talk. Chad made me this way. I am fucking dudes like they are a piece of trash. I don't have any feeling when it comes down to sex.

John got up to put his clothes on. It took about an hour. When he was finished, he told me that my dick is the best and that he wanted it every day. When he could barely take it, I was going to give the slut what he wanted.

Chad called me three days later talking crazy and stupid. It was something I didn't want to hear or give a fuck about. I was trying to get my fuck on. John called me later the next night. He loved calling at night. He was my bitch and my booty call. In my mind, I knew what he wanted. He asked me to fuck him good again. I asked him that if I can cum in his mouth. He said that I could and that he would take it all down. I agreed to have him over.

John was upset with me when I didn't fuck him. I let him suck my dick and let my cum flow down his throat. Then I made him leave my room. That bitch thought he was staying the night. I don't let those kinds of people stay the night. I consider him to be a free fuck. By staying the night with me, it was like paying for a piece of ass. I had to let John know that I fuck ass and don't pay. He was cool with that.

I called the limo to come and pick him up. I was ready for the pussy to go home. After all of this foolery was over, I really didn't want to be around Chad. He was causing me way too

Lust, Lies & Love

much pain. I could never get Sam out of my mind. He was a man of understanding, caring and love. I always ask myself why did I leave.

Chad and I went to lunch. We wanted to talk things over. Our relationship wasn't the best at the moment. The both of us were fucking different guys every night. I thought it was wrong, but Chad loved it.

John came over to the house because he had something to tell Sam and me. He wanted to move in with us for two weeks. His house was being renovated. We agreed to let him stay. Chad was happy because he was going to get him a good fuck. I didn't have a problem with it. I would do anything to keep Chad happy.

I moved John into our room. Chad needed an extra body to fuck good. Our guest room was open for John, but I wanted it. Chad wanted John to stay in the room with him. Things began to get crazy later that night. Loud sounds were coming from the room. There was a lot a moaning. I crept out of bed. The closer I got to the noise, the louder it got. I was wondering what the fuck was going on. The bed was cracking. The floor was dancing. The walls were sweating. Something wasn't right with all of these weird noises. As I began to walk towards Chad's door, I started to hear everything crystal clear. Chad was fucking John sick. I heard John say to Chad, "Fuck me harder daddy."

My eyes got big as hell because Chad was my daddy.

"Who's your daddy?" John was going on and on.

I couldn't take it anymore. I went into our bedroom and saw them having sex. I took my clothes off. The both of them started to fuck the hell out of me. My asshole felt like it was on fire. The both of them put their dicks in me at the same time. My poor asshole was hurting so badly. Chad and John got off me. They knew I was in a lot of pain. It was getting the very best of my body.

When they got off of me and out of my ass, I rolled over and started to yell. Chad looked at me and began to laugh. I wanted to kill his monkey ass. This body of mine needed a hot shower. Chad turned on the shower and held me in it. He washed me down softly. It felt so loving. He was himself again. We have been through a lot lately and this is what I needed for my man.

I wanted to have Chad an "I love you party". He really needed the party because I really loved him. I only invited Chad's co-workers and a couple of my new friends. It was about fifty people on the guest list.

The next day, it was time to party. Chad didn't know anything about the party. When we surprised him, tears began to flow down his face with love. I was happy for Chad because he was getting back to his old self. He was happy and joyful. His co-workers were nice, amazing and happy people. Someone asked me what the theme was for the party. I told him it was an "I love you" theme. Everyone thought it was a good theme. The party was wild, sexy and crazy. People were doing some weird stuff. They were sucking dick, eating ass and fucking. I could only shake my head. My body wouldn't let me do anything, but I was going to get it together. I wanted dick and ass in my mouth. My body was tired from planning the party.

Chad and one of his friends came into the kitchen. I needed them to take the food outside. While taking the food out, I began to get undressed and ready. The two of them came back into the kitchen. I was in my birthday suit just as naked as I could be. Chad told me to go and put on some clothes. My sexy look came across my face. Chad and his friend took me inside of the guest bedroom. They started taking off their clothes. They pushed me to my knees and slapped me in the face with their dicks. I started to suck as if the dick was going out of business. I wanted their dicks and balls all in my mouth. Chad was fucking my face so good and so was his friend. My lips smelled like a dick and musty balls. I wanted to throw up. The smell was getting to me. The friend should have washed his stinky body before he came over. I was horny and crazy. I bent over and let the friend bust5 this ass wide open. It needed to be open, wide and sore.

I needed some good dick the most. Chad's friend's name is Ced. His dick was musty as hell, but I had to have that big dick. Anything that big can make my body fold. I so needed all of it. Daddy knew how to work that dick. I don't know what got into Chad, but he started to best my asshole down. He was jumping up and down in this ass so good. It was talking back to him. My baby couldn't handle this good ass.

Chad was sweating and shaking. I started to take to take it easy on him. Ced was sitting in the chair jacking off. My mouth loved it.

Lust, Lies & Love

When I saw Ced about to cum, I jumped off of Chad and started licking the head of his dick. When he started cumming, I started riding his dick. That crazy man started fucking me like a horse. My asshole was pounding. I kept my mouth close and took it.

Chad took Ced's dick out of me and began to eat me out and lick my hole. This mind of mine was in another world. They were giving me the special treatment. The kitchen had become the sex room. We had to hurry up and get back outside.

We were gone for too long. I must admit that they know how to have some good sex. Everyone was looking crazy when the three of us came outside sweating. When you have been fucked my two big dicks, you would be sweating like a horse too.

Ced and Chad were ready to eat. After fucking me so good, the two of them worked up an appetite. I fed the both of them. Everyone was outside having a blast. Ced had my ass hurting so badly, but I enjoyed it a lot.

After everyone left the party of the year, I got on the phone and called some of the guys. I told them about the time we had. A couple of them were very upset with me. I haven't called or invited them to the house. In my heart of hearts, I was done with them. The guys were my heart and soul, but they didn't care for Chad. If they didn't like Chad, they didn't like me. I am really going to miss the guys. I think my time and love for me have faded.

Chad knew I was having a bad day. He decided to take me to Atlanta. I wanted to know why he was taking me because there was nothing for me there. Chad thought it would be a great idea for me to visit the guys. My heart skipped a beat. My mind went to left field. My eyes were blurry from tears. I couldn't believe Chad wanted to make things right between the guys and me.

When we got to Atlanta, Jack was the first person we met. He was so happy to see me. He told me that he has been taking with Chad. My heart was pounding because I knew the conversations weren't the best. I was very wrong. Jack said the convo was the best. He really got to know Chad and that the guys would love to have a relationship with Chad. That was the best moment of my life.

Jack and Chad planned a dinner for everyone. We wanted to know how everyone felt about Chad. I got the results I so desired. Everything went amazingly well. We did so much together.

Lust, Lies & Love

I didn't want to go back home because I have missed the guys so much.

The next day, Chad and I had to leave Atlanta. Work was calling. No one wanted us to leave, but they understood that we had to go. Before we left Atlanta and the guys, Chad wanted everyone to know that he loved and cared for them. That was the sweetest thing he could have said to any of my friends.

Since Chad was good to my friends, I was going to give him some of this good and tight ass. His dick was in need of some good loving. Instead of going straight to work, we went to the house. I gave Chad the best sex of his life. I started off by taking a hot bath. Then I laid on the bed naked and started playing in my asshole. I can see Chad fill out the front of his jeans as he was rising with excitement. He was hard as a brick. I put his dick in my mouth and started sucking it slowly. I jacked it with my soft hands. Slob was running all down his dick. His eyes began to roll from left to right then to the back of his head. My man was feeling like a king.

I let Chad put me into the bow and let him fuck the silly out of me. My body was happy as hell. He had me moaning and my toes curling. My body was weak and my mind was somewhere else. I love Chad's dick and Chad loves my ass and mouth. Sleeping was not on the menu.

After that great sex class, Chad was becoming a better person. I knew he liked to have a lot of sex. He wanted me to join this group sex that his friend was having. I was up for it because I wanted to keep him happy.

I was nervous about the party. I knew a lot of people were going to be there. I didn't know what to say.

Jack called and asked me about the sex party. I told him I was going. He started laughing. I wanted to know why he was laughing. Sam was going to be at the party. My ass got so wet I could barely stand up to talk. I knew I was about to get some good dick. If anyone could make my body fold it was Sam. He knew how to hit the right spots.

The next day it was party time. As Chad and I started getting ready for the party, the manager of Chad's second business called. They needed him at his shop. Someone broke into his bike shop. He was very hurt because he was only in business for six months. I felt sorry for him. His business was going so well.

Lust, Lies & Love

I went to the party late because I had to drive Chad to the airport. He was so upset that he couldn't attend the party or drive himself to the airport.

Sam was standing outside with a couple of guys. My heart was pounding with love. I got out of the care and started walking very sexy like. Sam grabbed my ass with those soft hands. I looked at him and said, "Hello daddy. How are you?"

"I'm good baby," He said it with such ownership.

I started to feel a certain kind of way when he grabbed me. We walked into the party together. People were drinking, talking and having sex. There was a big dick, a fat ass and a huge pair of balls stealing my attention. I went to the bar for a couple of drinks. My mind wouldn't let me think or focus.

Sam came and got me from the bar and took me into this room. He began to kiss on me. I noticed there were other people in the room as well. I didn't care because I was ready to get fucked. Three guys came up to us. They wanted to know if they could join us. I told them that they could. The four of them stood in a straight line. I got on my knees and went down the line sucking dick by dick. My mouth couldn't control itself. I was sucking like a thirsty horse. They had me deep-throating their dicks and sucking their balls. My jaws were hurting so badly, but I didn't stop. I loved it.

Sam bent me over and let there of the guys fuck me at the same time. My mouth and asshole were full. They were banging me like crazy. My asshole was so open and wide. The four of them had me where I couldn't move. They were giving it to me.

After they were finished freaking me, Sam and I made some real love. He was licking my feet and didn't stop until he got to my dick. He put that warm moist mouth on me. My mind hit the floor. Then he got on top of me and started to ride my dick and play with my balls. I enjoyed it. He lowered himself to his knees and I hit him from the back. I put my hands on his shoulders and started fucking him crazy and came all over his fat ass.

My ex-lover was tired but happy. His ass made me want to get back with him. I missed that warm, sweet, good-feeling on my big black curved dick. I remember when I use to fuck Sam in the mouth and he just sat there. I am going to miss that freak.

Lust, Lies & Love

After the party, I asked Sam to come to my place. I wanted some more ass and dick. I was ready for my body to fold. He wanted to take a shower before having sex. I was ready to get freaky.

When he went into the bathroom, I walked behind him. He was laughing, but I can tell he is horny too. He ran the shower. My horny ass pulled his pants down, put his dick in my wet mouth and started sucking. He has some good dick on him. I didn't want to release his dick from my mouth. He pushed me onto the floor and told me to spread my legs open. He put cubes of ice in my asshole. It was cold, but he warmed it us with his tongue. He started sucking on my asshole making a loud smacking noise. My good ass was cumming back to back. He sucked it all up. MY ass started to tighten. My legs were just there; they couldn't move. Sam really did the damn thing.

As soon as we finished filling each other up, Chad called. He wanted to update me on the status of his business. I told him that the party went well. He also wanted to know if I fucked anybody. I told him that I did three guys and Sam. He was okay with it because he was going to fuck my ass crazy when he got home anyway. I was ready for it. That's my daddy.

Lust, Lies & Love

Sometimes I feel like I am only Chad's piece of ass. I knew he loves me and cares about me.

Sam left to go back home. Chad came home not soon after Sam left. He didn't come alone. He was with a light-skinned guy that he introduced as his cousin. I have never met or seen this person before. I believe Chad.

I called my chef over because Chad needed a great dinner. I know he is tired of work and the people. Tim came over to the house and started to prepare dinner. The three of us were sitting in the living room. I notice Chad and his cousin Jay kept making eye contact. I didn't know what was going on. I went to the bathroom. My mind needed to be cleared.

When I returned to the living room, Chad and Jay were having sex. Chad had Jay's legs up in the air and was fucking him like crazy. My mouth dropped because I thought Jay was his cousin. I stood and watched the whole movie. The room smelled like ass and raw balls. I wanted to throw up. I ran out of the house and called Jack.

I told him about what was going on. He wasn't surprised because Chad's family believed in having sex with each other. Jack asked me if the guy was Jay. I shook my head and told him yes. Jack agreed that they were always having nasty and raw sex. I couldn't believe it.

After I got off the phone with Jack, I went into the house and watched them fuck. I started to cry. That shit was nasty and flaw. When Chad saw me crying and heard me yelling, he stopped freaking Jay and ran over to me. I told him that I am mad at him because he was fucking his cousin. He looked at me like how did you find out about my family fucking each other.

He wanted me to join, but I refused. Chad pinned me down and let Jay fuck me and slap me around. My world was crushed and hurt. Jay was freaking me good, but I don't do family. Chad was yelling to Jay to fuck the shit out of me. He told him to make me feeling every inch of his dick. I felt his dick and balls inside of me. My ass was in pain, but I took all of it. I was trying to please Chad, but the sex was getting out of control. My body wasn't the same nor did it feel the same.

His friends and family were fucking the hell out of me. Either things were going to get better, or I was going to leave. I took a trip to Atlanta. I needed to be with the guys. When I got up with everyone, I wanted to cry. I told them about Chad and his cousin. They were sick to their stomachs.

Sam was upset and wanted me to come back. If I could I would. Sam was once them my world and my all. While in Atlanta, Sam treated me with care. The two of us laughed and cried together. That was something Chad was lacking. I was going through so much with the business and Chad. I gave Sam my Atlanta business. I only have a love for Sam and he deserves the best. I surprise him with the business. He couldn't believe it. We went on a lovely boat ride and had dinner. We cuddled the night away. He did things for me that Chad has never done. Sam use to eat my ass out so good. He knew how to make me shake. I missed the good times with Sam.

Chad was very upset when he heard about my escapades with Sam and my giving him the business. He wanted to know why. I told him Sam put half in. Chad knew I was lying because he knew that I put in everything. I wanted Sam to have a better life. He treated me like gold. I wanted to treat him like a king.

Chad and I went our separate way, but I wasn't for long. We needed to find ourselves. Things weren't the same for Chad and me. He was a different person. Sam heard about us.

Lust, Lies & Love

He wanted me to come and live with him for a month. That's what I did. I always felt the love in Sam's arms. Sam and I wanted to try to reconnect. We were falling back in love with each other.

Since Sam and I were both freaks, I wanted him to fuck me rough without any lube. I wanted to feel real pain. When I asked him to do it for me, he agreed to fuck me dry. The both of us started sucking each other's dicks, licking each other's balls and kissing. It was so amazing to be loved again.

Now it was time for the wonderful rough sex. Sam began to put his dick inside of my tight ass. I was holding my teeth together. My toes were crossed. My fists were balled. My mouth was closed tight. That shit was killing me so bad. Sam wanted to stop, but I wanted to feel the pain. My baby was freaking me like fat girls love cake. My whole body was stiff and sore. He did the works to my body. He had me tired, speechless and out of it. My baby gave me what I wanted and more. I felt Sam's entire big black pretty dick inside of me.

After we finished doing the grown folks, Sam went into the bathroom and ran me a hot bubble bath. He washed me. He was the very best. I wanted him back. Before I got out of the tub, I gave Sam some good head. My man worked hard on this body. I had to repay my boo back. Sam's love is so amazing and priceless. I enjoyed myself with him.

The next day, Sam took me on a shopping spree. I wanted to fall over and cry. He was the sweetest of all. He got me everything I wanted and more.

Not long after, Sam started to get tired. The shopping spree ended early. I took Sam back to his place. As I was going into the kitchen to eat, Sam asked me to make him some tea. I got worried because he only asks for tea when he is not feeling well. Sam came into the kitchen. I notice that he is sweating. I put my hand on his forehead. He was warm. He had a fever. I ran frantically around the house looking for something that he could take. Sam could not get sick. I gave him some meds and hot tea. I put Sam to bed.

After I put Sam in bed, I heard a knock at the door. It was a good friend of Sam's. His name is Chase. He was sexy. I told him that Sam wasn't feeling well and that he needed to rest. He wanted to know who I am and my relationship to Sam. We went to brunch. We talked to get to know each other. Chase is a real estate broker. I loved that about him. He was a good friend of Sam and his family.

I explained to Chase that I am Sam's ex who keeps Sam on his feet. He felt more at ease once he knew my relationship with Sam. Every time Chase opens his mouth to speak, my dick gets harder than ever. I want some of that dick.

Since Chase was in town, he invited me to his hotel room. We had drinks. We listened to music and talked about everything. My eyes kept zeroing in on Chase's dick. His print is big and thick-looking. He kept giving me drink after drink.

By the tenth drink, I was good and drunk. I couldn't stand straight or talk clearly. Chase helped me into his bedroom. It was more of a penthouse than a hotel room. I lay down as Chase took my shoes off. He left the room. About ten minutes have passed. I was dozed off by the time he returned to the room. I felt something crawling on my face. I thought that I was imaging things. When I open my eyes and look up, I see Chase rubbing his big dick across my face. I wanted to fall out because his dick was way too big. I grab his dick from my lips and put it in my mouth. I don't think it going to fit. His dick choked the hell out of me.

Lust, Lies & Love

I kept sucking for what seemed like hours. That dick was still rock hard.

Chase stopped because of Sam. He was in the moment. I told him to fuck Sam. He was sick and I needed some dick. Chase told me to remember that he fucks and doesn't make love. My ass tightened when I heard that. I didn't want to go back to Sam after that good love making. Chas gave it to me. I didn't feel bad about making love to Chase. Sam was sick. I had to get it in and more. Chase didn't want to leave me because he was falling in love with me. The dick was good, but I couldn't be with him. I was with Chad.

After Sam started feeling well, Chase and I went home. Chas came home a week later. I told him about the trip. He was happy for me. Once we had a long sweet talk, everything was going well. Our business started to pick back up. Our lived were about to change. Chad bought new cars, houses, and more cars. Things couldn't get any better.

I notice a lot of guys coming to the house for Chad. He said that they were his friends. I didn't believe it because every time I walk into our bedroom, he was fucking one of them. That was the shit that got to me. Chad always claims that everyone is his friend when indeed he just wants to fuck each and every one of them. I got a trick for him. I am going to invite some of his friends for dinner. Whenever they come over to eat, drink and talk, I am going to fuck them one by one since they are just his suppose-to-be-friends. Chad knew how to get under my skin. I have to watch him fuck stank dick, sour ass, and raw balled men. I even have to kiss him while his breath smelled like shit. Now it is time for me to start fucking and sucking like crazy. Chad was only good for the word love.

I was ready to make some music. Chase stood me up and got behind me. He started licking my asshole. My knees were buckling as my body got weak. His tongue had my asshole so wet. I couldn't take it at all. My body fell onto the bed lifeless. He spreads my legs wide and eats me silly. Everything on my body was moving crazy.

After the good eating of the ass, Chase turned me over and started making love to me. His dick felt like feathers. His lips felt like snow. The inside of his mouth felt like a warm heater. He had my mind gone. His head game was the best I have ever had. He took his dick out of me. Precum drips everywhere. I catch it as it was falling. My mouth was full of love.

Lust, Lies & Love

I got into the doggie style position and started throwing this good ass back. Chase was yelling so loudly. Good ass makes your say some crazy things. I was throwing and riding so good. His dick was going the job. Then he picks me up and starts making love to me against the way. He was dicking me upside down. The only thing I could do was hang there. My inside felt amazing. Chase hit new spots I didn't think I had. Every time he hit that spot, my ass came like crazy. My body got so weak from being upside down. I was Cumming like crazy and getting dicked down so good. He made mad love to me.

I wanted our relationship to work, but Chad has done too much for me. I didn't leave because I knew things were going to get better. To release my stress, some of the guys wanted to attend a sex party. That was the best thing I heard all week. We all went to the party. I was ready to do some freaky things. There were shirtless men with big dicks. My heart pumped ten times faster the normal.

When I went into the bathroom, a guy was standing up looking into the mirror. I wasn't paying him any attention. He wasn't my type of man. As I begin washing my hands, the guy got behind me and started kissing me on the ear. My fat ass was getting wet and tight. Things were about to get happy. I pulled my pants down and bent over sideways. I let him eat me out. His tongue and lips felt so good. He ate me out for an hour. He had me weak as fuck. I pulled my clothes up and went back into the party to enjoy the guys.

Chad came with some friends. I laughed because one of the guys was Sam's brother. I couldn't believe my eyes. We acted like we didn't know each other. If we were to be in each other's faces like we knew each other, Chad would have known something was up.

Everyone begin to drink. Laugh and talk. When we started having too many drinks, I pulled Sam's brother to the side. We talked and drank. I was horny and wet. We went into the bathroom. I took his dick out and sucked on the head of it until he released his load into my mouth. It was so tasteful.

As I rose from the kneeling position, Chad and Sam walked into the bathroom. I finished just in time. I wanted more. The three of them gave t to me. Chad bent me over, tied my arms to my ankles and let everyone fuck my ass so good. The deeper they went, the better it and the more I came. I told them to fuck me weak and silly. They fucked me for a couple of hours. Life couldn't get any better. Having three men fuck me at once is amazing. I felt everyone in the bottom of my stomach, but I didn't care because that is what I wanted. Sam didn't love it as much. He wanted me to himself. Sam was sexing me with love and care. He had my body in love. I didn't spend time with the other guys. I was busy fucking and sucking. My body needed some good loving.

After we all left the sex party, Chad and I went back to our place. We needed to think things over. I began telling Chad how much I missed Sam. I am still in love with him. Chad looked at me crazy and sad. He told me to come into the bedroom so we could really talk. I went to sit on the bed. Chad beat me in the face. He had my face black and blue. Ten minutes into the cruel beating, Chad kicked, slapped and punched me. My body was hurting like hell. Chad beat all the love that I had for him out of me. I knew it was time for me to leave Chad. People wanted us to stay together. My mind couldn't sleep or rest.

I called Sam and told him what was going on. He was very upset and angry. Sam wanted me to send him pictures of my face. When I sent him the pictures, He went crazy on the phone.

Lust, Lies & Love

Sam wasn't happy at al. My face had him crying. I waited until Chad went to sleep and left the house for Atlanta. Sam was waiting for me at the airport. He saw the hurt and pain on my face. He started to cry when he saw me. We went back to his place for some comfort. Sam made me feel the best. Some of the guys came over because they heard about what happened. They were hurt and sad because they never thought Chad was that type of guy. Jack didn't want me to go back to Chad, but I had to. He was the love of my life. Jack came and took me on a friendship date. We talked about everything that was going on in my life. The more we talked, the more I cried and cried. I couldn't stay in Atlanta for long.

Chad wanted me back home. When I returned home, Chad wanted to work things out. We wanted to be one again. I packed my bags and moved to Las Vegas. Sam was starting up a new business there. I knew things were going to be the best, Chad wanted to know where I was because he hasn't heard from me in a couple of weeks. I told him that I went to Vegas for work. He believed me because I am always working. My plans were not to go back to New York. I had to better myself and Sam.

Lust, Lies & Love

Sam moved with me to Vegas. I was only going to be in Vegas for six months. I didn't want Chad to come and visit. He didn't mean much to me anymore. I loved Sam with all of my heart. He was my boo thang and more. Vegas was treating us with care. Sam wanted to buy a club here. He didn't want to go back to Atlanta. I was willing to do whatever in order for things to happen. I put in over eighty thousand because I wanted him to live out his dreams.

A couple of weeks into the lovely and amazing Vegas, Sam was a club owner. He owns a men's strip club. The night before the grand opening, we walked around the club holding hands in love. Sam wanted to do some freaky things. I climbed up the pole and slid up and down it while Sam fucked me while I was upside down. That dick felt so amazing. I felt it going inside of my ass. Sam beat my ass down so good. It seemed like his dick got bigger because I couldn't take it anymore. The more I slide down the pole, the harder he was beating my ass up. Through it all, I really enjoyed the sex. Sam really made my day and more.

Leaving Vegas was going to be very hard. Sam was there. I didn't want to leave him alone. My last week in Vegas, Chad and I had sex, at least, five times a day. I had to keep his dick pleased. He had to keep this mouth and ass feeling good.

When I got back to New York, I didn't want any sex or love from Chad. I only wanted peace and happiness. Had didn't see me the first four days. I reserved a hotel room. I didn't want to see him. Chad called every day, but I didn't answer any of his calls. I needed some space from him. Sam called the days that I was at the hotel. He was so horny. He missed me too. I wanted to give my boo some phone sex. Sam had me playing in my ass, moaning and sucking a fake dick. The more I moaned and sucked, the faster Sam jacked off. His dick was hitting the phone. I knew he was about cum. I wanted all of it in my mouth and face. I missed Sam's loving and the way he dicks me down. Sam had a dick that was made of gold. That's why my mind was so crazy about him.

Chad sent a limo to the hotel to pick me up. It took me about two hours to come downstairs, I wasn't ready to see him. When I arrived at the house, things weren't the best between the two of us. Chad found out about my moving in with Sam. He wanted to know what was going on with Sam and me.

Lust, Lies & Love

All of the guys told me to tell Chad the truth. Tears were flowing down Chad's face as I began to speak. I had to let him know that I was falling out of love with him and that Sam makes me complete. He couldn't believe that words that were coming out of my mouth.

Later that night, Chad wanted to do something special for me. We went out on the town, took a nice boat ride and sexed the night away. While we were having sex, my mind was on the Sam the entire time. The way he use to sex my body up and down clouded my mind. Chad started off by licking my toes and kissing his way up to my balls. He licked my dick up and down.

Chad's mouth and tongue felt so good. I pushed him off of me. I laid him on his stomach and ate him from the back. His ass was sweet and tasteful. My tongue felt like it got stuck in his ass because it didn't want to come out. Ass juice was dripping in my mouth. My throat loved it. Chas was riding my dick so good that his balls and dick were hitting my thighs like crazy. The inside of his ass was warm. I was enjoying it because I wanted a nut.

After I got my nut, things were done with us or that's what I thought. Some of the guys came to New York. I was so happy to see them. They wanted to go to Vegas to visit Sam. I was up for it, but Chad wasn't a happy camper. He didn't want me to go because of Sam. They promised Chad that they will take good care of me.

When we got to Vegas, it was time to fuck the city away. Sam met us at the hotel. I began to cry when I saw him. My baby looked amazing and sexy. Everyone got ready and went to the town. We had a blast. We were drinking and having sex everywhere.

Sam and I left the town early. I needed some dick in my tight hole. Sam wanted to have a threesome. I was ready for it. He asked me to find someone. I asked his brother. He had a shocked look on his face, but he was ready to make things happen. The both of them had big dicks. Sam placed one of my legs on the wall and bent me over. The both of them fucked me at the same time. I wanted to fall to the floor, but I couldn't because their dicks were holding me up. They were banging the hell out of me. My ass was talking to me in Spanish. They drained me dry and stiff. I couldn't take any more dick. So I began to suck the both of them off. Sam came so much that it was running down my lips. It was thick, creamy and white.

Lust, Lies & Love

Sam's brother put his dick in my mouth. Everything began to flow down my throat. I took it all for the both of them.

After we got finished making love or should I say fucking, my body felt like a brick. It was hard. My ass was red and my mind was just there. I didn't feel bad about fucking two brothers. They wanted this good ass. I gave it to them.

Jack and Matt came to the hotel. We were taking so long. They wanted to know what was taking us so long. I told them that we were having an amazing threesome. He shook his head because he wanted me to himself.

After we went out on the town, we partied like black stars. I am going to fuck Matt so good. His ass made me cum just thinking about it. I love when Matt rides my face. His ass is so fat. Whenever he rides my face, I hold his waist tightly as his bounces up and down as I such that asshole so good. Everyone thought I was acting funny the first night. I only wanted some good dick in my mouth, ass, and face. The guys don't understand me, but they will be fine. We thought that we will rock the second night while in Vegas. Sin city belonged to us. Whoever I fuck in Vegas will stay in Vegas.

Lust, Lies & Love

Calvin met us at his friend's club. We haven't seen him in so long. When we got into the club, some of the guys wanted to drinks, pop pills and smoke whatever. I had drinking and fucking on my mind. Somebody needed to eat this ass out. I got drunk with the guys and had a blast. Calvin was so happy to see everyone. He was once my sex bitch. He has some good ass. Jack, Matt and the other guys wanted to chill with their friends. Calvin wanted to go back to the hotel. We went back to have some alone time. Calvin began to touch on me. He had my mind wondering. I was ready. I couldn't wait to eat Calvin's big, black, sweet, juicy ass. I wanted Calvin to fuck my tongue with that ass and me shake.

As we began to watch television, Calvin started kissing and licking on mine. My eyes were rolling like a train. I thought they were going to pop out of my head. The feel of his lips and tongue were getting the best of me. I couldn't control my body. My legs began to open. My mouth widened. My mind was loose. Calvin was doing me just right. We didn't go all the way because Chad kept calling. The hotel's phone wasn't working. My phone was dead. I had to use Calvin's phone. Chad knew whose number it was. He wasn't happy. Calvin put the phone on speaker. He wanted to hear everything that Chad had to say. Chad was being so rude. Calvin yelled out and said, "I'm fucking your man and his ass is so good."

Chad hung up the phone. I knew he was mad as hell, but he will be okay. Calvin and I were only good friends.

After our first week in Vegas, it was time for everyone to go back home. New York isn't where I want to be. Chad was home. I didn't want to see him. When I got back to New York, Chad had all of my clothes packed up. All of the boxes were outside waiting for me. That's when I lost my mind. He could have called one of the guys to come and pick up my things. I wanted to kill that long-faced bitch. I was good to his stank ass yet he treated me like a no good dog.

I called Calvin and some of his friends to help me move. I moved to Atlanta. The guys were happy. My life was about to happen for the best. Sam called a couple of days later because he heard about Chad and me. Sam wanted me to move to Las Vegas, but I didn't know what to do. Calvin wanted me to spend some time with him. My heart was in between to two. To get my mind off of everything, the guys took me out. They wanted me to enjoy myself and to feel free. I didn't have much fun. I had so much running through my mind.

Everyone was having a blast at the club. I was sitting in the corner looking sad. Things were making me crazy. As the club began to fill with people, my head started to spin. Smoke, lights, and people were everywhere. I had to leave early because I couldn't take it. Calvin came back to Jack's place. We were staying there for the moment. Calvin wanted to talk and make things better. All of the guys came back early too. They were drunk, high and crazy.

Jack and Calvin began to act funny with me. The two of them wanted a threesome but didn't want to have it with each other. They really didn't like each other, but I was about to change things. This big ass of mine needed some dick in it. The both of them were going to give it. Calvin took matters into his own hands. He sat down in a chair and let me do the work. I put strawberry cream all over his body. I licked on his balls and sucked the head of his dick. Calvin pushed my head down on his dick. I began to gag, but I took it. It wasn't ten minutes into our having sex that Calvin began to cum.

Lust, Lies & Love

It was lovely, amazing and wonderful. Jack was looking with an ugly smile on his face. He already knew that he was going to get a good fuck. My mouth, ass, and body were all for him. I couldn't wait to let Jack have his way with me. I will suck his dick all night if I had to. Jack was the best with that mouth. He made me shake and wiggle. I was tired of fucking all the guys and Sam. It was time for me to find my own place. My body was ready for some thug dick. Someone who was going to fuck my back out and more.

Since Chad and I weren't together, I was going to let a couple of thugs fuck me front ways. Matt had some thug friends who were strippers who came over. They were some of the sexiest ladies alive. Two hours later, the thugs came over. We had drinks, naked pussy, and ass to play in. They ladies began to dance on the poles. Dicks were sticking up everywhere. My eyes were still the entire time. I made sure everyone was getting wasted. I wanted some thug dick. They guys bodies were buff and sexy. I can just taste dick in my mouth.

When the guys started to fall over, the ladies were happy than ever. We all found a sex thug. We pulled their clothes down and sucked their dicks. We were sucking so good that their body started to move. My guy woke all the way up. He put his hands on my head and started to control my neck. The bitch had me where I couldn't move. His dick was all in the back of my throat. He had a dick with a curve in it. That always had me hooked.

After the thug got finished fucking my face, he later went to my fat ass. The thug opened my asshole up and began fingering my hole. It was feeling so good. It really went down when he stuck his dick inside of me. My ass and lips began to tighten. My asshole started opening. My body was like a new born, just lifeless. I enjoyed the way he made me feel. My name should have been a nasty boy for that night. I was doing whatever with whoever.

When the party was over, Matt and I took his friend home. His friend was the sexy thug. When he got out of the car, he wanted us to check out his new place. It was amazing and lovely. I glance over at the bar to see a bottle of patron. My body was ready to get pretty boy wasted. Matt was ready to go, but I was going to stay for some fun.

After Matt left the house, Ted who is Matt's friend, began to drink shots of patron. I think I had too many. My body wanted some sex. Ted gave me the eye. I was trying to play hard to get, but it didn't happen. He started kissing all over me and loving on my body. He was so different one on one. His sex game was on point the entire time. The bed was white and calling my name. I got naked. Ted put a strawberry with cream in my asshole and sucked it out and ate it. He was a real freak.

After he took the strawberry out of my ass and ate it, he put peach cream on his dick and stuck it inside of me. My asshole was hurting like fuck. Ted was doing his thing. He had the biggest balls I have ever seen. They were so pretty. I thought that I will put them down my throat. Those balls were big, hanging and choking me. I tried to take it like a pro. Ted saw I wasn't sucking his balls right so he decided to put his dick and balls in my mouth. I couldn't think straight. I wanted to cry because it was too much pain for me, but I wanted it.

After we got finished making music, we cuddled throughout the night. When we woke up the next morning, I had ten missed called from Chad. I didn't call him back. He called ten more times. I finally answered the phone. He wanted me to come back home. Bad and good time started running through my mind. I wanted to go back, but I was scared. Chad was once my best friend, lover and my pride and joy. Without him in my life, I didn't mean anything. My heart began to split for the best. I had Chad and Sam on my mind. Things had to get better for me. Chad wanted me to leave the next morning. I did just that. My life felt like a ticking time bomb.

I got back to New York. Chad surprised me with so many gifts, trips, money, cars and more. My baby was back the best loving and caring for me. The both of us went out for dinner and drinks. Everything was going well until Chad's last ex-walked in. My body started to heat up with fire. The old bitch was looking at me sideways. I wanted to take action. I knew Chad would have been upset.

As we began to eat our dinner, Chad's ex-boyfriend bent down sand gave Chad a kiss. My fucking mind began to get loose. I could have hurt that bitch. Chad thought it was funny, but I didn't like it. Keeping my mouth closed was hard.

After the little rat left, I gave Chad a piece of my mind. He tried everything to calm me down, but he couldn't. He got the best of me. That was the final straw or that's what I thought.

Lust, Lies & Love

When we left the diner, I had evil all on my face. Chad told me to stop acting like a pest and to join the fun. I had his fucking fun because I am not freaking you and the ex at the same time. He wanted a threesome with his ex. Chas was having too much fun with his life. Sometimes I regret leaving Sam. He was my everything and more.

Our guest room was nice, lovely and cozy. I went inside of there for sleep. My mind and rest needed rest. I went into the kitchen for something to eat. A couple of Chad's friends were sitting down. I asked myself why. I thought that friends visiting at night was over, but I was wrong. Chad only wanted his friends over for sex. They gave him whatever he wanted and more. I thought I had enough. A couple of Chad's friends went into our bedroom. They were drinking, talking and having fun. In my mind, I wanted to kill them. How can they speak to me, but still fucking my man? That shit was wrong. Chad had another thing coming.

Since he wanted to freak his friends, I am going to fuck his dad. Two can play that game. Chad's dad has always had a crush on me. He is an older guy, but he is cute as hell. One of Chad's friends got sick. The guy lived out of town. Chad was going to visit him. I was happy as fuck because he has to travel ten hours and the dad was coming to visit. It was going to be the time of my life. Chad's dad's name is Parks. I was going to let Parks fuck the hell out of my body. Before Chad left the house, he told me his dad was arriving today and that I shouldn't be late picking him up from the airport. How could I be later to pick up a soon-to-be fuck? Chad gave me a kiss before he walked out. Mr. Parks called me because he had a two-hour delay. That was amazing to me because I needed to get this ass of mine together. I had to wash, tighten and shake it together. My ass needed to be clean and fresh.

After I got out of the shower, Mr. Parks was calling me to pick him up. A big smile came across my face. As I was pulling up to the airport, I saw this sexy, tall, huge black guy. He was looking like wow. I rode by him twice. It was funny because the guy was Mr. Parks. He laughed when he got into the car. The only thing I could do was laugh and say hello. Chad called when I was leaving the airport. He was making sure I picked his dad up. Chad also wanted me to take his dad to get something to eat. I didn't because I had something for him to eat and get full.

Lust, Lies & Love

When we finally got to the house, I told him I was sorry for not getting him any food. He said that it was okay because he was going to eat me. My eyes dropped to the floor. Mr. Parks was making my night. Since he was a nice and amazing guy, I went into the bathroom and ran a hot bubble bath. I helped wash him up. Mr. Parks' body was soft and sexy. I wanted to hold him tight.

The two of us sat in the bath tub for about three hours talking about life and Chad. We had a wonderful conversation, but he really didn't want to talk about Chad. So we stopped the Chad conversation short. Mr. Parks began to look into my eyes. My body was ready for daddy.

His dick was bigger than that of a Pepsi bottle. I knew I couldn't take it, but I was going to try. He was the guy who loves to make lovable sex. We started off by kissing each other. He laid me down and rubbed me with feathers. He licked me down my spine. He knew how to make a man feel lovely. He began to kiss my thighs with his soft lips. I thought I was in paradise. I tried to keep them closed, but they flew wide open. Mr. Parks got between my thighs and went to work. Daddy knew how to make love.

Lust, Lies & Love

Before we got finished making love, I let him eat me out for about an hour. His tongue was wet and thick. All I could say was "Shit. Eat me daddy."

That tongue had me yelling like a little bitch. He had me climbing up the wall and shit. He was making love to me as if I had a pussy. He said that my asshole was wetter than ever.

After it was over, I called my chef over to cook daddy something to eat. He needed something amazing and different. Daddy had the nest breakfast ever. I helped Mr. Parks get his things together. He had to leave because of work. Chad was okay, but his father was the best. He ate his ass like no other. I am going to miss that good dick.

After Chad's dad got home, he gave me a call. I thought that was sweet. Mr. Parks wanted to come back to New York, but Chad was coming home. I enjoyed everything about Mr. Parks. When Chad arrived at the house, Sam called me. I didn't know what to do because I really wanted to talk with Sam. I missed him a lot and wanted to get back with him. Sam only wanted me to love and care for him. That was something really didn't do. I am not paying for it by being with Chad. Sam gave me that world and more. I left Sam for the wrong reason.

Chad wanted some friends to come over for drinks. I knew he wanted to fuck the night away.

Since I was being stupid for Chad, I was willing to let his friends fuck me good. It was ten of them. I was going to take five at a time. I had to make Chad happy. Chad put date rape pills in everyone's drinks. He had them horny, out of their minds, and ready to punish my asshole. The five of them started off by standing over me naked. Crazy thoughts were racing through my mind. Two of them put their dicks in my mouth. I could barely think, but I was enjoying it. The other three forced their dicks in my asshole. I was in pain. Everything was splitting and in pain. Chad sat back and watched the horrible show.

After ten minutes of crazy sex, I couldn't feel my body or mind. I felt lifeless. Something in my mind was telling me to act a fool, but I didn't. I wanted to upset Chad. He told the guys to fuck me to sleep. I couldn't believe him. My head began to spin. My heart was hurting. My life was almost over. They were hitting nerves that shouldn't have been touched.

After they got finished fucking the dog shit out of me, my body dropped to the floor. He stood over me and began to Jack his dick. Cum was all over my face and mouth. Tears began to flow down my face. Chad laughed and walked over me. I wanted to say wow. I stayed on the floor for the entire. My body shut down. Chad went out with the guys. He came back to the house with two of them. They all had a threesome in front of me. That bitch was the rudest of them all. Chad finally helped me off the floor. He looked at me in my face and said, "Bitch, you are stupid for leaving Sam. He was a good man to you. He gave you what you wanted and he loved you. I only wanted you for sex. That's what I got from you."

My heart was broken because I knew I had a good man. After Chad gave me those bad words, I called Sam and told him about it. He sent me a ticket to come to Vegas. I ran to the airport with the clothes on my back. Chad treated me like shit. I had to leave him.

As I was getting on the plane, my soul began to cry. I had enough of the monster. The flight wasn't long. I was ready to see y baby, Sam. He was the real man for me. Sam never hurt me.

When I arrived in Vegas, I ran into Sam's arms and gave him a kiss. He was my love, my strength, and my peace. I felt so loved when I was with Sam. My baby only wanted the best for me. Sam and I had a long conversation. We were thinking about getting back together. I knew he was going to say yes.

After I began to blink my pretty eyes and licked my sexy lips. Sam wanted to be a couple again. I was so happy. I was about to be back with my baby. Chad called and asked me to come back home. I laughed because it was so funny. How can he ask me to come back after how he treated me. I wanted to tell Chad that he is a stank bitch and that I am on something bigger and better. So, therefore, he could go and fuck himself. I didn't tell him those things because I was going to be the better person. Hanging up the phone on Chad made me feel so good. He didn't know how to take it.

Now it's time for Sam and me to go back to his place. We are going to dance the night away. I am going to ride his big dick so good. My body couldn't wait to get into Sam's bed. Sam was driving so fast and out of control. He was ready to fuck this good ass. I was willing to give it to him.

We are finally at Sam's place. He opens the door and picks me up. When we got inside of the house, I went straight into the bedroom and started taking off my clothes. I was ready

Lust, Lies & Love

for some good dick. Sam folds my legs back against the wall. He eats me out. I was moving around like a loose worm. The dick was so amazing. Chad's stupid ass was calling while we were having sex. So I pick the phone up and let Chad hear me moan. He was yelling so loudly into the phone. It was his loss and Sam's gain. Sam was hitting all of the right spots. I was throwing this ass so good. Sam tried to slow me down, but I kept going. I love to hear Sam yell like a little bitch.

When I lay on my stomach, Sam got on top of me and went to work. I was feeling cum flowing all down my legs. Sam had so much back up. His body was shaking so fast. I thought he was going to go into shock. I was putting this ass on Sam so good.

After we made love, a couple of the guys were at the door knocking. Sam and I couldn't believe it. We haven't seen them in so long. Jack was so happy to see the two of us back together. They were ready to party the night away. Everyone was looking amazing and young. I knew the dicks were pretty and sweet. I wanted to suck a couple, but that couldn't happen. My Sam was too good to me. I couldn't cheat on him again. I am so over Chad, but I must admit that he was a good fuck to me. My life is happy, amazing and lovely. Sam and I were a family again. He meant life and more to me. I am in love with Sam and he is in love with me. Sam is going to be my baby for life.

Lust, Lies & Love

CHAPTER 7

Sam and I are back together. We are living the good life. I moved from New York to Las Vegas. It was a big move, but I was loving it. Sam's business was picking up. He was also helping me start up my own business. Things were a lot different for us. We had to get that trust thing back between the two of us. I did a lot of things to hurt Sam. The one thing that I loved about Sam is that he is always there for me.

We moved into a three bedroom, two bathroom, apartment. It was very pricey. My heart was backfilled with joy and peace. Having my backbone into my life was the best thing ever. We only spent three days together before Sam has to leave for work. I was going to miss my baby.

Lust, Lies & Love

The day before Sam got ready to leave, I had to give him some of this good ass. It was tight and hasn't been fucked in a couple of months. I bent this ass over and let Sam fuck the life out of me. I squeezed the hell out of this asshole. I let him beat these lips up. I yelled out "DADDY!" My baby got some fire dick. My tired ass went straight to sleep after Sam got finished with me.

When the both of us woke up the next morning, it was time for Sam to leave. Tears ran down my face. I had to be strong for the both of us. Sam didn't want to leave because we were just getting back together. Before he walked out of the house, he asked me to hold things down. He was going to be gone for two months. My mind couldn't take it, but I was going to make things work.

Our apartment was very lovely. The office space was small and amazing. Sam called the supply people to come over. We needed some new items. When the office van arrived at the house, it was this nice-looking guy. He later got out and knocked on the door. I didn't have any clothes on, but I had to let him in.

When I opened the door and looked up, it was this young man who was taller than the green giant. That was a turn on in my book. The two of us went upstairs to the office. I wrapped a towel around me so that he wouldn't be looking at me. It didn't work because the closer we got to the office, the towel was falling off of me. As soon as we hit the top of the stairs, I was fully naked. The supply guy was looking like I am going to fuck you. I bent over to pick up the towel and told him that I was sorry. He told me not to worry. We were flirting, but I wasn't going to cheat on Sam. I had business to take care of. The supply guy's name is Smith. I was so surprised that he didn't try to touch me.

Since I was bending over and down, that was his little peak show. After Smith left the house, I called and told him that everything was done. He was happy. Business was about to start for me. The two months that I was going to be along was going to kill me. Without Sam being beside me, the pillows and I were going to make it happen.

I stayed in Vegas for a month before flying out to Texas. Sam and I were both missing each other. Texas was hot as fuck. I only stayed for three days. Sam knew I couldn't do the heat. IT was very hot. I was ready to get back to Vegas and work. Sam was going to be in Texas for another month. So I called the guys. I wanted them to come and visit. I have really missed them. Everyone was excited about coming. The trip was going to be a six-day, seven-night trip. We are going to have an almighty blast. Everyone took a week off of work. I was so proud of the,

When the limo arrived at the house, I noticed other people were with them. In my mind, I wanted to know who these guys were. Jack told me who they were. My mouth dropped. They were the exes of each of the guys. I asked myself what was really going on. They were still good friends with each other My ears and eyes couldn't believe it. My lovely heart invited everyone into the house. I took them on a mini tour and showed them to their rooms. I didn't kick it with the new guys as well. They were too much for me.

Later that night, we began to play all types of games. The drinks were coming fast and I was ready to fuck. One of the guys began to take all of his clothes off. I wanted to take him to my room and fuck him so good. The guy had a body of a model. Everyone wanted more to drink, but I couldn't take it anymore. I was getting horny and Sam wasn't there to fuck me good. We were still playing games and drinking. All of the guys were getting naked.

Lust, Lies & Love

My body was ready, but I couldn't. Jack came over to me and put his dick in my face. I moved him. It was hard for me to do it. Watching the other guys have sex wasn't easy. Their dicks were huge. A couple of them were fucking some of the asses inside out. Many of them were making noises that made my dick rise. I began to jack my dick. The only person I can think of was Sam. The more I thought of Sam, the more I jacked off. I was feeling a rush that I have never felt before.

After the amazing sex show, everyone showered and went out on the town. I stayed home because of work. Sam called and told me to come outside. Someone wanted to see me. When I opened the door, it was Sam. He looked sexy and wonderful. I was so happy to see him. Sam came home early because work was slow. Every time I touch him, his dick got hard. I had to take it out of his pants and put it in my mouth. His dick makes me gag, but I enjoyed it. Sam fucked me differently this time. He was fucking my asshole like a punching bag banging the hell out of me.

When everyone came from the club, Sam was so happy to see everyone. Some of the guys were drunk as fuck. Sam wasn't too thrilled when he saw the new guys. I had to keep him calm. He wasn't trying to bring any new people into the circle.

Ten minutes into the conversation, Sam was feeling all of the guys. He didn't know what type of guys they were, but he really got to know them. Once of them was a real estate agent which was a plus because I was thinking about buying another home in Vegas. Sam didn't know. I wanted to surprise him.

The guys' trip ended very fast because Sam and I needed some quality time. My baby needed to be loved and held. Things were getting better for the two of us. I loved the way Sam pound my asshole. He has my ass lips jumping with love. The love I use to have for Sam was coming back. Sam was always my world, heart and soul. I am so happy to be back with my baby. Sam and I had to return back to Atlanta for a business trip. My heart didn't want to go back. We were doing just fine. I didn't want anyone to miss it up.

As we were getting off the plane, we saw Chad at the airport. My stomach dropped to my ankles. Someone told him that we were going to be in town. Sam and I walked pass him as if we didn't see him. Chad called out my name so loud, but yet I kept walking. Chad took me through too much pain. Sam wanted to fight Chad, but I wouldn't let him.

When we pulled up to the hotel, there was a sideways look on Sam's face. My mouth didn't open until we got into the hotel room. I asked him was he okay. He said kind of. Chad was a flawless bitch knowing that we weren't friends anymore. My phone began to ring. I was Chad. I didn't answer because there was no reason. Sam started punching holes in the walls. That bitch was going crazy. I knew it was time to give him some good ass. My body was bent over. He began to eat me. It was so good. My knees started clapping together. I knew I was going to hit the floor.

After my ass was ate out so well, I got up because Sam just needed a sample. We left the hotel an hour later to attend the business meeting. I was weak as hell, but I had to attend the meeting. Sam was so shocked when we got to the meeting. Chad bitch ass was teaching the class. The only thing I could say was what the fuck. I hoped that Sam was going to keep his cool.

After the meeting was over, Chad walked up to us and told us to have a good day. Sam wanted to fuck that bitch up on the spot. My baby did good and kept his cool.

Lust, Lies & Love

After we left the meeting, I had to call all of the guys. Sam was having a bad day. I knew they could cheer him up. Everyone went to Jack and his secret friend's place. We told everyone what happened. They were mad as hell because they didn't like Chad.

Since we were back in Atlanta, I thought I should have my baby a get-together. His mind needed some fun. I always have something up my sleeves. My plan was to get him a big dick stripper. He needed some big dick in his mouth and ass. It took us two hours to plan the party. I was more ready for the stripper than anyone. Big dick, balls and a lot of cum were turn-ons for me. We got everything together, blindfolded Sam and sat him front of the stripper.

When we took the blindfold off of his face, he was in shocked and very surprised. They guy got fully undressed and began to dance all over Sam. The stripper's body was flowing like water. My ass was wet as fuck. He laid Sam on the floor and started kissing him from head to toe. He began to suck his dick happily. I loved it so much. The young guy was fucking the hell out of my man. Our money wasn't going to be a waste. Sam enjoyed it.

Lust, Lies & Love

I joined in the action. The guy fucked so good. He had me where I couldn't talk or move. The dick was so amazing and true. Jack and Calvin paid the stripper some extra money. They wanted to see us get fucked at the same time. The two of us were ready as hell. I needed some dick in my stomach and ass. Sam had a big dick, but I needed a monster inside of me. We started off by sucking the stripper off at the same time.

The bitch was moaning for days. Sam was deep-throating that dick so good. I couldn't let him outdo me. So I put all of the guy's dick and balls inside of my mouth. His body was stiff as fuck. That mouth of mine was awesome. He laid the both of us on our backs and spread our legs open just to fuck us one by one. I grabbed onto his nipples as he held my shoulders tightly and tore my ass up. I was feeling his dick all up in my chest. Sam told me to jack off, but I didn't have to. The stripper was fucking me so good that my dick was cumming on it's on. Dude came three ties inside of me and twice in my mouth. I couldn't seem to get enough of dick or cum.

After he couldn't go anymore, I got on top of him and started bouncing on the head of his dick. He was telling me to stop, but I didn't. I wanted more cum inside of me. I felt sorry for Sam because the stripper was too weak to fuck anyone else. Jack made sure that Sam didn't go to sleep sadly. He took it upon himself to fuck Sam. I thought it was sexy. My body laid down and watched Sam get fucked. It wasn't all that, but I enjoyed it. My baby was getting dick from everywhere. His asshole was wide as fuck.

After they finished with hi, I thought maybe I would fist fuck him. That was the funniest night of my life. Sam couldn't take it for nothing. He had to shit. I made him hold it. I had to teach him about fucking everything that walked. Sam is my baby, but sometimes you have to teach your bitch about fucking around.

When I got finished with Sam, I took a shower and left the house. Calvin was calling me. I had to go and jump in that ass. Calvin knew I was trying to be faithful to Sam, but he didn't care. As I was driving to Calvin's place, my heart was on Sam so strong because he meant the world to me. While on the way, I called Calvin and told him that I couldn't make it. He was mad as fuck. He began to moan in the phone getting me horny as fuck. I couldn't drive or think. I had to make it to Calvin's.

Lust, Lies & Love

When I arrived at his apartment, he was naked and ready for a good fuck. I sat on the couch. He took off his robe and bent over in front of me. He opened his ass. My dick was hard as fuck. I got down on my knees and ate him out. Calvin was shaking his ass while my tongue was all in his hole. Dude was riding the hell out of my face. We didn't fuck because Sam was on my mind. I wanted to make love to him.

When I was walking out of the door, Calvin began to slow dance to my favorite song. My body was ready to make love. I kept walking. If Calvin kept dancing so beautifully and slowly, then something was going to happen.

Once I got into the car, Calvin called me wanting to know why I didn't make love to him. I told him that Sam was on my mind. He said that he understood, but I knew he didn't. On my way home, the only person I could think about was Sam. That's my baby until the end.

When I got into the apartment, Sam was sleeping like a baby. I took matters into my own hands while he was sleep. I pulled the covers back. I took off his clothes and lick him with everything I loved. The long tongue of mine was going to wake him up. It's thick, powerful and very long. Two minutes into my

Lust, Lies & Love

licking him so good, he woke up moaning. Things were about to get good. Twenty minutes later, I took my tongue out of Sam's asshole. It was wet as hell. He put his finger in his tight ass and fingered himself. I sat back and watched. My dick was sticking up like a light pole all hard and stiff. The more I watched him play in his ass, the more I wanted to make love to him.

After he got finished doing his thing, he was ready for me to stick my dick into his soft ass. I put it in and took it out. I had to tease him for a couple of minutes. Sam was getting mad. He got up and went into the kitchen. When he came back into the room, he had a bottle of whipped cream, a cup of cherries and some cake sprinkles. The freak was about to come out of my baby. I sat up on the bed because something was about to happen. He pushed me back on the bed and sprayed my dick down then put a cherry on top. He went to work on this dick. My eyes couldn't stop rolling in the back of my head. The feeling was phenomenal. Sam rolled his tongue around the head of my dick. I was about to cum, but I held it.

After sucking my dick so good, Sam went down to my balls. He started licking them while jacking me off. His hands were moving in a circular motion while jacking me off. I loved it. Sam was a real freak.

When we finished making music, the two of us went to sleep. My body was very tired. I woke up the next morning with sex on my mind. My dick wanted to have a threesome with Sam and Calvin. Something is telling me that Sam is going to go for it. I was right. We sat down and talked everything over. Sam was more ready than I was. This dick of mine was ready to fuck some ass. These balls were ready to smack against some soft ass. We went over to Calvin's place.

When we got there, he had drinks ready for us. Sam wasn't a big drinker, but he will drink the night away for me. We gave Sam six shots of patron. He was drunk as fuck out of his mind and everything else. We already knew we were going to misuse Sam's body. Calvin wanted to fuck Sam with no lube. I was up for it because he was drunk and didn't know any better. Sam's ass stayed wet as if it was a waterfall.

After we got finished fucking Sam loose, it was time for me to attend my first business trip. I was only leaving for three days. Sam wasn't sad because three days weren't that long. I was going to miss Sam. He is the love of my life and more. The business trip was going to help us get through our rough times.

As I was getting on the plane, Sam blew me kisses which I thought was so sweet. The trip was taking place in Florida. I loved it because I needed some heat in my life. The flight was long, but it was crazy. A young man asked could he sit with me. I shook my head. We talked about life. He was sexy as fuck. I wanted him to wrap his thick lips around my big dick.

When the guy got up and went into the bathroom, a wide smile came across my face. As time went by, I noticed he was still in the bathroom. Forty minutes later, I got up to see what was wrong. When I opened the small door, he was bent over in pain. I didn't know what to do because he was acting so weird. Five minutes into his acting weird, my body was beginning to walk out. I felt something pulling me back like I was a child.

When I turned around and looked, it was the young man. He had his dick hanging out of his pants. I wanted to cry because his dick was so small. I got on my knees to suck it, but couldn't. His dick smelled like horse shit covered with ass juice.

After that, I went down to his balls. They were sour and spoiled. I could have killed that raw ass bitch. I just knew I was going to suck a dick. He asked me what was wrong. I told him that his dick was stank as fuck. I walked out as if nothing happened. My ass sat by the window and went to sleep.

Two hours into the trip, I felt something wet on my big dick. The guy was giving me some amazing head. My legs were kicking the seat in front of me. This young bitch had me going crazy as fuck. My dick was hard. My balls were wet. My heart was racing. The more he began to suck my dick, the more I was about to cum. I took both of my hands and put them on his head. I held his head down and came all in his mouth. My sweet bitch took all of it down for the team. I laughed at his nasty ass. You can tell the bitch will do anything for a piece of dick.

After that tired punk gave me some good head, I went back to sleep. That bitch was the best on the plane. We are now landing in Florida. I am going to the meeting with a smile on my face. The limo picked me up and took me to the hotel. I had to check in and get ready. The meeting was in the hotel conference room on my way to the meeting. I

Lust, Lies & Love

was tired, but I couldn't turn back around. The meeting was very important.

When I walked into the meeting, there were only a couple of people. Everything and everybody was fucking ugly. My ass didn't learn anything because the people were making my damn skin crawl. Since I didn't have anything to do, I thought I should take one of those ugly bitches back to the room and fuck them until a pretty smile come across his face. I always heard that an ugly bitch had the best ass. I saw this tired ass guy who was at the meeting. My dick invited him back to my room. The both of us introduced ourselves. His name is Mich. He was ugly as fuck, but I was going to fuck him good. We started off with a glass of wine. Mich was a very smart guy. He was just ugly.

After the wine and the amazing conversation, I showed him to the door. Hew act like he didn't want to leave. So a freak like me asked him to stay the night. He agreed. I knew the night was about to be on. I put on a movie and let him enjoy himself. I told Mich that I was going to take a hot shower. He was sitting in my living room looking like an old dick.

When I went into the bathroom, my body didn't want to come back out. That face was a mess. The water was running for about twenty minutes before I got in. After those minutes were up, I thought maybe I would get in. The water was feeling so good. I didn't want to get out. I was getting horny as fuck. I knew it was time for me to get out of the shower. I didn't dry off because I was going to let Mich lick me dry. I walked into the living room naked. Mich's eyes got big as fuck. This dick was hanging like a horse. Mich's mouth wouldn't close for anything. So I took my dick and put it in his mouth. My dick wanted to feel his throat and all. I only put the head of my dick in his mouth. He choked. That made me mad as fuck. I took it out and told him to open his mouth as wide as he could. I put my entire dick down his throat.

Tears began to flow from his eyes. He was shaking like a jumping monkey. I took my dick out and told Mich to put his hands on the end of my couch. He arched his back while standing spread eagle. I was going to fuck some sense in him. His asshole was tight as hell. I didn't take my time. I threw this dick in him. He was yelling and crying. It was the first time being fucked.

Since he wanted to yell and cry, I had something for that, My dick started fucking him harder and deeper. The ugly bitch was speechless and couldn't move if he wanted to. I tried to tongue fuck the scary-looking fuck. He couldn't take that. I knew it was time for me to fuck him good and let him go his way. He had some good ass. That hole has never been touched. I had to play in it. I was going to cum in his mouth. He was ready for some sweet cum. Mich's whole face was white. I laughed and told him to go back to his room. He could barely walk back to his room. I wanted to help him, but I was tired as fuck. He called me while he was walking back. I didn't answer because that was only a fuck thing. We weren't friends or coworkers. That was something he needed to get into his head. I wanted some ass. That's what I got. That dumb bitch's mouth was wet as fuck. I'll be getting some more of that as before that meeting is over.

Sam's bitch ass called me because he wanted to know how things were. I told him good and that I was ready to come home. Sam began to go crazy on the phone. That's because he needed some dick. I was ready to go back home and play in that tight ass. My baby knew how to work it. We all got an email saying that he meeting was going to be cancelled on the last day. I had to fuck that ugly ass Mich before I left. The night before we left, everyone went out for dinner. Mich was getting so wasted. I couldn't believe my eyes. Two hours into our amazing dinner, Mich was drunk. We all thought it was funny as hell. I took it upon myself to take Mich back to his hotel. He was only four doors down from me. Instead of taking him to his room, I took him inside of my room and put him in the shower to wake him up.

When Mich came to himself, he didn't know what happened. After I told his crazy ass, he laughed. I left him lying down in the living room and went into the bedroom. We had a long night. A couple of minutes later, Mich was walking into my room. He said he couldn't sleep. I told him to get in the bed with me. I noticed that he only had on a T-shirt. He put his head under the covers because he was cold. I turned over and didn't think twice about it. I felt something wet touching my dick. It was Mich's mouth sucking my dick.

That ugly flower can suck a good dick. I loved it. I was only feeling mouth and tongue. He wanted me to fuck him. He got on top of the desk and bent over the edge of it. I put his legs up and fucked him good. Mich was nutting like crazy. I can tell it was his first good nut.

Lust, Lies & Love

He began to call me daddy and tell me that he loved me. I couldn't fuck him any longer. That bitch was going crazy. It was his first good dick.

When we woke up the next day, that ugly monster was lying beside me. This is a bad episode of coyote ugly. I was scared as fuck because I never woke up to a monster. I wanted to chew my arm off than wake him up. In the back of my mind, I wanted to push that ugly bitch out of the window. He asked me to walk him back to him room. My heart wouldn't let me say no. So I told him to let me go back into my room. I needed a trash bag to cover his face. He laughed. He thought I was trying to be funny, but I was dead ass serious.

An hour later, it was time to go back home. My world was so happy. Sam couldn't wait to see me. I was ready to see him. Everything went well with the business trip. I really enjoyed myself. Now it is time to go back home to get my fuck on. My ass is home waiting and I am ready to fuck it. Sam's ass had a taste that always left me speechless. I am missing me some good. It is now time to take a nap. When I open my eyes, I want to be landing in New York.

Lust, Lies & Love

Ten minutes later, the plane was landing. I saw my baby Sam. He looked so sexy while waiting for me. I jumped into the care and started kissing on him. I wanted to make love. Sam started driving fast as fuck. My baby was ready for some good dick.

When we pulled up to the house, the both of us ran upstairs and took off his clothes. We fucked. Sam's ass was tight as hell. It took me five minutes to get my entire dick in. Once I got this dick inside of that ass, it was on for the entire night. I rubbed Sam down with strawberries and wine. I started licking him from his asshole to his ears. Every part of his body was tasteful. I threw Sam's legs back and put my dick in his ass. I made love to him. His ass was so good that he made my toes fold. I got off of Sam and let his mouth go to work. His lips were feeling so amazing on my dick. I had to face fuck him. My baby was deep-throating my dick so good.

When I took my dick out of his mouth, it was wet as fuck. I wanted to be nasty while fucking Sam. I thought it would be a good idea to fuck Sam until he had to shit. I put my dick in his mouth with the shit on it and made him swallow every inch of it. I knew he was willing to try anything. My eyes asked hi softly. Sam

Lust, Lies & Love

has always wanted me to fuck him nasty. I didn't feel back about it because this is what he wanted. My dick was trying to choke the hell out of Sam. The nasty bitch always wanted some good dick.

Before we can get finished fucking, there was a knock on the door. Sam went to the door with the stank mouth. When he opened the door, it was Rich. He was a really good friend of Sam's. Rich and Sam came into the room. I was naked and ready to fuck the both of them. Sam jumped into the bed naked while Rich just stood there and looked.

The both of us helped Rich take off his clothes and threw him on our bed. His dick was big as hell. I had to suck that dick. Sam started playing in his ass while I was sucking his dick. He had balls for days. The more Sam was playing in his as. I sucked Rich's dick faster. Sam wanted a threesome, but I wanted the dick to myself. Rich didn't waste any time. He bent me over and fucked me. I felt that dick all in my stomach. The only thing I could hold on to was my ankles. He had me Cumming without me jacking my dick.

Rich's dick felt like it was a ball inside of me. It was big as fuck. His balls were beating the hell out of my thighs. He put on of my legs behind my head while standing. That shit hurt like hell because of his pounding meat in me. The more I moaned, the more that twelve and a half inch dick fucked me. I couldn't take his dick, but I didn't let him know it.

After we got finished fucking so good, my asshole was wider than fuck. I couldn't sit or stand. I could lie down on my side. That fuck got the best of my ass. Sam was moaning and ready for some good dick. Rich and Sam have never fucked before, but I was about to change that. I opened Sam's mouth and put Rich's dick inside of it.

Since he wanted some dick, I gave him some. Rich made love to Sam. I think they were falling for each other. I never heard Sam moan so softly and nicely. Rich's dick was making Sam moan lose his mind. The word yes came all across my face. Rich was about to take my silly bitch away.

My hands were ready to pack Sam's clothes, but that didn't happen. Sam was just in the moment. I am thinking about moving Rich in for a couple of weeks. The dick is good. I need to keep it for a while. Sam's dick is okay, but Rich had that good. I am putting Sam in the guest room because I need some good dick. Sam agreed to moving into the guest room.

Lust, Lies & Love

Things were about to spice up for the three of us.

Sam's birthday was coming up. I wanted to have him a sex party. Chad always threw a nice sex party. I wanted to get Sam some strippers. My friend Mitch was a stripper. He was the best. I called him up because I knew he would come through for me.

Before I planned the party, I called a couple of the guys to see what they had to say. Everyone thought the strippers were a good idea. I called Mich up. He was happy to hear from me. We haven't talked in so long. Once we began to talk about the party and our lives, Mich asked if I would give him some ass. He said he wouldn't charge. I laughed because he already knew he was going to get some ass.

At the party and after the party, it took us a week to plan everything. So I went to visit Mich for two days. He fucked the shit out of me both days I was there. I almost forgot how that dick felt. It felt so good going in my warm ass. I missed that dick so much. Mich knew how to lay that fat pipe down.

After he got finished with me, my insides weren't any good. My asshole was hurting like a bitch. My ass wanted to ride that big dick, but I couldn't because I was hurting so badly. It was time for me to leave Mich and fly back home. I had a party to plan.

When I got back to New York, I called a couple of the guys so they could help me plan Sam's party. Sam didn't think I remembered his birthday. How could I forget about his special day? We all were ready to see some dick and ass.

The day was here. We were ready. Jack blindfolded Sam and sat him in the middle of the floor. Everybody waited on the stripper. When Mich came into the room, he only had on a red bow. We took the blindfold off. Mich slapped Sam all in the face with his dick. It was big as fuck. Sam didn't know what to do. Mich was dancing all over him. Sam was acting all coy, but we knew better.

Once he put that dick on Sam's big lips, it was on from there. Sam was touching, sucking and ready to fuck. Mich put on a show. Dude had dick for days. His ass was so round and smooth. I wanted to put his ass in my mouth. It looked sweet and ready to eat.

Since Sam and everybody else were looking all surprised, I took my clothes off and spread my body like an eagle. Then I bounced my ass against Mich's dick. His dick was getting hard as fuck. My ass was wet. A couple of minutes later into our playing around, I felt something hard and thick slide in my ass. It was Mich's big ass dick. He packed all of that shit inside of me. I thought my ass was going to fall out. I was seeing things that weren't there. That dick had me so gone. The only thing I could say was what the fuck is going on. That big dick bitch had me in another zone. I loved that shit. He made his dick jump inside my ass. I was hurting like hell, but I took that pain. It was worth it. Mich bust this ass open. I threw it back. He was every man's dream. Sam didn't take dick very well. He couldn't take the pain. I wanted to beat that bitch ass. I enjoyed me some good dick.

Before Sam left to go back home, we had sex for the last time. I was crazy because he was sitting in front of us watching like a sad puppy. He already knew I was going to get me some of that dick before he left.

When Mich and I finished having sex, Sam and I took him to the airport. My body wanted to hold Mich and let him fuck me dead. I didn't want him to go because the dick was so good. The guys really enjoyed themselves.

After the amazing party was over, we all went back to our work and fuck lives. Sam was a hardworking man that strived for the best. I fucked every day for about three months. His ass was good, but loose at the same time. The bitch has been fucking other dicks. I had something for him. I will send Sam on another trip. Then I will invite his best friend over and fuck him crazy. That is exactly what I did. Same went to Mexico for a week. He was so happy about the trip. His sister went with him. I knew they were going to have a blast.

After I dropped Sam and his sister off at the airport, my fingers danced across my phone's keypad dialing Ted's number. He is the best friend. He couldn't believe I called him to come over. My ass wanted some new dick.

When Ted came into the house, I was naked. His mouth dropped to the floor. My dick wanted to pick his lips up. I asked him was he okay. He nodded. My back needed some lotion. So I asked Ted will he apply some on me. He agreed and rubbed my body down softly. His hands were soft and amazing. H went from my back to my asshole. My body was shaking for that dick.

A couple of minutes into his rubbing me down, he laid me on my back and threw my legs back. He sucked my asshole. Every part of my body was crying for help. His lips were feeling lovely. I turned over onto my stomach to let him on top of me. I spread my legs open and let him get in this ass good. He went crazy on this ass. He was fucking the hell out of me. My asshole was loving that big dick. His dick seems like it is getting bigger as he is fucking me. I felt Ted's dick all in my deep throat. The dick was so good that I had to take it to the bathtub. That bitch had my head under the water so I couldn't move. He was holding my head down with his big hands and fucking me good only letting me up to catch a breath. I was moaning like a little bitch. I couldn't help it because he was working that dick.

After we got out of the shower, I called to order him something to eat. Only good dick will make you do crazy things like that. When Ted got finished eating his breakfast, he wanted some more sex. I gave it to him. My body was hurting like hell, but I wanted more dick. Before Ted and I were about to have sex, I told him to fuck me like it was his last time. He laughed. I Knew it was about to be some trouble. He wanted me to do a slow dance for him.

The dance was nice and freaky. I played in my ass while I danced. My eyes met Ted's. I saw that his dick was sticking straight up. My ass was wet and ready. I thought I had a waterfall inside of me. He enjoyed it all. The bed was calling my name, but I couldn't make it. Ted pushed me on the floor. He told me to open my mouth and suck his dick. It was so big that I could only fit the head in. That bitch ass had already bust my ass open. Now he is trying to kill my mouth. He had me gagging for my sweet life. Every time he was about to cum, his dick would get extra big. My throat was ready for it to come. I was going to take it all down for the team. Ted wanted me to suck his dick until he came.

Ten minutes into my sucking his horse dick, this hairy bitch tried to face fuck me. I punched that bitch's dick to let him know that it was too big. He didn't want to hear that. My crazy ass tightened its lips together and started sucking like it was my last dick. He couldn't take the lips and nutted instantly. Of course I couldn't let any of the juices go to waste. My throat enjoyed all of it. He put on his clothes because it was time for him to leave.

Lust, Lies & Love

Before he left my place, he looked at me and said that he couldn't believe that I let him fuck me. He was worried that I wouldn't because of his relationship with Sam. I laughed. I told him that he was not the first friend of Sam and that he would not be the last. I loved new dick. He couldn't do anything but laugh.

I let Ted drive my car because I needed to taste that dick again. Dude was driving all off the road. I was giving him some deep throat. He came all over me. My mouth and ass didn't want that dick to leave.

After leaving the airport, my body went home for a good nap. Ted put me to sleep. Sam called later that night. He wanted to know what I was doing. I told him that I just left the airport. He wanted to know why I was at the airport. I told him that I took Ted there. Now he is acting like he has amnesia asking Ted who.

"Your best friend, bitch." I hissed at him.

I told him that Ted came over looking for him, but he wasn't there.

"We did fuck and it was good as hell too."

"Lying ass," Sam said with a chuckle.

Lust, Lies & Love

Sam thought I was lying about fucking Ted. I had to hurry and get off of the phone with him. He was killing me with that nasty-sounding voice. Sam and his sister came home early because of Sam's suspicions of Ted and me.

When he opened the door, I wanted to punch the little sissy for being stupid. He was trying to cry and act all upset. I didn't want to hear that. So I took out my dick and put it in his mouth to shut him up. The sad dick face went from crying like a monkey to sucking like a pro. Sam just needed some good dick to put in that hot mouth. His head game was so good. He kept my dick wet and on point.

Jack called me because Chad asked about me. That's one dick that I really missed. Chad would fuck me in a way that other wouldn't think about. I am going to take another business trip to Atlanta. I want Chad to fuck this ass once again. He made my ass wet just looking at it. When he put his dick inside of me, my body just melted.

I told Sam it would be a great it would be a great idea for me to open up my own fucking business. I love to fuck. It is something I really enjoy. That slow bitch wasn't hearing that, but I was going to make it happen. I am the type of dude that love sucking and getting fucked by a big dick. Sam can have all of the money. I just want a good fuck because my ass wanted to try out some new dicks. Sam kept telling me no. I knew how to fix his stupid ass. I took him into the kitchen and fucked him so good.

"Baby, you can have whatever you want," Sam yelled as I pounded his ass.

My face had a glow of happiness on it. Since Sam didn't want to go into the business with me. He called and asked his dad to help manage everything. I was so fucking happily because his dad and I had a great fuck. I need a big older dick to tame me. Sam couldn't do it, but his family and friends could. His dad came to visit so we could talk more about the business. He was about everything and so was I.

We needed something to eat. I sent Sam to the store. His dad stayed with my freaky ass. As soon as Sam walked out of the door, we started fucking. I didn't hear Sam come back into the house. He dropped the food off into the kitchen and walked into our bedroom. His eyes got big as fuck when he saw me fucking his dad. His dad saw him and told me to keep going. I was fucking that old fuck as if he was a young man. His ass was tight. His dick was big. He knew how to work that body. Tears were flowing down Sam's face.

I looked at him and Sam and said, "If you really love me like you say you do, then you will join in and help me beat your dad's ass up good." I bit my lip to make it appear a bit sexier because I knew what I was asking is a lot.

We both put our big dicks in dad's asshole. We had that asshole so wide and deep. Dad was taking both dicks with no problem. His asshole was better than his son's. He was cumming like a train. I took my dick out of his as and lowered myself to the floor. I let him drop his load all over me. I loved it. Sam tried to move, but I made him keep fucking his dad. He needed some new ass. He was fucking his dad as if he didn't know him. My crazy ass was for him to fuck him harder. I told him to bust his dad's ass wide open.

Sam began to pump that ass hard as hell. His dad was trying to get up, but I wasn't having it. I held him down and let Sam fuck him like crazy. The dad's asshole was red as fuck. I felt sorry for him. Sam was tired as hell. My lips and tongue played with dad's ass. I had to make him feel better. We never talked about the suppose-to-be-business. We were giving him the real business. The both of them drained the hell out of me.

The three of us took a shower and went to sleep. We woke up the next morning and took dad to the airport. On our way back home, Sam asked me would I have a threesome with his friend, Amir. Of course I agreed. That dude is fuck as fuck. Before we could get home good, Sam was on the phone calling Amir. He didn't answer so Sam left a message.

Chapter 8

As we were pulling into the driveway, Amir was calling Sam back. I was happier than ever. Sam talked to Amir about the threesome. He agreed to it. I knew things were about to get hot. Mr. Amir came over two days later. He was ready to fuck. He was one of the sexiest men alive. My mouth wanted to eat Amir up because his body was unbelievable. Amir went into the bathroom to take a shower. When he came out of the hot shower, he only had on a T-shirt and a pair of basketball shorts. His dick was big as hell. I wanted to put it in my mouth. The three of us went into the living area for popcorn and soda.

Sam's outfit looked like a sheet. That shit wasn't sexy at all. Amir turned me on with those shorts. Sam asked me to go into the kitchen to get drinks. When I got back to the living area, Sam was naked as a fucking jay bird. I wanted to beat his asshole inside out with my big dick. Sam's ass was sitting upright. I knew his asshole was wet as fuck. The three of us began to talk and laugh. Amir was looking so good that I wanted to laugh my dick in his mouth. Sam was ready to do some things. Amir's dick was eleven inches. A bitch like me could easily take eleven inches. Sam was the one that couldn't take dick.

After all of the talking and laughing, it was time to fuck. My ass wanted Amir's dick for a couple of months. I was going to get it. Sam kept saying that he was ready for the threesome, but the simple fuck can't take a big dick. I told Sam to fuck the threesome and that I am about to let Amir fuck me silly. When he finishes with me, he can do whatever he wants with Sam. Amir put me on my side and fucked the shit out of me. I was taking all of that good dick. Mass was wet as the red sea. The way Amir was fucking my big ass I thought I had a pussy because he was moaning the entire time.

After I got off of my side, I got into the doggie style and let him have his way. I felt his dick in my throat and mouth. Amir had a dick that only a bad bitch could take. I was that bitch. He was fucking me easy, but I had to tell him to fuck the hell of this ass, It needed to be punished. I don't know why I said that. He tied my arms and ankles together. He was taking his time. Then he banged the shit out of my body. I couldn't feel my damn ass because he was sexing me so roughly.

Sam wanted to join, but I didn't need a silly fuck messing up my sex game. I am a real freak who loves to suck dick, lick balls and eat ass. I take all of his babies down my deep throat. I am just a nasty ass bitch. I made sure Amir got a couple of nuts. That punk ass was going to remember me. Amir sexed me so good that Sam had to wait for an hour.

Within that long hour of waiting, my ass was getting horny as fuck, but I was going to let Sam enjoy himself. Now it's time for Amir to fuck my dizzy ass boyfriend. Amir's dick was going to kill Sam's little asshole. I told Sam to not make a sound while getting fucked. I told him to take it like a pro. If he didn't, I was going to beat his ass. He wanted a big dick. Now he is going to have one. Amir only put half of his dick in Sam. I thought Sam was about to fall out. So I told Amir to put it all in.

Lust, Lies & Love

When he did, Sam's eyes were getting big as hell. The bitch kept his mouth closed, but tears were coming down his face. I wanted to hit Sam in the face for crying like a bitch. Amir was fucking him good and he was crying.

After Amir got finished with Sam, I couldn't take it. I had to jump back on that dick. My sore ass wanted more. Amir was fucking me so good and fast. It didn't take him long to cum. The ass was so wet and good. Amir had to be home the next day.

We called our driver to come and pick him up. Before he left, he wanted to thank us for inviting him over and giving him a good fuck. I was going to get some more of that dick. Amir is now gone and my bitch Sam is looking at me stupidly. I told him in a very soft voice that he should have taken that dick instead of running from it. Sam looked at me sideways. I made that flat face dick sucking punk open his mouth. I put my dick inside of it.

After he got finished sucking me off so good, my friend Jared called because he wanted to hang out. Sam didn't want me to go. He knew what type of person Jared was. As I was getting ready to go out with Jared, Sam unzipped my pants and put my dick in his mouth. I wouldn't take it out. I was mad as hell. Jared and I were really going back to his place to fuck. Sam stopped all of that. He went to sleep with my dick in his mouth. My nasty ass waited until went to sleep and came in his mouth. Cum ran down his mouth. I was laughing so hard.

When Sam woke up the next morning, he wanted to kill me, but he knew better. Sam and I wanted to open a business together. I wanted to open a fucking business, the one where you stay home all day and the clients come over. You fuck them for a couple of hours. Then they pay and leave. That would wonderful business. Sam is going to visit his dad for a couple of days. I will be working and going on a fucking spree. I had so much work to catch up on.

Jack and some of the guys were calling as I was trying to do some work. I had to stop working and answer the phone. They were going to be in town for a couple of days. They needed a place to crash. I told them to come and stay, We were going to have a blast. Sam is gone and that's more ass, dick and mouth for me. I didn't see any of the guys in the afternoon. They all had business meetings to attend.

Lust, Lies & Love

After the meeting, everyone came back to my place for some fun. Everyone was so happy to be together. It's been a long time since I have seen them. I had to make my famous drink for these dick suckers. They were drinking like crazy. Those deep throat men were thirsty. Deep throat men and I get along very well. My dick loves to feel the back of that mouth. Everyone began to talk loudly and yell out of control. I knew they were ready to be fucked. Jack stood in front of me. He put his hands around my throat and began to slap me in the face with his dick. That shit was turning me on. Jack's dick was big and thick.

My mouth was ready to go to work. All of the guys had big dicks. It was only five of them. I wanted all five to fuck me at once. I needed a good workout. We all went into my bedroom to watch television, but that didn't happen because my freaky ass started to take my clothes off. Ad soon as I took my underwear off. Dick was running all up in my ass and mouth. I was stuck like Chuck. Calvin was fucking me hard as fuck. Matt was choking that hell out of me with that big dick.

After Calvin got finished with me, I was walking bowlegged and pair-toed. They were just getting started with me. Three of the guys stuffed me into a chest with head and arms first. Then they stuffed my legs in it. The only thing you saw was ass. It was all in the air. They took turns freaking me. My ass was hurting like hell. I tried to take three dicks at once. It was a killer, but I managed. Their nasty freaks came all over my back and ass. It felt so amazing running down my body. They fucked me good. I went into the bathroom to take a break. I pulled the shower curtain back. To my surprise, it was two of Jack's friends in the bath tub fucking. Big boy was throwing that ass back. The small dude couldn't handle it. The big boy stopped throwing that ass and started to ride the dick. He was going a split while he rode it. He was a bad bitch. He made the small guy cum in no time at all. I only watched them have fun.

After the two of them finished, my mouth grabbed the small boy's dick and started sucking. He asked me where can he cum. I told him in my mouth because my throat wanted to taste him. The guy has so much cum. I took it like a real pro.

After he came in my mouth, I made him fuck me backwards. My ass was jumping for dick so I got it.

Lust, Lies & Love

I woke up the next morning and couldn't walk. They fucked me wrong, stupid and silly. Ten minutes later, Sam called for me to come and pick him up. The airport was twenty minutes away. I told him to catch a can because my ass was hurting. He asked why. I told him because his friend fucked that shit out of me. Sam called me a nasty ass bitch. My heart laughed. I told him that he is right. I am a real nasty ass bitch because I fucked his dad and his brother. I also told him that when he gets home that I am going to fuck him too.

All of the guys left before Sam got back home. When Sam walked into the house, he didn't see anyone and thought I was lying. He gave me a big smile. He started hugging my dick with his mouth and didn't want to let go. He missed his baby so much. His baby was my dick. I didn't miss him at all. Something was telling me that Sam had been fucking. His ass was stank as fuck. I put my fingers up in his ass. They came out smelling like shit. His asshole was opened wide as fuck. I was going to beach his stank ass. My dick was the only one that could play in that ass. Sam's asshole was tired as fuck.

After I got finished fucking his mind up, it was time for me to go and hang out with some friends. I couldn't believe Sam went out and let some big dick fuck his stank ass. He is a nasty bitch. Sam had a couple of friends that were coming to visit. Sam said they were really nice. I couldn't wait to meet them. My ass needed some amazing loving. I wanted to make the guys feel at home because I am going to fuck that hell out of them unless they all have big dicks. Sam was getting everything ready. I was getting my ass ready. Sam knew that fucking is in my blood.

Whenever he brings his friends around me, I am going to freak at least two of them. It is now time for me to go and pick up the guys. When I got to the airport to pick them up, my dick got big as fuck because they were so sexy. I wanted the dark-skinned guy to fold me over the front seat and fuck me like a dog in heat. He is sexy. I knew that dick is big.

When we got back to the house, Sam was so happy to see them. I left the house and went to the bar. My mind needed a break from everyone. When I got to the bar and grill, I saw this guy that Sam introduced me to. His name is Zona. He is a lawyer in Atlanta. Sam always talked about him because he was a really good friend. He bought me four drinks.

Lust, Lies & Love

He was trying to get me wasted. I had three shots of patron before he came.

After all of those drinks, my body began to get hot and horny. Zona was a very nice man. He made my heart love even more. I could take any more drinks. The both of us thought it would be a good idea to go back to Zona's place. He informed me that we were going to lie down, cuddle and go to sleep. Things didn't go as planned. Zona and I ended up playing the night away. I lay on the bed naked and began to touch myself. Zona loved it to the max. I turned onto my stomach as Zona started eating my ass. Then he put his dick inside of me. It took my breath away. He had my insides feeling like feathers.

After I got off of my stomach, Zona put me against the way and fucked me standing up. My ass and stomach were happy. I felt all of that dick in me. My legs began to get weak, but I worked it out. I wanted to fall on the floor, boot my ass up and let him fuck my ass crazy. My body never felt that feeling. He fucked me in ways that words can't explain. My little boo got that good dick. His lips felt like the skin of a baby.

When it was time for him to cum, he let loose all over my face and body. I thought I was in lover's world. When the two of us got finished having sex, we slept the lovely night away. Zona held me. That made me feel special. My heart didn't want to leave, but I had to.

Sam was at home with the guys. I knew they were having a blast. Now it is time for me to share my love. When I walked into the house, Sam and the guys were having a fuck feast. The only thing I saw was ass and dick. A bitch like me was ready for whatever. I was good and only fucked Sam. He was so happy that I didn't have sex with any of his other friends. That's what he thought because Zona fucked the hell out of me. I helped Sam's bitch ass take off his clothes. The bitch was stank as fuck. I had to teach him how to wash his musty ass. My dick wasn't trying to fuck anything with a stank asshole.

After we got finished talking, he took a bath. The bitch was still sour. He let the wrong dick fuck him. I had to take him to the doctor because his ass was tasteful. My mouth was missing it. Sam had an infection. I couldn't take it.

A couple of days later, he was better. I did my baby a favor by getting on my knees and let him face fuck me. The head of his dick was so good. Sam fucked the inside of my mouth with his head. It was so big that I could barely take it. My baby was back to himself.

Three days later, I had a business meeting to attend. I want me to go, but I had to keep the money coming in our household. The trip was going to be amazing because I was going to meet a long lost friend. He was once the love of my life. Pat was my business. I was going to take care of him. Sam knew something was up, but couldn't put my finger on it. I knew his mind was wondering, but I didn't care. I wanted and needed a new man anyway. Sam's bitch ass was good to me, but I wanted a bigger dick. Pat was the right guy for me. He was all man and more. I needed someone like him in my life. The two of us went to Spain on my suppose-to-be business trip.

When we got into Spain, Pat surprised me with lavish gifts and more. My heart wanted to cry because Pat was treating me like a king. He took me out on the town and got e more gifts. I had to give him some of this good ass. My hole was jumping for some amazing dick. I was falling in love with Pat. He treated me with the utmost respect.

When we got back to the hotel room, I was ready to make love to him. His body was like tea. His lips were like baby wipes. Pat like that weird sex that I didn't care for. He started off by putting candle wax all over me. He licked it off with his tongue before it became solid. He tried to put his finger in my ass. The bitch was going crazy. I was trying to make love and to not fight.

Before we did anything, I had to stop him because he was going wild. I had to sit him down and let him know that I am trying to fuck, but not fight. His mind was gone. The trip ended early.

Sam was so happy to see me back home. My dick fucked Sam so good. His ass tasted divine. Sam rode the hell out of my face. I couldn't taste anything but ass juice. My boo was working that thang. Sam wanted to call Jack and the rest of the guys after sex. We haven't seen them in a while.

Everyone was happy to hear from us. We are in our New York home, but we are taking the guys back to our Vegas home. We all want to spend some money and live it up. I had to get everything ready before I invite the guys. It took about one week to get it together. We were renting the house out of the summer. Sam was so ready to go. So was I. The guys always believe in giving up the ass and dick. I have fucked almost all of Sam's friends and family. Sex was my hobby.

The guys came over. Things were about to happen. I hugged everyone. Sam was like a kid in a toy store jumping up and down as his friends arrived in the house. My dick started jumping up and down because I knew my dick was going to jump into someone's mouth. I pulled Sam to the side and told him I wanted to fuck Jack. He gave me a crazy ass look. Fake tears began to run down my face. Then he agreed that I could. The fake tears left quickly.

While everyone was in the kitchen talking about whatever, I called Jack into our bedroom. He wanted to know what was wrong because I was looking sad. That was my way of getting what I want. Jack put his arms around me and asked me what was wrong. I leaned forward and gave him a kiss. Jack took his dick out and put it in my mouth. I started sucking his dick as if I was a crackhead in need of a fix. I couldn't get enough because it was big, thick and good. My mouth deep-throated Jack's dick so good.

When Jack and I had sex for the millionth time, it was very different because we usually fuck like crazy. This time we made love. He was moving his dick very well. Jack had my mind in la la land. His dick was the best ever. The both of us really enjoyed that moment. Jack wanted to make love all night, but I needed for him to bust my ass open. That love shit felt good, but I needed him to beat this ass down.

After we got finished making love, Sam walked in and stood beside the bed. Jack left. I told Sam to take his clothes off. I wanted him to beat my asshole up. That's what he did. Sam had me moaning loudly and crazy. My asshole was hurting so badly, but I took it for my baby. He had so much cum running down my ass. I enjoyed all of my baby inside of me. He came so much in me that I had to push a lot out of my asshole.

After that good beat down, my body was weak as fuck. Sam surprise me by giving himself head. My eyes got big as fuck. I couldn't believe that freaky bitch. He started doing things that I have never seen him do before.

Since Sam wanted to give himself head, I pushed his head all the way down and made him gag on his own dick. All of my bitches are nasty as fuck. They love doing nasty shit that's crazy.

Lust, Lies & Love

Sam and I went into the kitchen after we got finished fucking. My ass was sticky and wet. Swear was all over my face. The guys knew we had been fucking hard as hell. We should have invited everyone to join in. I needed more dick inside of my ass, the bigger the better for my asshole. The guys enjoyed the food and wine. We made sure they were treated with love. Some of them wanted to play a new sex game. My tired ass didn't want to play because I was fucked out. They didn't want to hear that. They wanted some of this good dick and ass. I watch everyone play before I joined in. Dick and ass were all over the room. My eyes were about to pop out of my head. If I could have put every dick in my mouth, I would. Everyone's dick was pretty as hell. My body wanted them bitches to haze the fuck out of me. This ass needed to try something different.

As they begin to play the next sex game, I saw Jack and Matt in the corner playing with their big dicks. My mouth was ready to give the both of them a good sucking. I didn't like the game as much. I went over to Jack and Matt. We were talking about fucking each other. It was not long into the conversation that I put the both of their dicks in my mouth and went to sucking. My mouth was packed as fuck. The two of them had me stiff and pause.

Sam came over and stood over the three of us. I didn't stop because the dicks were good. He couldn't take just looking and not joining in. The nasty bitch took it upon him to jack his dick. Matt took his dick out of my mouth and started sucking Sam's dick. I thought that was stupid. I didn't let Matt suck for long. My mouth was enjoying that dick. Sam was mad as hell when Matt got up. I laughed, but not for long.

Sam stood back over us until he came. I had cum running all down my face. My mouth stopped sucking Matt and Jack's dicks. I got up and punched the hell out of Sam. The bitch tried me for the last time. Jack and Matt were very shocked because they have never seen me act a fool. Sam already knew I was tired of fucking him. My ass wanted some new dick. My hands wanted to kill the bitch. Our relationship was once based on love, but now it is all about sex and only sex. The dirty bitch thinks that I really love him. My ass loved dick. Sam wanted to work things out, but I wasn't having that. The single life was my best friend. Our business wasn't going well. I was taking a toll on Sam. He was getting behind in his bills. He didn't want to do the sex business because he didn't want me to work there. Sam knows that I know people. We he realized it, he rethought about it. He asked me to work the business and be good. I told him that I am always good at fucking and sucking. Sam looked at me and walked away.

Three months into our new business, we were making some good money. Everything was going well. Sam started spending money as if we were making millions. I told him that I was going on a trip with one of our clients. He asked me why. I told him to get away and enjoy each other. He wanted to know who the client was. I gave him another name because the person was his oldest brother. We have never fucked. This is something the both of us wanted to do. Sam paid for everything and more. Jan is Sam's oldest brother. Dude is fine as fuck. We were going to have a blast only. I don't think Jan likes men, but he is very friendly. He was worried about Sam finding out about his going on the trip. I took care of all that.

When the two of us arrived in Mexico, Jan was ready to hit the beach. We went straight to the hotel to change clothes and then head to the beach. Jan had a beach body. I wanted to eat him up. We enjoyed the water for about two hours.

After those hours were up, the shower was calling our names. We went back to the hotel. I turned on the shower for Jan. As I was watching, I heard Jan call my name. He needed me to wash his back and the back of his legs.

I washed his back. He turned around to play with his dick. I dropped the rag and walked out. He grabbed me by the shirt and told me not to tell Sam because he had a wife. He just wanted to fuck a man for the first time. I shook me head. I was speechless. My ass wanted the dick, but I couldn't get my mind off of his wife. I didn't know he was married because he never talked about a wife. I told Jan that I couldn't do it, but the more he touched me, the more my body wanted him. He kisses all over me.

My dick was getting hard as hell. All of my clothes came off. I let Jan make love to me. He worked that dick like no other. He put me on top of my head and gave it to me. He took his time and made mad love to me. I was falling in love with him and the dick. The sex was so good. Jan had me speaking in an unknown language. His lovemaking was the best.

Lust, Lies & Love

After we got finished having sex, He told me he as to leave his wife because I made him feel like a man. Tears began to flow everywhere. My heart was filled with joy and love. I couldn't do it because of Sam and the wife. Making love to Jan was crazy, but the best at the same time. My mind told me I was wrong, but my heart told me to let him love me. This trip was the craziest ever. I fucked my man's brother and fell in love with him. Jan didn't care about Sam being hurt. He wanted to be with me. My mind was in a crazy place. The sex is what fucked up my mind. Good dick is hard to come by. When you get it, you better keep it. Jan's dick was good, but I can't keep him. He is a married man.

We enjoyed our trip. I am still speechless about what happened. Before we parted ways, Jan told me that he wanted to be with me. I couldn't say anything because I was in shock. Jan stayed on my mind for a very long time. I wanted to stay on the trip forever, but I couldn't.

When I returned to my home, the driver helped me carry my things into the house. I have him a tip and left. I dropped everything in the kitchen because I was hungry. Sam wasn't anywhere around to make me lunch. As

Lust, Lies & Love

I begin to make something to eat, I heard a voice say "Calvin please stop."

Sometimes I think my ears are playing tricks on my, but not this day. I walk into my bedroom. There was Sam on his knees sucking the fuck out of Calvin's dick. When he looked up and saw me looking into his face, he was frozen. I laughed because I was about to let Calvin fuck Sam's ass with no lube.

Since he wanted to fuck around on me, Calvin was going to make him pay for it. Calvin's dick was hella big. Sam told me he was sorry. I laughed. I wasn't trying t hear those bitch ass lies. I saw a video camera on top of the television. Calvin asked me to turn it on. He wanted to record Sam crying and begging him to stop. It took Sam about ten minutes to take his clothes off. He didn't want to feel that bid dick inside of that dry ass.

Calvin tied Sam up to the bed and put his dick inside of his dry ass. He fucked him silly. Sam started yelling and tried to move. His restraints restricted his movements. Calvin fucked Sam until he started bleeding. I looked and told Sam he would be fine. Sam was lying on the floor in so much pain. I didn't care because I was about to fuck Calvin. His fat ass is what I needed.

Lust, Lies & Love

When Calvin came out of the bathroom, he bent down to make sure Sam was okay. That's when I took out my dick and put it on his lips. He started sucking my dick as Sam watched. His mouth was the best. I enjoyed that shit so much. I lay beside Sam. Calvin straddled me and rode my dick. My ass was moaning like a bitch. His asshole was tight and warm. I threw Calvin's punk ass off of me and started fucking him doggy style. The bitch was throwing his ass back so good. He was making me work for that nut.

Sam couldn't do anything but look and cry. That still didn't stop me because I wanted some good ass. After I got finished fucking Calvin doggie style, he put his legs behind his head. I was standing all the way up in that ass. His asshole was wet as fuck. He was yelling and wanted me to go deep. My dick felt the inside of his stomach. Calvin was a real ass freak. I rather fuck him than Sam. Sam's bitch ass couldn't take dick. When he tried to take a dick, he always cried like a fuck boy. My big dick needed to feel a grown man. Calvin was that man.

After Calvin and I finished fucking, I got Sam off of the floor and put him in the bed. I left him there. Calvin wanted to please me a little more. His ass and dick were good enough. He always had my mind gone.

After round two, I was ready for Calvin to leave. I wanted to cum and go to sleep. He wanted to stay the night. I wasn't with that at all. I had to let Calvin's punk ass know after I fuck him. I always send them home. He understood and went home.

Two days later, Sam started feeling better. This wasn't his first time getting fucked with no lube. Whenever he does stupid things that I don't like, this is what he gets. Sam told me that he was sorry for fucking and sucking Calvin's dick. I told him no to be a sorry bitch, but just be careful. I looked at Sam's asshole. It was a hot mess. Every time I tried to touch it, he always cried. There was some cream on the table. He asked me to rub some on his asshole. It was lube. Sam didn't know I change out the bottles.

As I was putting the lube on his hole, I slipped my dick into his ass and went crazy. Sam was yelling, crying and acting a fool. I was laughing while on top of him. Sam couldn't believe I fucked him while he was in pain. He knows that I love sex. He also knows that I am having fun with his ass.

Lust, Lies & Love

A couple of minutes later, Jack called to check up on us. I didn't want to talk. Sam got on the phone and told Jack everything. After he got off of the phone, I fucked him even harder. He wasn't supposed to tell anyone. He is my piece of ass to do with as I please. I am going to fuck him however the fuck I like.

Not long after that, Jack was calling back. I believe the bitch wanted some dick. He was in town and wanted to come over. I told him to come over because Sam and I were very bored.

Two hours later, I heard a knock at the door. It was Jack's sexy ass. He came into the house with an evil look on his face. I didn't care because Sam belongs to me. He is my bitch. The bother of them started talking about what happened. I walked by and laughed out loud. That made Jack mad as fuck. He called me into the room. He wanted me to tell Sam that I was sorry. These are the words I told Sam. I told him that I was sorry for fucking the hell out of him and to forgive me. He accepted my apology, but Jack wasn't pleased with it. I got up and left the room. I didn't want to fuck Jack up.

My phone rang. I didn't answer. Those two bitches were working on my last nerve. Sam felt better. I went into the bathroom to get his medicine. They always put him to sleep. Sam took the three pills and drunk some water. Five minutes later Sam was asleep.

Jack was looking at me sideways. The punk wanted some dick. That's why he was acting funny with me. I didn't want to fuck him at that moment. My dick was stank. My balls were musty. Since he was acting funny with me, I will fuck him with musty balls and all. Jack enjoyed the nasty smell. He deep-throated my dick so good. I didn't stop him because he wanted to suck my dick so I let him. I always knew that Jack was a nasty bitch. He knew that I fucked Sam and didn't bathe. He didn't care because he wanted some dick. My dick could have fucked Jack all night. He knew how to fuck and how to suck as mean dick. I loved when he goes all the way down and gag. It feels so good.

It was time for me to leave all of these bitches alone. I needed to find me some new dick. My ass needed a dick that knows how to make me fold inside and out.

Sam asked me to stop fucking around on him and to worry more about the business. I listened and did what he told me to do.

Lust, Lies & Love

The next morning, I flew to Atlanta. Sam and I had a business there. We haven't been there in so long. Things weren't looking good. IT took me about two months to get everything back in order. I was trying to hold our business and our Atlanta business down, but the fucking business got the best of me.

Now it's time for me to get back to the money even if it means fucking my clients in order to get it. I will because I need it. Sam was so happy that things were getting back on track. It was time for me to start back taking care of home. We moved back to Atlanta. We still had our homes in Vegas and New York. We were going to rent them out to some friends. The guys didn't know we were moving back. I think it was for the good. IT will be more money for the business, more ass, more dick and a long of amazing people. Sam wanted our relationship to be like the old times. We once had a bond that no one could break.

Once the guys found out that we were in Atlanta, things were about to be on. They love to work and party. That's what I loved about them. We rested for two days then went to work. Sam was glad to be back around his friends. The only reason I got along with them is that they let me fuck whenever I got ready.

Lust, Lies & Love

Sam stayed with his friends for three days. Our apartment was getting worked on. Jack wanted me to stay with him. I didn't know he was single. We talked about his relationship for an hour. I felt so sorry for him. Tears were running all down my face. Hack is a very good man.

After our talk and the tears of hurt, Jack thought that we should have a drink. He knew how to kick things off. After the first drink, I told Jack to make our second drink stronger. That's what he did. IT was actually a little too strong, but I got what I asked for. I made a face after each sip and Jack noticed. He asked me was the drink okay. I told him that it would be better if he let me fuck. His eyes started glowing with happiness. I wanted to take his mind off of his old relationship. I licked Jack on his chest and stopped at his dick. My tongue played in his pee hole. He was squirming everywhere. He couldn't take the tongue. Then I put his dick down my throat. It was big as fuck, but I took it.

After that, Jack stood and fucked. We fucked the night away. Jack will always be me down bitch. Whenever I wanted to fuck him, he always gave up the ass the dick. I only had two more days with Jack. Sam and I had some business to take care of the next day.

Just when we thought things were getting better, our store manager left the store. She didn't let us know anything. We were mad as hell, but everything worked out for the best. Matt came through for the both of us. We were so happy.

After everything was over, I went back to Jack's place. I had a long and crazy day. When I got into the house, I noticed that Jack wasn't there. There were candles, rose petals and wind strategically placed in the bathroom. Jack walked out of his room naked. His dick was swinging side to side as he walked. My eyes rolled in the back of my head. He told me that he set this special moment up for me. I couldn't believe it. My heart started to sing out in love. Jack was the man of my dreams and more. He wanted to be my main dude, but that couldn't happen.

When I got into the bathtub, Jack started feeding me grapes followed by sips of wine. We both loved it. Jack touched me in a caring way. I was getting horny as fuck. He went under the water and put his head between my legs. He was sucking my dick. The only thing I could say was shit. His mouth was powerful as hell. The more he sucked me, the more my mind was running away. I wasn't going to catch it. Jack was fucking my world up.

When he came up for air, I bent over on the side of the tub and let him eat me out. His lips were soft as fuck. His tongue was fucking the hell out of my asshole. It was so good that tears started to flow down my face.

When he heard me crying out loud, he put me on my back and made love to me. I was moaning and saying daddy. Jack's dick was the best ever. Jack was going to make me his.

After we got finished making love, Jack got out of the tub and went into the bedroom. When I got out, dinner was ready for me. That's my type of guy. Jack wanted to fuck me on top of the dinner table. I was willing and fucking ready. That was a dick I had to have. He took all of the food off of the table. My crazy ass got on the table and put my legs behind my head. I made my asshole move in and out. Jack loves that freaky shit. My nasty ass put a banana in my ass. Jack bent his head over and started eating the banana out of my ass. He is such a freaky bitch. We were going all out for it.

After the Chiquita moment, it was time for me to ride Jack's big dick. I was jumping up and down as if I was a monkey about to eat. His dick had a curve to it. I mostly rode sideways. I felt every inch of his dick inside of me. Jack kept Cumming back to back. My ass was wet as fuck.

After Jack got finished Cumming, I went straight to sleep. The funny thing is that I was still on Jack's dick. When I woke up the next morning, Jack was fucking the hell out of me. His mind was gone. I think it was my fault because I put this ass on him so good. It was time for me to leave Jack's place.

Our apartment was ready so we could move in. Sam was so happy about moving in. We had so much stuff to move by ourselves. I called a couple of the guys to help. Of course they agreed to help. I was going to pay them with my dick. Fuck each of them one by one in the asshole. It won't be the first time. Sam knew I wasn't going to help out. My body was made for working and fucking and not for moving stuff into an apartment. That was too much for me to do. I am not use to manual labor. I lift legs, not chairs.

Jack had so much sweat on his face and chest. I wanted to let him fuck me with all that sweat on him. MY bitch was looking so good. He kept giving me the eye. I couldn't shoe much love because Sam and the guys were there. Everyone looked at me crazy when I went to get Jack something to drink. He was the only one sweating. He needed something to drink. Sam's bitch ass came up to me asking where his drink was. I told him that it was at the fucking store waiting on him.

He started acting crazy in front of everybody. I wasn't going to have that shit at all. Sam got worse as I looked at him. Things were about to get out of hand. I punched that bitch in the mouth and made him walk to the store which was twenty minutes away driving. The guys needed something to drink. Sam was mad as hell, but I didn't care because I told him that when he plays pussy then he is going to get fucked. That's what happened to him.

When Sam got back from the store, I laughed at his dumb ass. He would do anything for some dick. I wanted to leave Sam for good and be with Jack. Sam wasn't making me happy anymore. Jack knew how to make me happy and more.

Since everybody had a long day of moving, I thought it would be a good idea to take everyone to the bar. We needed to have some fun and a couple of drinks. We all wanted to relax.

Lust, Lies & Love

We pulled up to the bar. A couple of our Vegas friends were there looking good as fuck. My dick was ready to fuck some ass. I was planning on getting wasted. The drinks were going to make me sin the night away.

We were at the bar for about fifteen minutes, and I was already drunk. Sam had to sit me down. When I woke up the next morning, I realized I was naked. Sam fucked me while I was drunk. Payback is going to be a bitch. I fixed Sam a drink and put a pill in it. I am going to let all of the guys fuck him at once. He didn't feel it because the pill put him to sleep. The little dick bitch fucked me while I was sleep. Now I had to get him back.

Sam woke up a couple of hours later hurting like hell. The guys gang raped him. I enjoyed it all. I didn't try to stop anyone. He needed that ass beat the fuck in. I loved when Sam's friends suck on my balls and dick. Their mouths and tongues are always so warm. They know how to keep me happy. Out of all the guys I have fucked, Sam's dad was the best. He was the only one that could make his dick jump inside of my ass. When he is fucking me, he makes his dick jump even faster. That shit hurts like hell, but I always take it like a pro.

Lust, Lies & Love

Sam wasn't into the fuck fame like me. Sam's sister, Kathy, had a fire ass husband. I always told her that he likes men. She never believes me because he is so manly. I had to make a believer out of her.

Sam and Kathy went to dinner with the family. She left her husband home alone. That dick was mine. I wanted him to make my head hit the headboard and to give it to me rough. His cum needed to drop in my face like raindrops. Something was telling me that Grey had some good loving. I wanted him to dick me down.

Sam called and told me to go over to Kathy's house. Grey was there by himself and wanted some company. That was the best thing I have ever heard from Sam. My stank ass took a bath and put on some nice clothes.

When I arrived at Kathy's house, Grey only had on a T-shirt. He was about to take a shower. He went into his room and put on some clothes. I told him I didn't have a problem with his being naked. He said great and took all of his clothes off. I almost fell out when I saw his huge dick. It had to be twelve inches or better. That is my kind of man. Only big dicks can go in my ass.

Lust, Lies & Love

We were looking at each other for almost an hour. I couldn't keep looking at his sexy ass. I thought about getting to my knees and sucking him off. That was way too much dick to go all the way down my throat. I went with my plan B. Plan B was to put all twelve inches in my asshole. That shit was feeling good as fuck. Grey knew how to fuck some ass. I jump off of that dick and let Grey fuck me while I lay on my stomach. He put his entire dick inside of me. I thought his dick was going to come out of my mouth. MY insides were bawling up with madness, but I didn't care. My ass wanted some good dick. Grey had my legs stiff as hell. My heart was beating at over a hundred beats per minute. I thought I was going to pass out. The head of his dick was the size of half of a baseball. It took me forever to get all of it inside of me. I was hurting like fuck, but this is something I wanted.

It was time for Grey to sum. MY mouth opened up to let him shoot his load in it. It was so much. I took it all in. My mouth was filled with dick and cum. Grey told me to let the cum flow down my throat.

After everything was done, Grey didn't know what to do because I was the first piece of male ass the he has ever fucked. He had never been with a man before. I knew it was good. He was Cumming like crazy. He told me that my ass was better than his wife's pussy. My head game was the best. I can teach the wife a thing or two or three or four. Licking a dick is not like sucking a dick. I am going to let Grey fuck me again. When I want something, I get it.

We went into the living area to watch television. It wasn't ten minutes when the front door opened. Sam and Kathy walked in. Grey didn't have on any clothes. I had to play everything off while Grey went to put some clothes on. The both of didn't think anything of it. Sam kept looking at me. I asked him what was wrong. He told me that I looked drained. I told him that I wasn't feeling well.

We left and went home because I didn't want Sam to play detective and try to figure anything out. Grey texted me while I was on the way home. He told me that it was the first and the last time, but he really wanted to fuck me again. I told him that I would be back over. The text read in all caps: YOU WON'T AND I MEAN IT.

Sam turned back around because he left his wallet in Kathy's car. When he went into the house, Grey came to the car and told me that he enjoyed fucking me, but it can't happen again. He told me that I had his mind gone. I told him to fuck and that I will be back over.

Grey called me a simple bitch. I got mad. I went into the house, took the condom off of the bathroom counter and put in on Kathy's pillow. Sam and I left for the night. Kathy called me because she wanted to know whose condom was on her pillow. I told her Grey and I used it while he was fucking me. I told her that Grey loves men, and he fucked me like no other.

Kathy gagged when I told her. She told me to stay away from her house. I told her that when she kisses Grey on the lips that she will be tasting my ass. She started to lose her mind. Grey wasn't upset because he wanted to be with me. A good ass and mouth will run any man crazy. I made sure that dick was jumping while inside of me.

The first day I saw Kathy's husband I knew he was a DL brother, on the down low. He always told me I had an ass to die for. That's when I knew he liked men.

Grey and I started doing business deals together. We were doing any and everything to get closer together. Grey always called me over when Kathy went to work. We would fuck the day away in their bed. He never washes the covers because he wanted Kathy to sleep in my fuck juice. Grey was going to be mine.

Two days later, Grey called me back over. We started taking and had a couple drinks. One thing leads to another and we ended up in the bedroom. Kathy walked in and caught us fucking. I was riding Grey like he was a bucking bronco. Kathy started fighting Grey while we were fucking. Something came over me. I hit the fuck out of that bitch. We were trying to fuck and she wanted to fight. That's what I call a simple ass bitch. She should have fought the both of us, but the bitch knew better.

After she got finished crying and yelling that she was hurt, she told Grey to pack his bags. He had to get the fuck out. I told her that was wonderful because he could come with me. Now ain't that a bitch. Grey moved in with Sam and me. My friend needed somewhere to stay. We had an extra room. I am always putting Sam in the guest room whenever guests come to stay. The guest needed to be in the room with me. That will give us a chance to fuck all night.

Lust, Lies & Love

Kathy was hurt about what happened. Things weren't going well for the two of them. I thought that I would step up and take over. Sam didn't know what was going on. Grey didn't want Sam to know at the moment.

Kathy came over and had a talk with Sam. They were in the guest room talking really low. I am glad that they were having a nice talk. Grey wasn't happy with her slow ass. I made Kathy leave because Grey and I were ready to get our fuck on.

When she left our house, Sam went into the guest room. Grey and I have been fucking hard as fuck. My head was hitting the headboard. My legs were tied to the bed poles. He was fucking me so well. Sam heard the loud sounds that I was making. He didn't come into the room or call my name. Grey's dick was feeling so amazing.

After Grey and I got finished fucking each other, that crazy bitch, Kathy, came over. I don't know for what reason. She lost her man, and I got him. She was acting all hurt, but I didn't care how she felt. She still wants him back after she caught us in her bed fucking while I was riding her man's dick. We love each other. I have been there for him. Her man has me whipped. He is mine now.

Lust, Lies & Love

Kathy started to fake cry. I laughed out loud and told her to cry me a river. Sam wasn't happy when he found out what was really going on. He wanted to beat my ass. Sam left me for good. He was tired of the cheating, the lying and the heartache. He wasn't going to be missed. The bitch was stupid as fuck. Grey is my new boo.

Kathy wanted to kill the both of us. I wanted to have a talk with her. So I took it upon myself and called her. The two of us met up at a local bar. She wanted to know what made me do what I did. I told her that Grey was sitting in front of me naked. I couldn't take looking at his big dick. Things went from there. Kathy was a lady who understood things, but not this time around. She was really mad at the two of us. I had to cut our talking time short.

Sam and I had to go and take care of some business orders which didn't take long. Kathy called me an hour later because she wasn't finished talking. She asked could she come over. I told he she could. I felt that things were about to go bad. The crazy bitch kept asking me WHY.

"Why what?" I asked with my lips turned up. "Why I fucked your man in your bed or why are we together?"

Lust, Lies & Love

"Both," She said quietly

"I am the type of bitch who breaks up happy homes and who fucks the one I want. Does that answer your question?" I asked exactly.

I got a nasty look from Kathy

"You nasty bitch."

I laughed back and said matter of factly, "I know because we fucked on your wedding night."

CHAPTER 9

Grey and I are finally together. He is mad at me because I told his wife about us having sex on their wedding night. I wasn't going to say anything, but the bitch tried me stupid. I had to tell her what she wanted to hear.

Kathy wanted her husband back. My heart couldn't let him go. She was a very rude old bitch. She only wanted him for his money. Grey loved Kathy, but he was confused. He didn't know if he wanted dick or pussy. Something inside of me wanted to let Grey go. I wasn't going to share the love of my life. Kathy wasn't going to get him back. She acts very slow in the mind. She caught Grey and I having sex. The monkey still wanted him back.

Lust, Lies & Love

My life was fucked up. Kathy tried to make me lose my damn mind.

After I sat her ass down, the two of us talked about the Grey situation. Grey walked into the kitchen while we talked. He gave me a kiss before he left the room. My eyes lit up with joy. Kathy's mouth dropped to the floor. I laughed. Grey told me to get up and go to the store. He wanted some strawberries and wine. I knew he was going to eat my ass so good.

When I walked back into the house, Kathy was naked as a jay bird. Her pussy lips were hanging out. Her meat was brown and stank. Grey didn't want that nasty musty shit. I had that clean ass for him. My cakes are pretty, big and ready to eat. Grey didn't want that loose pussy.

After I got Kathy's sour faced ass out of my house, Grey and I made love. He put my legs into the air, cuffed my hand to the bed and ate the hell out of me. My ass was so wet. I wanted to crawl up the wall and back. He was giving me some good loving.

After Grey un-cuffed me with his powerful hands, I took over the sex party. He lies on his back. I open his legs and start sucking his big balls. The smell of them had me going insane.

Lust, Lies & Love

It took me a couple of minutes to put them in my mouth. They were bigger than usual it seemed.

Later into our lovemaking, Grey bent me over the bed and started fucking me hard as hell. I didn't know what was going on. He went from making sweet love to fucking me like a horse. My asshole wasn't pleased with him. He made me put my fingers in my ass while he was fucking me. That hurts like hell. His dick was bigger than ever. My fingers didn't make it any better.

I asked him to stop. He started to pound my ass harder. I wanted to cry, but I held every tear. I laid there and let him have his way.

Fifteen minutes later, we heard the front door open. We kept on having sex. I looked up and Kathy was watching us shocked and surprised. I wasn't because I didn't care. My lips started on Grey's dick. He told me to open my mouth so that he could cum inside.

Kathy's bitch ass couldn't take it. She knows that I am a freak in the bedroom. She is boring as fuck. I had to liven things up. Kathy was very old-fashioned. Dick sucking and ass licking weren't in her blood. That's why the bitch couldn't keep her husband. I tried to teach her, but it wasn't easy. In order for Grey and I to have some one on one time, we moved back to New York. Kathy didn't want to see her husband and me happy.

After being in New York a couple of days, I called all of the guys to come over for dinner. Some thought we were only in town for a couple of days. They had no idea that we had moved back. Jack didn't say anything to me. He was still upset with me. The punk didn't want me to leave Sam. If he was so upset with me, then his monkey ass can have Sam and fuck some sense into his small head.

Jack started yelling at me. I should have put my big dick in his mouth. His throat is deep as hell. He would have loved that. Everyone left our small gathering and went home. Grey didn't get made. He was ready to fuck the night away.

Since Jack made Grey mad as hell, I had to go and get my baby something to drink. His mind wasn't happy. Every time we get into a fight with the guys, Grey always fucks my insides crazy. My legs were telling me to run for the border. I knew better than that. I always endure the pain. I will do anything to keep him happy.

Lust, Lies & Love

Before Grey got ready to fuck me, he called two of his friends over. Things were about to get ugly. The other two friends are his fucking buddies. They have fucked me in the past. I didn't want them to touch me. He would call the ugliest men over to fuck my ass. The two of this smelled like dog shit. The first guy took his dick out. It was greasy as hell. Grey made me suck on that nasty dick. I wanted to gag so badly.

While I was sucking the guy's dick, Grey tells me that the guy just finished fucking someone else. My mind went into right field. He is such a nasty bitch. I was sucking someone else's shit. Grey was going to pay for it.

The guy's dick felt so good, but he wasn't clean. I notice he had gray hair around his balls. Something wasn't right with that picture. The other guys wanted to eat my ass. I bent over and let him do his thing. All of his teeth were missing in the front. I didn't care because those gums were feeling great.

Grey stood back and watched the dummies make a fool out of themselves. My asshole was ready for a real dick. Grey had the dick and I had the ass. I could only take eight inches of Grey's dick. His dick was twelve inches long and thick. He asked me to take all twelve inches down my deep throat. It was the hardest thing ever. He knew I loved him with all of my heart and soul. My business wasn't doing well. Grey thought that I should join his new business. He was the owner of G's porn. His business was making a lot of money. I needed it so badly. Fucking the clients wouldn't be weird to me. Sucking dick and getting fucked is what I live for.

After talking it over with the guys, I was going to go for it. My first night was a little crazy, but I managed. Grey had me in the VIP room. In order for you to work in the VIP room, you had to be a bad bitch. I was the worst of them all. Everyone was pretty, but they couldn't fuck like me. I took all types of dick in my ass and down my throat. I was down for it all.

When I went to work the next day, Grey call me into the office. Two clients wanted to have some private time with me. My ass was happy as fuck. Older men pay a lot of money to fuck.

Later that night, I went into the private VIP room. The old men were naked and ready to fuck. I started playing with the heads of their dicks. The two of them were getting harder and harder. Then I put both of them into my mouth. MY neck was stiff. They had me where I couldn't move. Not long after that, they fucked me good. I couldn't believe how they were making me feel. One of the men was fucking me upside down. My stomach felt all of his dick.

When I started moaning, he fucked me harder. The old bitch had some good dick. The second guy's dick was bigger than the first. I never saw such an old man with a big dick like that one. It took him a while to put it all inside of me.

When he finally got it in, my ass was ready for whatever. He put my head inside a case and tied my legs and arms to a chair. He fucked me flawlessly. I never thought two old dirty bastards could fuck so good. They will pay you their life if they have to.

Grey was very pleased with the pay. I requested for the two of them to come back next week. They knew how to fuck. I guess it gets better with age. Grey had so many guys wanting to be with me. He wanted to make money for his business. I was willing to help. My baby was happy to have me on board. I had to make the money because I wasn't going to let the money make me.

After my shift was over, someone called me from a private number. Something told me not to answer. Whoever it was kept calling me over and over. I finally answered the call. It was Sam calling because he wanted a private dance. My mouth dropped to the floor. How dare he call me for a quick fuck. I wanted to kill him. I called Grey and told him about the call. He told me to take the job. I knew Sam was going to pay well. He wanted some good ass. I wanted the money.

After Grey and I had our conversation about Sam, I call Sam so we could talk about a price. He was willing to pay five thousand dollars for one hour. My eyes crossed all kinds of ways when I heard that. Dollar signs flashed in my eyes. I was willing to let Sam fuck me all night. Grey wasn't going to let me go alone. Chris went with me over to Sam's place. Chris is Grey's brother. When the both of us arrived, Chris was looking all crazy and started acting funny. I didn't know what was going on. Chris had me scared as fuck.

Before we entered the house, I asked Chris what was going on. He knew Sam because they use to fuck around. My mouth hit the floor. Chris told me that he was sorry. I told him not to be. I am only her to make money.

Sam was happy to see the both of us. I asked Chris if he wanted to join. I knew he had a big dick. He said no at first. I had to let the young man know that I fuck brothers and all. He was happy to hear those words. He didn't waste time taking off his clothes.

When I looked down at Chris' dick, I was speechless. His dick was bigger than Grey's dick. My throat was jumping for some dick down my throat. Sam was sitting back with a smile on his face. I knew something crazy was about to happen. Chris ripped off my clothes and pushed me onto the bed. Then he opens my ass up and starts to eat me out. His tongue had me so wet. It was hitting all the right spots.

After Chris finished tongue fucking me, Sam bent me over the bed and started fucking me. I was on cloud nine. I had two dicks in my face and ass. Chris made me feel amazing. He made real love to me. His dick felt like no other.

Sam wasn't into it because he didn't like to share. I felt sorry for him. Chris' dick had me in another world. Later that night, Chris and I went back to my place. When the both of us enter the house, Grey was sitting in the living room with his dick out. I couldn't believe he didn't try to put it back in his pant when Chris walked in. The two of them were both freaks.

Lust, Lies & Love

Chris started laughing. I got on my knees and tighten my lips around him. I sucked on Grey's dick leaving Chris shocked. The dick was so good that I forgot that Chris was in the room. The more I rolled my tongue around Grey's dick, the louder he moaned. Chris was getting hotter by the minute. He began to play with his dick. I wanted Chris' dick in my tight ass. My hole was ready for some penetration.

Grey got up and led Chris to me. The inside of my ass was in so much pain. I thought Chris could only make love, but he tricked me. After he was done with me, Grey stepped in and took the fuck over. We screwed each other into the early morning. My body was tired as hell. Chris left early because his boyfriend was on his way back in town.

Grey left two days later. He had to take care of some court issues with his wife. The bitch didn't like me at all. While Grey was gone to take care of business, I took it upon myself to fly to Atlanta to see the guys. They were happy to see me. Life was different without the guys in my life.

We partied for the old and the new. I enjoyed my two days. When I got back home, it was time for work. I haven't worked in two weeks. I was ready to dance, fuck or whatever for that good money. Grey had some of the best paying men for me. It was about four that wanted to fuck me at the same time. Since the money was good, I gave them what they wanted. My horny ass let all four of them fuck me simultaneously. I was mad as hell because their dicks smelled like shit. They even had small dicks. I got the hell up. Those bitches made me mad as hell. I don't like a stank dick. I wanted to fuck them up for life. I got my money and got the hell on. Grey didn't pick a good group of me.

When I got to the house, Grey asked me how everything was. I told him not to say anything to me. How could he bring me four guys with little stinky dicks? He was lost, but I got myself together. I sat down and explained to him what happened. He was mad as hell. That was bad business for him.

Now that I cleared the air with Grey, we went into the bedroom and made love. He knew how to make me happy. The movement of his dick had me shaking. I loved it so much.

Two weeks later, Grey had to travel to Texas. He was starting a new company. He wanted me to come with him. I couldn't because I had work of my own. Grey didn't want to leave.

Lust, Lies & Love

I needed Chris to come and fuck me stupid. As soon as Grey walked out the door, I was dialing Chris' number. I didn't get an answer. Five minutes later, He was calling back. I asked him to come over and check out my dishwasher. The crazy thing didn't want to work. I went to the bathroom and turned on the shower. My ass needed to be fresh before Chris came over.

As I was taking a hot shower, I hear a loud knock. It scared the hell out of me. My sexy ass got out of the shower naked and went to the door. When I opened it, Chris' big dick ass was at the door looking sexy as ever. He wanted to know how long the dishwasher has been acting crazy. I told him for about a couple of days.

As he was checking out the dishwasher, I started rubbing on my bare naked ass seductively and suggestively. I started playing with his dick. Chris pushed me off of him. He was trying to work in peace. I wasn't worrying about his working. I wanted that big fat dick inside of me. He was getting fed up because the dishwasher was showing signs that it wanted to work. Chris had so much sweat on his body. I wanted to lick him up and down.

Lust, Lies & Love

After he lifted himself from the floor, I gave him a bath cloth to wipe his face. He was tired. I helped him take off his shirt and shoes. As I was unzipping his pants with my teeth, the phone starts ringing. It was Grey. I answered the phone while continuing to unzip Chris' pants. He pointed to the phone. I told him that it was Grey. Why in the hell did I say that name? Chris put his big dick all down my throat. I dropped the phone so fast and completely forgot about Grey.

Chris threw me to the floor and put my legs over his shoulder. He started eating my ass so good that I buried my fingernails deep into his skin. His tongue had me cumming, everywhere. I couldn't hold myself together.

After ate me out so good, I thought that I would be a little nasty. I turned Chris over onto his back and opened his fat ass cheeks. I put whipped cream down that crack of his ass and licked it all off. I had him squirming like a fish out of the water. Then I turned him back over and started sucking his balls. I had to go out with a bang.

While I was sucking his big balls, I was jacking his dick at the same time. He couldn't take it. He threw me on my back and put my legs up while he fucked the hell out of me. I tried to

Lust, Lies & Love

get him off of me, but I couldn't. He started to fuck me harder. My ass wasn't any good now. He was fucking me angrily. I couldn't stand or move. He got the best of my ass.

Before Chris left the house, he looked me into my eyes and told me that he was the brother with the biggest dick and the one who knows how to fuck you good. My body was sore. I was lost for words. I was able to sleep soundly for the rest of the day.

When I woke up the next morning, Grey was standing over me with a dozen roses. I was so happy to see him. He lifted me from the bed and gave me a big hug. My body was hurting so badly. I couldn't tell him why my body was hurting. I kept smiling as if nothing happened. Grey was gone for two weeks. I thought he needed a romantic dinner and bath. I ordered a nice dinner for him. He was so happy.

After dinner, I ran him a nice hot bubble bath. Grey was relaxing so good. His body and face were on point. The more I looked at Grey, the more I saw Chris' face. That dick had my mind in a bag. I got into the bathtub and joined Grey. It was time for me to fuck the shit out of him. He had his head lying on the wall of the tub. His legs were spread open. I went under the water and started sucking his asshole. His ass lips were soft and sweet. My tongue was rolling all up in his asshole. I couldn't stop myself. It was so good. Grey's eyes were rolling in the back of his head. My dick was getting hard as fuck. I knew it was time for me to get into that good ass. He loves to get fucked while lying on his stomach. I couldn't do it that way because he reminded me too much of Chris. I sweet talked him into lying on his stomach. He did want to but he didn't want to miss out on this good dick.

As I began to stick my dick inside of his ass, Chris' face kept popping up. I knew this was going to be an ugly night. Chris got on his knees and put a deep arch in his back. His ass was sitting upright. I didn't waste any time. My hands opened Grey's ass wider. I shoved my dick I his ass and went to work. This dick was fucking him super stupid. Grey couldn't move. He started to cry aloud. I didn't care because I was thinking about Chris.

After I got finished fucking Grey so stupid, he looked me straight into my eyes and said that I was fucking him like I was fucking someone else. My eyes got big. My lips fell to the floor. I gave in and told him that I fucked his brother. He didn't get mad because that's how they get down. I felt a lot better. I never went to work while Grey was gone. Chris had that good dick. That was my daily workout. Grey knew I was going to be faithful. He is very understanding. I wanted life to be better for us, but he couldn't seem to leave the porn business. It was making the both of us money. My soul wasn't into it anymore. I wasn't going to leave Grey if he didn't stop. That was his business and I respect that. I was missing my Atlanta friends.

I took a three week trip to Atlanta. Grey didn't come. I was so happy because I was going back to my old days. Those days consisted of fucking all of the guys. Grey wouldn't mind because he knew how I was. All of the guys were happy to see me. I haven't seen Jack in forever. He was at the house when I arrived. We had unfinished business to take care of. Jack can suck a dick like no other. He always let me put my cum all down his throat. The bitch was nasty just like me.

Everyone wanted to take shots all night. I was ready for it. Once I get good and drunk, I will be fucking, sucking and eating ass all night. Jack is the main person that I wanted to fuck. Every time we fucked each other, I always have his asshole talking back. It gets so wet. Jack asked me to come into the guest room. I knew he wanted some of this good dick. The two of us went into the guest room. Jack wanted to talk about Grey and me. My dick was ready to fuck.

We talked for about ten minutes. Jack will talk all night. I couldn't take it anymore so I threw Jack across the bed and pulled his pants down. I ripped his boxers off and started eating his ass. My tongue was going all up in his asshole. I was trying to make my tongue touch the inside of his stomach. Jack was moaning like a little bitch. My hands wanted to slap the shit out of him. I didn't because I knew the dick was good. I turned Jack over on his side and put my dick n his tight ass. I went to work. That punk was yelling for days. He couldn't take dick. The faces he was making were ugly as fuck. That didn't stop me from fucking that ass so good.

Jack was asking me to stop fucking him so hard. I looked into his weak face and laughed. Jack was a nice guy, but I had to slap the bitch across the face for telling me to stop. He already knew that was my ass. I was painting the hell out of that tight hole. I had to punish him.

After we got finished fucking, Jack could barely move. I felt sorry for him because I fucked him with no lube. That asshole was moving all kinds of ways. We went back into the living room. Hack was walking so slowly. Everyone was looking crazy and stupid. I was so ready to get back to Grey. I was missing the love of my life. He meant the world to me. Grey knew he was my pride and joy.

Every time I fucked any other guy, I always tell Grey because he is very understanding. We were running a porn business. I was going to fuck friends and all. As I was leaving Atlanta, I met this guy by the name of Post. He was a very nice looking guy. Post was a lawyer back in New York. We started talking a little more. Our conversation was very stimulating. It was love at first sit.

Before we went our separate ways, the two of us exchanged numbers. I was really feeling Post. When I got onto the plane, my mind couldn't stop thinking about Post.

When I arrived back home, Grey wasn't there. He was still gone on a business trip. I called Post to see how he was going. I couldn't believe my ears. He was back in town. His law firm is based in New York. Since Grey wasn't here, I thought it would be a great idea for Post and me to meet up. Things were getting lonely for me. Grey wasn't here. My heart needed someone to love. I knew Post was that guy.

Mr. Post had a limo waiting for me outside. My eyes lit up with joy. The two of us went to a romantic dinner. When we walked into the restaurant, all heads turned our way. Our look was to die for. Post pulled out my chair like a gentleman. He pushed me back up and started to sing one of my favorite songs. My heart dropped to the floor. Post knew how to make a girl happy.

The food was wonderful. The night was amazing. As we were leaving the restaurant, Post grabbed my arm with a soft touch and looked into my eyes.

"I don't like you. I love you." Post bit his lip as the words escaped his mouth.

Tears began to flow down my face. I was trying to pull my feelings back, but it didn't work because I was feeling him a lot. While we were on our date, Grey started calling me. I didn't want to answer the phone. When I answered it, he was so happy. I could only imagine what his excitement was about. He was coming home in the next couple of hours.

Lust, Lies & Love

When I heard that bad news, my body became stiff. Post and I needed to spend more time with each other.

"What the fuck!" I whispered under my breath.

Of course Post was the concerned date. He asked me what was wrong. I shook my head and pretended like nothing was the matter, but he didn't believe that. When I told him, he got so upset. I had to make it up to him.

We went back to my place. I gave Post the best sex ever. I started off by taking his clothes off. I got to my knees and sucked his dick. He thrust his hips so he could go deeper into my mouth. My eyes were rolling into the back of my head.

After I finished sucking him so good, he threw me on the end table and bawled me up. He started fucking me. My body was stiff as fuck. I felt all of his big dick. Post was fucking me stupid. He was making sure Grey wasn't going to get any of this good ass when he came home.

Post finally got me off of the end table. He picked me up and threw me onto the bed and tied my body up. I knew he was about to fuck the dog shit out of me. As he was twisting the ropes in perfect little knots around the bed posts like a diligent boy scout, my asshole was tightening up. Post turned me over onto my stomach. He tied me up again and put his dick inside of my ass. He fucked the shit out of me. He had my legs spread wide open. I couldn't feel or move my body. He was doing me so hard and deep. The inside of my ass felt like a hot train.

Two hours later, Post was done. I lay there with a sore look on my face. Post gave me a kiss and left my house. The inside of my heart was overjoyed. Five hours after Post left the house, Grey was driving up with a smile on his face. He was elated to see me. I couldn't smile back. I was still in so much pain. He wanted to know how everything was. I told him that everything was wonderful.

Grey was the type of guy that believe every and anything I told him. Since he was gone for two weeks, I invited a couple of the guys over. Chris, Jack and Post joined us for dinner. I introduced Grey and Post to each other. We had a dinner/sleepover party. Everyone was getting along great. My mind was in a different zone. I have slept with all three of the guys. I didn't know how to react around all of them, but I managed. The three of them had the best dick ever.

Lust, Lies & Love

Chris kept saying that he was so hot. Grey got up and lowered the air. I knew he wasn't hot. The bitch wanted some sex.

After Grey adjusted the thermostat, everyone started taking their clothes off. All I could do is shake my head. They were about to have a welcome back home sex party for Grey. Post looked at me with a smirk on his face. He knew he was about to get some good head and ass.

It was time to get this party on and popping. Everybody was fucking each other. Chris was fucking me and sucking Post's dick while he was standing over me. Grey was sitting back as his dick got hard from watching the action in the room. I enjoyed all of Chris' dick. He can fuck so good.

We were all being freaky. I put blindfolds over everyone's eyes. Post wanted to see Chris and Grey fuck each other. I looked over my blindfold and pushed Chris onto the bed and watched him fuck Grey. I was a nasty bitch. Chris thought he was fucking Post until he took his blindfold off. He realized that it was his brother, Grey. I couldn't do anything but laugh. Chris didn't stop fucking Grey either. He was on those pills. Grey was yelling so loudly because Chris was fucking him silly. It was a turn on for me

Lust, Lies & Love

After everything was over, my tired ass was ready for some sleep. Before I went to sleep, Chris made everyone drinks. I notice my drink was super strong. It had me feeling weird. Chris had extra shots of something in it. I blanked out after I downed a few.

When I woke up the next morning, Chris' dick was in my ass. Grey's dick was in my mouth. Those two bitches drugged and fucked me sorry. They knew I wasn't mad because I always need a good dick.

Grey wanted to cook breakfast for everyone. I felt like something wasn't right. A crazy look was over everyone's faces. They guys wanted to know what was going on. I asked them to leave because Grey and I needed to talk. My heart was feeling something.

While everyone was packing, I knew my heart was right. Chris began texting me because he wanted me to know something about Grey. My mind didn't want to keep texting, but my heart needed to know. Chris told me that Grey went to visit Kathy in New Jersey. I guess she was the business trip. I didn't get mad because the bitch is his wife.

When everyone left the house, I asked Grey how was the trip. He said that it was good and that he had an amazing time. I went on to tell me that it was a lot of work. I started to fake losing my mind. I asked where the business trip took place. He told me that it was in Atlanta. My smart ass mouth blurted out before I knew it.

"Do you mean that it took place in New Jersey?" I hissed with a twisted look on my face.

Why in the hell did I say that? His mouth dropped to his big dick. He started to explain, but I wasn't hearing it. Once you are a fuck boy, then you will always be one.

Kathy came to the house a few days after our spat. She was ready for a divorce. The bitch couldn't take it anymore. She wanted to take everything from Grey, but that wasn't going to happen. Since Grey didn't have a lawyer on his team, I called Post. He was a great lawyer and lover. Post agreed to take the case. I was to make sure that bitch, Kathy, left with nothing but her life. The house, cars and businesses were all going to Grey. I was going to make sure of it.

We all went to court a couple of weeks later. I knew the judge because we once fucked around. He was very nice to Grey. On and off for two weeks, Grey was in court. After everything was over, my baby won the case. I didn't feel sorry for that tired face looking heifer, Kathy. She was now single. I have her ex-man to myself.

As we were walking outside of the courtroom, the bitch looked at me and fixed her mouth to say something.

"I guess you are happy now?" Kathy shouted with her hands on her hip.

"Bitch, I been happy. You have a good day."

I smiled as I walked past her pathetic self. Since Grey didn't have to pay Post, I paid him for doing a good job. Post and the judge wanted sex for working so hard. My hot ass was willing and ready. I let the two of them fuck me at the same time. This ass of mine was getting dicked down so good. The judge was fucking my ass backwards. His dick wasn't big, but he knew how to use it.

Post ate my ass so good. I was that ride or die bitch that would ride for my man. Grey thought it was time for him and I to get our life back on track. Things had been crazy for us. It was for the best. Grey closed the business down. It wasn't for him anymore. He started doing real estate. That was something he always loved but never pursued.

Happiness eclipsed Grey's face when he started real estate. It didn't matter what he done because I was happy for him. My hot ass wanted to work and fuck all day. I knew the fucking all day wasn't going to happen. Grey really loved me. I needed to change. It was going to be very hard. My lifestyle was living life to the fullest.

Grey and some of the guys were planning a trip to Japan for my birthday. I was ready as ready could be. My body was ready to be licked, sucked and fucked. All of the guys needed to come. The more dick my ass gets, the better I feel. Everyone agreed to come to Japan for my birthday. I was so proud of Grey. He and the guys were the best.

When we arrived in Japan, everything looked so amazing. The guys were stunned by the view. The four of us toured the city before we went to dinner. I was enjoying Grey and the guys.

After we left dinner, we went back to the hotel. We were living it up. I was having the best birthday ever. Chris' best friend, Charlie, flew to Japan. We didn't know anything about him. Chris told us that he was a very nice guy.

Grey and Chris went to the airport to pick up Charlie. Jack and I stayed at the hotel. We were getting our thoughts together. We wanted to know more about this Charlie character. The guys weren't happy about new people entering our circle. Grey called and told me they were on their way back. Jack and I were getting nervous.

Ten minutes after the phone call, the three of them walked into the house. Charlie was a tall sexy guy. Chris introduced to us. He seems like a cool guy. I knew it was time for a meet and greet. I had all of the questions. The five of us formed a circle and grilled Charlie.

First we told Charlie a little bit about each of us. Then we found out a little about him. He is twenty-nine years old. He is a real estate broker. He is single. When I heard the word single, my eyebrows raised. I knew I had to get that.

It was time for us to have a couple of drinks and relax. The interrogation is over. We all noticed that Charlie likes to walk around naked. His dick was big as fuck. He had a horse dick. We all wanted to taste that dick.

Lust, Lies & Love

Some of the guys were drinking way too much. I had to take the bottles away. Charlie, Grey and Chris were drunk as fuck. I didn't get mad because I wanted everyone to have fun.

The night began to get crazy. Charlie and Chris were touching each other. Jack and Grey took me into the master suites to watch television. It wasn't anything on. I noticed that Grey was playing with his dick that way he does when he gets bored. My mouth couldn't take it. I pulled his dick all the way out in front of Jack and started to suck it real good. I had Grey moving around like a worm. My head game was so powerful. I sucked dick like no other.

As I was sucking Grey's dick, Chris and Charlie walked in. I kept sucking. My mouth was wet as hell. I needed more dick. Since Charlie was new to the group, he was the first person I let fuck me. I felt his dick all in my stomach. It was thick, long and hard. He was cumming every minute. My ass was full and weak.

After Charlie filled me up, I let the team bang me all at once for my birthday. They were fucking me silly. The dick had me going crazy. They fucked me for a good three hours. My body was tired as fuck. That was such a turn on for Grey. He was a real freak. I really enjoyed Charlie. He had some real good dick.

Lust, Lies & Love

Jack wanted to go to a bar for some drinks. All of the guys went except for me. I chose to stay in the room and relax. My body couldn't take any more stimulation. I was enjoying being alone. The guys were having the time of their lives.

While in Japan, I had to take care of some business. Grey had some real estate deal in Turkey. I had to tie up some loose ends. Things were looking good for Grey.

When the guys got back to the hotel, I had to sit everyone down. They all wanted to know what was gong on. I told them that I had to leave because Grey had to business deal in Turkey. They were sad and upset. I didn't want to leave so soon. Grey understood and told me to be safe.

I left Japan the next day. Turkey was calling my name. When I arrived at the airport, it was a young lady named Jennifer waiting for me. She had a smile stretching across the width of her face to greet me. She speaks English very well. She was a very weird looking lady.

As we were getting on the bus, Jennifer started to act crazy. She yelled at the driver and slapped him. Then she looked at me and smiled again. The bitch was crazy as fuck.

Lust, Lies & Love

After that crazy ass ride, the two of us went to the hotel. It was so amazing and lovely.

I decided to freshen up a bit and get out and g on the town with Jennifer. She was ready for any and everything. She was my new ride or die bitch. The club was the first place we visited. Those people knew how to party. The bartender was fine as hell. I knew I had to take him back to the hotel.

The people were drinking like crazy and smoking out of control. They were kissing like there was no tomorrow. That was my type of club. Jennifer's freaky ass was in the corner sucking somebody's dick. The guy's dick was big as hell too. I mean she was deep-throating that dick so good. My hands wanted to push her out of the way and show her how to suck dick. I had to teach her that if the guy's toes don't curl up then she isn't doing something right. I make the toes curl and bodies shake. Jennifer needed to take some of my classes. She was good, but she needed to be amazing.

After Jennifer finished her anonymous blowjob, I wanted to slap the fuck out of her. She could have let me suck the dick too. Before we left the club, I went to the bar and left my number with the bartender's fine ass. Jennifer noticed that we were making eye contact.

On our way back, Jennifer asked me if the bartender was coming over. I told her that I didn't know. He can get it if he does. The bitch started laughing all loud and crazy. The driver was so happy to put her out. We had a ten-minute drive before we arrived back to the hotel.

While on the way back to the hotel, Mr. Ken who is the driver kept looking at me through the rearview mirror. I thought something was wrong. He kept looking like I owed him something. My mind began to wonder.

"How are you?" Mr. Ken asked as he gave me the eye.

"Wonderful. Yourself?"

"I'll be better if you give me some of that fat ass."

My eyes widened with surprise. I actually wanted to try the dick out. Mr. Ken opens my door and walks me to my room. He put my bags away. I didn't realize how big his dick print is. He had a walk to die for. His print was so huge that I couldn't take me eyes off of it. A bitch like me didn't want to let someone like Mr. Ken walk out the room without giving him any ass, but I had to.

Lust, Lies & Love

There was a knock at the door. It was Mr. Ken with his dick hanging out of his pants. My heart dropped to my knees. He forced his big dick down my throat. I enjoy every inch of it. He fucks my throat so good. I jump up and down for new dick.

"Can I fuck your ass?"

"No. You cannot."

Mr. Ken didn't want to hear that. He threw me on the bed and took my clothes off. He put his dick inside of my ass without any lube. My ass hurts like hell. Every time my body starts to fold. He fucks me harder. We had sex three hours strong.

After Mr. Ken left the room, I went straight to sleep. Jennifer and I had a long day ahead of us. When I woke up the next morning, Jennifer was standing over me. I yelled at her.

"What are the fuck you doing here standing over me like that? And how the hell did you get in here?" I said angrily.

"The door was open," She said innocent enough.

I didn't know what to do. My ass and dick were hanging all out. Jennifer looked at me with a smile on her face.

Lust, Lies & Love

"What are you smiling at?"

She pointed toward the sheets towards my dick. "You have a big dick." Then she held up her hands to give me a visual of my estimated length like the actors in the subway commercial. You can't get this foot long for five dollars.

My mouth opened so wide. Then I started to laugh. I shook it off and went to take a shower. We had several homes to look at. While we were looking at homes, I called Post to come and be with me. He agreed and I was happy.

Jennifer and I went to pick up Post from the airport later that night. He looks amazing. Jennifer looks at him like she wants the dick.

On our way back to the hotel, I thought it would be a good idea for me to sit in the back seat with Post. Ms. Jennifer didn't like it at all, but I didn't give a fuck. I was trying to suck some dick before we arrived at the hotel. Post's dick is thick, long and nice.

As we were riding, Jennifer stopped by her hotel first. She had to get some sleep clothes. I asked her about how long she was going to be. I had to see how much time I had for Post to bust one in my mouth. Since it was going to be a while, I went in to make my move.

Ten minutes have gone by since Jennifer has gone. Post and I started playing around. He took his fat dick out. My mouth went to work. He had dick for years. It was so good too.

By the time Jennifer came outside, Post had put me to sleep. When I woke up from my snooze, I felt something wet on my body. It was post licking my ass so good. His tongue felt amazing. I lay there and let him have his way. He was getting the best of me. His dick and mouth game had me gone. I loved this guy like crazy.

Jennifer was in the other room with her new new. He was fine. After Post and I finished making love, my hot ass went and knocked on Jennifer's room door. I had to see that fine ass man she was coveting. I was invited in naked and all. The bitch got mad because I was naked, but she knows how I roll. He-man was lying in bed on his back without any clothes on. His dick is bigger than all outdoors. I had to get that dick.

As I was going back to my room, Jennifer walks out of her room. She looks worried.

"What's wrong?" I asked.

"Someone had broken into one of our listings."

My heart dropped to the floor. That particular one is Grey's property. Jennifer told me not to worry. I was hard not to worry. Grey put so much into his house.

When Jennifer left to go and see what was wrong, I went back into her room. The guy was still sleeping. Nasty thoughts run through my mind. Something is telling me to go up to him and start sucking his dick. That's what I did.

When he felt my wet mouth, he started to push my head all the way down. I felt his dick in my stomach. He didn't realize it wasn't Jennifer until he opened his eyes. I thought his eyes were going to pop out of his head. He realized it was me. He didn't try to stop me or push me off. The punk enjoyed a good sucking. I wasn't sucking a good ten minutes until he was ready to fuck. He fucks me like no other. I had to get up after he finished. Neither one of us wanted to be caught. I felt sorry for Jennifer because she wasn't getting any dick.

Jennifer came back two hours later. Everything turned out fine. The next day Jennifer and I had a lot of business to take care of. Most of Grey's property was selling like crazy. I am so happy that his business is doing so well. My last day in Turkey was approaching.

Grey calls me. He wants to know how things are. I tell him that things are great. We didn't talk for long. Grey had a meeting to attend. The business is looking good for Grey.

Since this was my last night in Turkey, Jennifer and I go out and party. I am ready to get my party on. Jennifer has on a short red dress. She looks amazing in it. I want to pull up her dress, pull down her panties, and lick her pussy. That's how good she looks. In the back of my mind I was like Jennifer what are you thinking.

Before we left the hotel, I called Mr. Ken to come and pick us up. That piece of dick always has me wet. As we are getting into the car, Jennifer notices that she forgot her purse. She goes back and gets it. Mr. Ken is so happy to see me.

"Can I have some of that boy pussy?"

"What is that?" I asked pretending to be a naïve little virgin boy who secretly wants to get his ass pounded by a sexy stranger.

"Let me rephrase that. Can I have some ass?"

Lust, Lies & Love

My little voice was cursing Jennifer to come on. I never opened my mouth to answer the question. My bitch ass was trying to play hard to get. Jennifer came back five minutes later. I was saved by the little red dress. To the club we went.

Jennifer talked all the way there. I want to stick my dick in her mouth just to shut her up. I couldn't take all of that nonsense.

When we arrived at the club, I let Jennifer out. Mr. Ken needed to ask me a question. I already knew what he wanted. Since we are in front of the club parked, I only gave him some head. His eyes were rolling like crazy. His legs were shaking. I am giving it to him. The weak bitch came in five minutes. That was a waste of time, but I enjoyed it while it lasted.

Jennifer was outside of the car waiting for me. When I got out of the car, Jennifer looks at me.

"You are a nasty bitch because I saw you suck off the driver right there in front of me."

"Well bitch you should have turned your head. Have you ever heard of the word privacy?" I was being sarcastic. "Now let's party and have a blast."

Lust, Lies & Love

The club is larger than I imagined. Dick is everywhere for me. Jennifer is looking stupid as fuck. We walk up to the bar. Jennifer's nipples were hard. I can see them cutting through her dress. The bartender is ugly, but he is making all the right moves on Jennifer. He is making her hot and wet.

I left the bar because I had to find some thug dick. As I was walking towards the restroom, I see two guys standing by the wall. They are sexy was fuck. My body knows that they are thugs. I want both of them. I keep walking like I didn't see them. When I got into the restroom, I stand by the walls because I know there will be coming in. Not even a minute later, there are walking in. They are so sexy.

Now I try to leave, but one of the guys pulls me back in. He wants to know my name. I wouldn't tell him my name. I am scared now. The other guy asked if I could talk. I was mute. I still didn't say anything. The solution to my unresponsiveness is to put their big dicks in my mouth. They were thrusting nonstop. I started laughing. The first guy told me to get on my knees and suck his dick. I started sucking like there was no tomorrow. The other guy was eating my ass so good. I let them fuck me like I was a new slut on the block. My ass was hurting for the rest of the night. I was so ready to go back to the hotel.

Jennifer told me to go home and to be safe. She was leaving with the ugly bartender. I turned that bitch out. She never had that much dick in a week.

I called Mr. Ken to take me back to the hotel. When I made it back, he wanted some ass, but I wasn't able to perform. He didn't want to hear that. He was hard and ready. I called Jennifer to come to the room. She didn't answer her phone. Mr. Ken asked me what was wrong. I told him about the two guys who fucked me in the bathroom of the club we were at tonight. He was mad as hell. My happy ass smiled at Mr. Ken and turned over. I fell asleep almost instantly. I was worn out.

Before I knew it, Mr. Ken is on top of me with his clothes off. I tried to push him off, but it didn't work. My small body gave up. He puts me in the buck and fucks me silly. The shit was hurting so badly. He was using so much of his body weight. My mind wondered off somewhere else because the pain was unbearable.

After Mr. Ken finished tearing me a new one, he puts me into the tub and rubs my body down. He told me not to play with him. I was so ready when he left. I went to sleep in the tub. Jennifer and he friends came over and put me to bed.

I woke up to the two of them cooking breakfast, making coffee and singing to each other. I thought it was so nice. When I saw the guy from the bar with Jennifer, I had to do a double-take. I couldn't believe my eyes. He is the one whose dick I sucked. I was calling him ugly. I must have been drunk as fuck. He didn't say much to me. Jennifer is in love. I, on the other hand, was loving his dick.

After breakfast, it was time for me to go back to the states. Japan and Turkey treated me well. I didn't want to leave Jennifer. She is always the life of the party.

When I arrived back in New York, Grey was there to pick me up. He was so happy to see me. He told me that he had a special gift for me since I have been working so hard. I am so ready to see it.

After we pulled up to the house, Grey blindfolded me with a piece of cloth. The closer we got, the hotter I was getting. My baby told me to take the blindfold off. There sits a black on black Bentley sitting in the driveway. Grey has outdone himself. In the words of Mr. Ken, I had to give my baby some of this good boy pussy. It was wet and ready. Grey made love to me like no other. I felt every piece of his body. He made me feel loved and wanted. He had his way with me. I gave myself to him freely. My baby was nutting like a waterfall.

Grey started singing to me while we were making love. My heart began to cry with joy because I was back with my baby. He meant the world to me.

After we finished making love, Grey asked me if I had sex with anyone. I told him that I did. He didn't get mad because he knows that I am a freak. The two of us had breakfast in bed. Grey wanted me to take over the business for a while. He had some personal issue to take care of. I will do anything for my baby.

Two weeks later, everything was good on Grey's end. The business was going very well. When Grey got home from a ten hour work day, I wanted some sex. He was tired as fuck. I was going to put him right to sleep. He always takes a shower and gets into bed naked. Then he watches television. His body is sexy ad fuck. My mouth has to taste that dick, my dick.

Lust, Lies & Love

Grey is lying on his back with his eyes closed. I crawl over to him like a baby. He is sleeping so soundly. My tongue plays with the head of his dick. He wakes up from his fake sleep. I had his dick so wet. He couldn't take my powerful tongue. He bends me over and ties my arms to my legs. Then he fucks me so good. I was loving it so much. My ass was taking all of his dick. Grey was yelling like a young bitch. He knows how to work that dick. I have tons of cum draining out of me. Grey hasn't had sex in so long. I am not going to make him wait anymore. He punishes my ass so good. These cakes needed some rest and love. Riding a big dick like Grey's dick will wear you out. Grey is the best ever.

After out exquisite lovemaking, Grey went to sleep. My ass is powerful and is like no other. I let Grey enjoy his sleep without any more sexual interruptions from me. There is a lot of business things I need to work on.

As I am working, the phone rings. I look at the caller ID to see who was calling. It is Jennifer. I was so happy to hear from her. She had some properties for sale. It was time to wake Grey up to talk about business. Jennifer found four properties that needed to be sold. Grey is the go-to guy to buy and sell properties.

Lust, Lies & Love

Grey took the next flight to Turkey. He was ready to see what Jennifer had to offer. I told him to have faith and not to worry. Jennifer is one of the best.

When Grey arrived in Turkey, Jennifer gave me a call. I had to let the bitch know that if she tries to fuck my man that it is going to be trouble. She started laughing.

The next day, I flew my ass to Turkey. I can't stand a funny bitch. Grey's dick wasn't going to feel that inside of that stank pussy. When I arrived, Jennifer was happy to see me. She is my boss bitch. The three of us got into the car and listened to music on our way to our destination. We laughed at each other.

Grey didn't like one of the homes. A lot of work had to be done, but it was big. Since Grey was stressing over nothing, Jennifer and I took him to a wine bar. Wine is Grey's favorite drink. My baby needed a relief. We all started off with one glass. Grey and Jennifer started drinking glass after glass. I started to get worried. Grey can be a beast when he gets drunk.

It was time to leave the bar. Grey had ten glasses of wine. He was so feeling himself. Jennifer was on the table sleep. This nice guy

Lust, Lies & Love

helped me carry them to the car. He is sexy as hell. I thanked him and gave him my number.

It took me almost an hour to get them into the room. My body was tired as fuck. I lay the both of them down. I take a shower. As I was getting out of the shower, I see my phone blinking. It is the guy from the bar calling. He wanted to come over.

Since the two drunks were sleeping so well, I invited him over. When he arrived at my house, he had on a pair of basketball shorts and a t-shirt. The dick print was so big. My ass needed that so bad. The two of us went into the kitchen for drinks. His name is Mitch. He is a nice, sexy and amazing guy. We were having a good conversation. The drinks were making me horny. Mitch's lips were sexy. I wanted to feel them on me.

We went into the living area to watch television. Things were about to heat up. Mitch was licking his lips. I was getting hot. I know that Grey is in the bedroom sleep, but I didn't care. I needed some new dick.

Mitch started taking off his clothes. His body was amazing. His dick is big as fuck. I have been hitting the jackpot lately with these big dicks. His lips were plump and soft. A part of me couldn't take looking at him. I had to put my ideas into action. There were a couple of ropes beside my bed. Before I could reach them, Mitch had them wrapping my hands. He tied me up tightly. My body was stiff. I didn't say anything because I knew he was going to fuck me silly. Instead of Mitch taking his time putting his dick inside of me, he slammed it into my ass. I jumped in pain and excitement. I wanted to kill him. Mitch had me moaning so loudly. I fear that I am going to wake up the drunken monkeys so I stuff the end of a pillow into my mouth and bite down on it hard.

We went at it again hours later. It seemed like Mitch's dick has gotten bigger. My throat is hurting from trying to take all of that dick down. I was losing my mind. After we finished fucking, Grey and Jennifer woke up at the same time. I was good and sore. Grey wanted me to go into the kitchen to make him a drink. My legs could barely move.

As I was walking into the kitchen, Grey asked me what was wrong. I shook my head and staggered into the kitchen. He kept looking at me crazy. He asked why I was walking funny. I had to come up with something believable so I told him that I hurt my leg trying to carry their drunken asses to the room by myself. Grey was so hurt that I had to do that.

Mitch was in the living area killing himself laughing. My ass was hurting like crazy. Mitch put it on me good.

Jennifer had a bad hangover. She looks a hot mess. The bitch needed some good dick in her life. Everyone started worrying me about food. They wouldn't stop worrying me for anything so I stood in front of everyone and bent over. I opened my ass cheeks and told them that if they were hungry that they could come and eat. Mitch was the first person on his knees eating my ass out. Grey was looking crazy as hell. Mitch was in there doing the damn thing.

After he finished licking me, he lies down on the floor and fucks me in front of Grey. He was getting madder by the minute. Jennifer was speechless. I push Mitch off of me and so that Grey could fuck me. He banged me hard from the back. Mitch didn't like that.

Mitch stood over my face and started jacking his dick. I wanted his dick in my face. The louder I moaned, the faster Mitch was jacking his dick. A few minutes later, Mitch was Cumming all over my face. I was loving it. I couldn't take any more dick. My legs were hurting. My ass was sore. My body is done.

After this fuck fest, Jennifer took us back to look at the four homes. Grey purchased all of them. That is a very good thing. He is going to rent them out. His business is doing very well.

We enjoyed Jennifer and our stay in Turkey. Now it is time to go back home. Since I haven't seen my Atlanta friends in a long time, I thought I would be a good idea to pay them a visit. Grey couldn't because of work. I refused to call them. I always like to surprise them.

They were so happy to see me when I got there. Jack gave me a hug that was so tight. These guys are my babies. Everyone had to work that day. Jack took the day off in order to be with me. That was the best day of my life. The two of us went out to eat. We talked about old time. We genuinely enjoyed each other. Jack is one of my best friends. He was there when I didn't have anyone to depend on. I really love this guy. I treated Jack to a spa. He loved it. My feelings for Jack never changed. Jack means the world to me.

We went back to Jack's place. I was so surprised because Jack had rose petals and candles everywhere. My heart was filled with joy. I was falling back in love with him.

We took a hot bubble bath together. Jack fed me strawberries and gave me wine to drink. My day was looking good. At the end of the day, everything was amazing. We thoroughly enjoyed ourselves.

The other guys came home from work later that afternoon. I was very happy to see them. My mind couldn't stop thinking about Jack. All of the guys and I went out on the town. Everyone was ready to party and get our drink on. We were drinking shots like water. Matt was drunk as fuck. He knew how to get wasted. The other guys were dancing the night away. I was ready to leave the club. I needed to get on these tip toes and ride the head of a big dick. My ass needed some good dick.

Jack and I left the club early. We were ready to finish our date. When the two of us got back to the house, we started kissing, sucking each other's dicks and eating ass. The feeling was so amazing. Jack sucked the life out of me.

We went into Jack's room for sleep. I couldn't wait for the other guys. Jack had done his thing. I woke up two hours later and decided to fly back home. My feelings were getting the best of me.

As I begin to board the plane, tears run down my face. Love found me all over again. I think about how Grey is to tom. Then a lot of things start to run through my mind. I love Jack, but I am in love with Grey. Grey gave me a good life. He is my world and joy.

When I got back home, Grey was sitting in the living area. Tears were flowing down his face. I started to worry. He jumped up and started hugging me. Something wasn't right. The two of us had to sit down and talk this thing over. Grey wanted to thank me for being there for him when he didn't have anyone else to depend on. That was so sweet. He and I are meant to be together. We have been through a lot, but we are still here.

I always thought our relationship was open. He let me fuck whoever I wanted. I go on dates with other men. I travel with the best of them. Grey once told me that we didn't have an open relationship. He wanted me to enjoy life. I was loving it for the moment. The money was good. The dick was great. Fucking for free wasn't me. Some guys wanted to fuck for free. I thought that was crazy. I put my all into everything I do.

Lust, Lies & Love

Grey knew that I couldn't stop overnight. Since he has been so good to me, a very big surprise was coming his way. A friend of mine, Zack, is a male dancer. Grey has always been in love with male dancers. Everyone wanted the dancer to be a surprise.

I called Zack and the guys. Grey didn't have any idea what was going on. The party was going to be hot as fuck. It is now party time. Chris went to pick up Grey from the house. He had a hard time getting him out of the house. We waited an hour before the two of them showed up. Grey was blindfolded with a bath cloth over his face.

When Chris took the blindfold off, Zack was standing in front of Grey. He was naked and looking good. The guys were going crazy to see a new big dick. I was ready to get fucked. Grey was in shock when he saw Zack's dick.

After everyone partied and enjoyed themselves, I sent Zack and Grey into the room. They needed to enjoy each other. My baby deserves to be happy.

Chris wanted to go back to my place. I was happy as fuck. This time, I was going to charge him. The nasty bitch always wanted a free fuck. I had to sit Chris down and explain to him about the pay game. He didn't want to hear that.

After he paid me, he wanted me to start sucking his dick immediately. As I was going down his tree I noticed a sour smell. Chris' dick smelled like shit. I wanted to beat the fuck out of him. Why would I suck a dick that smelled like shit? Chris went into the bathroom to take a shower.

After he got out of the shower, his dick was fresher than a pair of Nikes out of the box. I started sucking the hell out of his dick. Chris made mad love to me taking me back in time. We both loved it.

Chris left the room to go and freshen up. He didn't close the door behind him. I started hearing this loud sound. It was Zack and Grey. They were getting it on. Zack was fucking the hell out of Grey. I knew Grey was in pain because he couldn't take a big dick.

After the fucking party was over, Grey came out of the room walking very slowly. Zack had beaten that ass in so good. He got what he wanted. Chris was laughing at Grey.

Everyone was starting to leave. As a boyfriend, I had to go and take care of Grey. His ass was in a lot of pain. When we got back to the house, Grey wanted to take a hot bath. I thought it would be nice to run the water for him. Grey was getting in the bath tub so slow. The punk was really in pain.

While Grey was taking a nice hot bath, I called Chris to come over. Grey was going to be in the bathtub forever.

Ten minutes after I called Chris, he was knocking at the door. My ass was happy as fuck. He walked into the house kissing on me. His dick was already hard. Since Grey was taking a bath, Chris and I went into my bedroom. Grey was a door down from us. We didn't waste any time. Chris took off his clothes. We went to work. He was dicking me down so good that I started calling his name aloud. It was just that good.

An hour into doing our thing, Grey started calling my name. I couldn't answer him because Chris was knee deep in my man pie.

After Chris got finished doing his thing, Grey was getting out of the tub. It was time for Chris to leave. Grey walked in a soon a Chris had left. He was still in pain. My dick didn't make it any better.

As Grey was getting into bed, I pushed him onto his back and spread his legs open. I ate his ass out and fucked the hell out of him. He started crying out in pain. I could see it on his face. I didn't care because I wanted some ass. The bitch made me fuck him stupid because he was crying. We don't cry while getting fucked just like there is no crying in baseball.

Grey was beginning to stop crying. My dick wouldn't let me stop. He wanted more. Grey was one of my best fucks. There were plenty of days when he didn't feel well. I felt sorry for him. Grey would let me fuck him whenever I wanted to. He wanted to keep me happy as I wanted the same for him.

After I finished punishing Grey, I let him go to sleep. He needed some rest. Since he has been so good to me, I went car shopping for him. I didn't go alone.

Jack called me and told me that Sam was in town. I didn't really care, but I knew that Sam would do anything for me. I called Sam up and met him at the BMW of America. He wanted to know who I was car shopping for. I told him that it was for Grey. His face turned red. He didn't want to hear it. I couldn't take it. The look on Sam's face wasn't pretty.

As Sam and I were leaving the car lot, He turned back around. I followed him. He went back to the car lot and bought Grey a brand new car. I was very speechless. Sam would do anything for me and that just proved it.

After we left, we took the car to Grey. His eyes widened so big. I told him that the car is his. He started crying. My heart wouldn't let me be happy. Sam was giving me the sad face. I had to make Sam happy. I told Grey to go and ride through town. He went running out the door.

As soon as he left, I started kissing all over Sam. He needed some real love. Sam held me so tight. He didn't want any sex at the moment. He just wanted to hold me tight. That's what I needed. I missed Sam a lot. He was once my everything. The more Sam was holding me, the more I was beginning to fall back in love. I really wanted to be back with him. Whenever things got rough in my life, Sam was always there.

The conversation we had brought up too many memories and a lot of tears. He was tired of living his life without me. My life paused for a moment. I had to get myself together. Sam started asking me things like will I ever love him again. I couldn't stop the flow of tears flooding down my face. That was a question I could not answer. My life is with Grey. He

Lust, Lies & Love

means so much to me regardless of all the men I fuck. We have come a long way.

After our heart to heart, the two of us went out for dinner. We had the best time of our lives. The dinner was amazing. Sam didn't want to leave, but I had to go. We got into our separate cars and drove away.

Sam called me with sadness in his voice. I couldn't take it. I wanted to tell him to come over and stay the night. As I pulled up to the house, Grey was walking outside. I told Sam that I would call him back later.

Grey walked to the car and asked me where I have been. I told him that I was out with Sam. He thought that was sweet. My slick ass had to come up with something really fast in order to leave the house. I had to reconnect with Sam.

After I made something up and gave it to Grey, things were looking good. I needed peace of mind. I dialed Sam's number. He answered the phone in two rings. I told him that I was on my way to come and see him. I heard the happiness in his voice. He was ready for some good loving. I was ready to give it to him.

When I pulled up to Sam's place, I noticed that there were three cars in the driveway. Now I

Lust, Lies & Love

am getting mad because this wasn't supposed to be a fuck fest. This was a one on one. Once I got up the stairs, Sam was already at the door. When he saw the look on my face, he wanted to know what was wrong. I asked him about the cars. He started laughing and told me that he had a surprise for me.

When I walked into the house, Sam had a candle lit dinner and a band playing as background music. Things couldn't get any better. My eyes lit up with joy. That was the best thing Sam has ever done for me. My love for Sam was getting stronger. I had to pull myself away. I didn't want to leave Grey. He understood me when no one else does. I love him for that.

The dinner and the band were so romantic. Sam made my night. After everything was over, Sam and SI went into his bathroom for a hot bubble bath. There was candles, roses and wine ready to be served. We started off with a glass of wine. The taste of it had my body in chills.

After the wonderful wine, Sam started licking me from head to toe. My body was in another world. Sam's lips had my body shaking. Then he put my dick inside his mouth. I was lost for words. All I could do is bite my lip in pleasure.

Lust, Lies & Love

Sam was working his lips on my dick. Sam opened my legs and started to eat me out. My ass was Cumming everywhere. The dick never got the chance to enter me.

Sam wanted to make me feel special. He did a great job. He didn't want me to leave, but I had to go. I have been gone from Grey all day. I knew he was looking for me. Sam was the best, but Grey's love was calling my name.

When I made it back to Grey, he was so happy to see me. I smiled as I opened my arms wide to embrace him. Grey fell into my arms. I missed my baby so much.

It was time once again for Grey and me to move. This time, we are going to better our lives and relationship for the better. Things needed to change for us.

After the two of us talked about moving, we called a couple of our friends to tell them the good news. Everybody had to work and couldn't make it. Grey and I didn't get upset. We understand priorities and work issues.

Since the crew wasn't able to come over, I wanted to surprise Grey with a special gift. We have been through so much. He deserves the best. Before planning a trip to Florida, I had a romantic night with Grey. My mind and heart

Lust, Lies & Love

wanted to do something very nice. Grey went to the store to pick up some bottled water.

While he was out and about, I went into the bathroom to run some water in the tub. I put rose petals and candles throughout the bathroom. Grey needed some good loving. This was going to be the best sex he has ever had. He has changed my life for the better.

I called Grey because I needed to know where he was. He was still at the store which gave me time to get everything together. I called this piano company to have someone to come over and play something for the two of us. I wanted it to be a special night for Grey. There was a piano player in the living area. I put a bottle of wine in the center of the bathtub. Love is in the air.

Grey walked into the house. Tears began to flow down his face. I love to see a man cry when the love is real. When we are fucking, that is a whole other thing.

As Grey started to walk towards the bathroom, I began to undress him slowly. His body is sexy. His love is real. I love him. I lay him down in the tub. I lick o his chest and work my way down to his dick. My lips start moving like a wave. My mouth was wetter than an ocean. I loved every minute of it. I had to make my baby feel good. Grey was shaking like crazy. I had to get a little nasty. He turned over onto his back and spread his ass cheeks open. My tongue went right into his sexy asshole. My dick was getting hard as fuck. I couldn't control myself. Grey was moaning loudly. My tongue was doing its thing. I only ate Grey out. We made love later that night. We enjoyed ourselves.

We were getting ready for our trip to Florida. Grey loved Florida's weather. We took a private place. Our friend, James, is the owner of the plane. He let us borrow it for a week.

Upon lift off, I noticed that Grey was sweating like crazy. This is the first time I have ever seen this. Grey started falling in and out of sleep. Now I was getting scared. We had an onsite nurse who was there. She noticed something was wrong. She came and doctored on him for about ten minutes. He finally came back to life. My baby was stressed over work. I felt sorry for him.

When we arrived in Florida, Grey was so happy. He loved the heat. It was time for us to have some time alone. Grey was treating our vacation like it was our first date. I was loving it so much. Our lives were getting back where it once was.

The hotel staff gave us first class service. After getting settled in, Grey and I went to the pool. We were the only two people there. Grey kept giving me the sexy eye. I knew what time it was. Since we were the only two in the pool, I took my clothes off so we could have a nude party. Grey gave me the best sex ever. My life was in another world. We only stayed in Florida for three days. Some work came up. I didn't want to leave.

Once we got back to our new place, things began to fall into place. Our open came to an end. We are now a monogamous couple. We stopped telling our friends all of our problems. We wanted our relationship to be happy once more.

I started traveling with Grey from state to state doing business. He meant the world to me. When people told me it couldn't be done, Grey showed me otherwise. He kept me going when I didn't believe in myself. I love him for that.

We traveled three months straight after we left Florida. Grey enjoyed it a lot, but I noticed tit was wearing down on his body. There were times when he couldn't sleep, eat or get up to go to work. I thought my baby was about to die on me. My heart couldn't take it. I tried to make him go and see a doctor, but he was being stubborn and refused. He always told me that he was fine and that he didn't need a doctor. He tried to convince me that he only needed some rest because he was just a little worn out.

The next day, I grabbed Grey some breakfast. While I was out, I researched some doctors and had one to come to the house and check out Grey. He thought the doctor was a friend of mine when he saw her. Grey was polite and offered, Kathy, the doctor something to eat. I went into the kitchen and got her a glass of iced tea.

When I walked into the bedroom, Grey's eyes weren't looking so well. Tears began to flow down my face. Grey told me not to cry because everything is going to be okay.

Kathy did a couple of tests on Grey. We will not get the results back for two weeks. I am hoping for the best. After Kathy left our home, Grey and I went to sleep. He needed some rest. I kept waking up during my sleep wondering the test results were going to reveal. I couldn't live without Grey in my life.

Lust, Lies & Love

He is my joy. He is the love of my life, my everything.

CHAPTER 10

Two days later, Grey took me out on the town. He wanted me to get my mind off of everything. We were having a blast. The drinks were good. My baby was doing his thing on the dance floor. He needed another drink. The dance floor wore him out.

As Grey walked up to the bar, I noticed that this guy was flirting with him. So I walked up to them. I overheard the guy asking Grey if he is single. Grey told him that he wasn't single.

"Hello, sexy who are you?" The guy asked me as I approached them territorially.

"I am the loved and the man of his dreams."

Lust, Lies & Love

I wrapped my arms around Grey as I said those words. Grey started laughing. The guy walked off.

I was ready to leave the club. I was getting horny as fuck. My ass needed some good dick. I knew Grey was willing to give it. I took Grey into the bathroom. I pulled his pants down and started sucking his fat dick. Grey was shaking like crazy. My mouth is powerful. Before we could leave the bathroom, Grey was Cumming everywhere.

This isn't over. I needed Grey to dick me down. His dick is like a horse's dick. He knew how to make my body fold. This ass is so wet and ready to be fucked good. I was ready to feel Grey's mouth on my body. I thought that we should try something different. I let Grey tie me up with ropes and cuffs. Before he tied me up, he oiled my down. It felt so good.

He entered me slowly. His dick was hitting the bottom of my ass. I wanted to cry. The shit was killing me so badly, but I took the pain. Grey lost his mind while fucking me. I was sore as hell when he finished. I couldn't walk to save my life. The shower was calling my name, but I couldn't make it. The life was going out of me.

Lust, Lies & Love

After we had our little party, it was back to business. Grey was happy again. He started to work himself crazy as ever. He always wanted to keep me happy. I told him that it is the small things in life that make me happy.

While Grey was at work, Kathy called wanted to speak with the both of us. We invited her over. She wanted us to know that some of the results were good. We were still waiting on two more of the tests. I am still nervous, but I tried to be strong for Grey.

After Kathy left, we went to dinner. We wanted to talk about what to do in case something happen. I tried to keep the conversation light and positive. I was interrupted by my phone ringing. It was Kathy. The other results came in sooner than we thought. We were anxious to hear the news.

Kathy began to cry on the phone. I knew it wasn't good news. My eyes started tearing up. Grey asked what was wrong. Kathy revealed that grey had cancer. Things weren't looking so well.

"WHY?" I yelled from the top of my lungs startling everybody in the restaurant.

Once I told Grey what the results were, he didn't seem to be sad.

Lust, Lies & Love

"Baby, that's life. I love you. You have been there when I didn't have anyone. You showed me, love. OI love you for that."

Those words were soothing to me, but that still didn't stop my heart from breaking. I was about to lose the love of my life.

Grey started treatment two weeks later. I was by his side every day. I was there through his painful, good and lonely times. We were going to get through this together.

I called the guys to tell them the news. They were all shocked. They came to New York a couple days later. When they arrived, they were still stunned beyond belief.

The treatment was too strong for Grey. The doctors had to change medications and dosages more than four times. Grey lost his appetite and wasn't eating well. He lost weight fast. The more I looked at him, the more I wanted to take his pain away.

Since Grey loved red roses, I went to a local market and bought him eight dozen roses, a dozen for each year we have been together. The five of us took Grey the roses. He was asleep when we got there. The guys stayed, but I had to leave. I left for a couple of hours.

Lust, Lies & Love

I couldn't eat, sleep or think. My world was a living wreck.

On day five, the guys had to leave for work. They were a big help. They assisted with bathing, feeding and walking Grey. They talked with him about the good and bad times we all had.

Kathy called to see how things were going. I told her that things were going as expected and that they could be better. She flew to New York to be with us. We were so thankful to have her.

When she arrived to see Grey, she pulled me outside and told that Grey had about three weeks. I blanked out. I saw black stars floating in the air. When I came to, I wanted to tell Grey. I decided against it.

Kathy and I went to dinner to discuss Grey's options. I couldn't eat nor did I want to talk. I wanted to be with Grey. Crystal, Grey's nurse, called me while we were out to dinner. She needed me to come back to the hospital as soon as possible. I was crying and yelling. I knew things weren't good. Kathy told me that no matter what happens I have to be strong for Grey.

Lust, Lies & Love

"Please don't let him see you cry. You have done your part." Kathy said soothingly.

When we got back to the hospital, the nurse told us to sit in the waiting room. I asked why we couldn't see Grey. She informed us that more test was being conducted on Grey.

"They're not doing any more tests. They have bad news."

That is not what I wanted to hear. We waited for three hours. I have been telling Kathy about our life story and that Grey and I have come a long way. Kathy was tearing up. She is so emotional. I give her a hug. She is such a nice person. When other doctors said they wouldn't see Grey, Kathy accepted us. She told me that her work is her life.

We waited in the waiting room for five more hours. I am so stressed out. I went to sleep on Kathy. Seven hours later, the nurse came to the waiting area. She told me I could go and see Grey. That was the happiest moment of my life. Being beside my baby made me feel love once again.

When I woke up from a long sleep, Grey was looking into my eyes. He scared me a little because I thought he was sleep. I just laughed. Grey requested something to eat. I fed him some fresh fruit which is his favorite. He was eating so hastily. Grey fell asleep before I could finish feeding him.

Grey woke up several hours later. He wasn't looking so well. I called Kathy to come into the room. She looked at me and told me that I had to stay strong because Grey was dying. Grey looked at me.

"Baby, I am about to leave you. I want you to be strong for me. You are the best I have ever had. I love you. If you ever find love again, make sure it is real love that the love we shared. You deserve it, and I am going to miss you. You have always made me feel complete and loved. Please keep me in your heart. When things get hard and you don't know what to do. Think about me."

I couldn't do anything, but cry. The thing that really got me is when Grey told me that I am his king after he kissed my lips. Grey slipped away from me as I held him in my arms. Kathy and three other doctors had to catch me. I was falling on the floor.

When I woke up later that night, I thought it was all a dream. Reality hit and I couldn't stand to stay in this house filled with memories of my lost love. I moved back to Atlanta. I needed the support of the guys in my life. I never gave up on myself. My life wasn't the same.

It took me ten years to find love again. He reminded me so much of Grey. Grey would have wanted me to be happy. I am always going to keep him in my heart. He will always be my number one. Grey was my joy, life and the love of my life. No matter what people say, I am always going to love Grey because he loved me. Grey and I had a relationship like no other. If I could bring him back to life I would. Once again, I love and miss you, baby.

The End.

www.ingramcontent.com/pod-product-compliance
Lightning Source LLC
Chambersburg PA
CBHW071148020726
47502CB00002B/328